The Dream

The Dream

Sarah J. Cadore

To: Michelle
Thank you and
best wishes

Sarah J. Cadore

iUniverse®

THE DREAM

iUniverse books may be ordered through booksellers or by contacting:

iUniverse
1663 Liberty Drive
Bloomington, IN 47403
www.iuniverse.com
1-800-Authors (1-800-288-4677)

ISBN: 978-1-4917-8910-0 (sc)
ISBN: 978-1-4917-8909-4 (e)

Library of Congress Control Number: 2016904507

Print information available on the last page.

iUniverse rev. date: 04/25/2016

To my wonderful mother, Anitta Veronica Smith, who was, is, and will always be my beloved queen

Acknowledgments

I appreciate deeply all my friends and relatives who took time out of their busy schedules to read and critique the early and final drafts of my manuscript. Without their encouragement and enthusiasm to see this book in print, I might not have pursued publication.

Thanks to my husband, my children, and my siblings, who always believe in me and have been my staunchest supporters. I appreciate your love.

Special thanks to Sister Teresia Mutiso, who gave me spiritual support at times when I really needed spirituality.

Prologue

The thermostat outside Stella's kitchen window read 99 degrees Fahrenheit. The blazing sun hung in the clear blue sky like a fireball waiting to explode.

Stella hoped for some relief from the unrelenting heat. But instead, the meteorologist on Radio XVYI reported another rise in temperature, in excess of 115 degrees Fahrenheit. Restless and unable to relax, Stella paced back and forth from her couch in the living room to the dining room window overlooking her driveway. She was awaiting the arrival of the technician, whom she had called fifteen hours earlier requesting service on her central air-conditioning unit. It was spewing hot air.

The day was particularly hectic for the electric and gas company, CEGSC, as every air-conditioned household in Haileysville was operating its AC at maximum capacity. CEGSC had its entire essential staff on call. Yet, with seemingly unending demands for repairs and requests for new installations, the company was still falling behind.

Stella had called CEGSC at least five times since her initial request, each time receiving the same answer. "Someone will be there within twenty-four hours, ma'am."

Becoming increasingly agitated, Stella decided to cool off in her Jacuzzi. She walked purposefully up the stairs, through her bedroom, and into the bathroom, where she turned on the cold water. She reached for the jar of jasmine oil from the tray at the foot of the Jacuzzi and added a liberal amount to the water. She closed her eyes and inhaled slowly. The exotic aroma of the jasmine oil enveloped the bathroom, creating an ambiance that further enhanced the already aesthetically pleasing decor.

The bathroom was painted sapphire gray, and there was a skylight immediately over the baby-pink Jacuzzi. The floor was accentuated with pink-and-gray marble, which continued into a baby-pink vanity and sink lying amid a gray, marbled surface with streaks of pink throughout. The faucets over the Jacuzzi and sink were of 24 karat gold. The light illuminating from the crystal chandelier that hung flawlessly from the ceiling over the vanity created a soft, radiant glow throughout the bathroom.

Stella's towels were a mixture of pinks and grays, each accenting the decor to perfection. The large inlaid, gold-framed mirror over the length of the marbled vanity exuded character and depth, while promoting a welcoming, sophisticated, romantic, and yet relaxed environment.

In addition to the jasmine oil, Stella added a generous portion of bubble bath to the water, dropped her clothing to the floor, and slowly stepped into the huge bubbles. As she immersed her smooth, tanned, tender body in the cold water, Stella felt, simultaneously, a sensation of relief and shock. It was as if she had stepped directly out of a sauna and into a pond at the dawn of spring. Never had she envisioned a moment where she could become completely smitten by a tub of cold water. She was in seventh heaven.

Stella turned off the tap, sat motionless in the Jacuzzi, and closed her eyes as she tried to erase from her mind the events of the day. Within minutes, Stella dozed off and was floating into space.

She landed in the middle of a large field covered by a sea of flowers. There were daffodils, lilies, roses of all colors and species, hibiscuses, and countless other blossoms, some of which she had never seen or could not recognize. The fragrant air was light, sensuous, and stimulating. The sun shone through the tall green palms and engulfed the ground like a sparkling waterfall, and the light breeze slightly brushed the petals.

Intoxicated by the beauty and aroma of her surroundings, Stella stretched out her arms, twirled, skipped, and ran through the field, absorbing every inch of its mystical splendor.

In her jubilant state, Stella reached out to embrace a tree but found herself holding the hand of a little boy whose face she could not see. A cluster of his dark brown hair draped limply over his face. He was as naked as a bird.

Stella was taken aback but showed no fear. She tightened her grip on the little boy's hand, and like friends, they skipped, hopped, and danced gleefully, in enjoyment of their wondrous surroundings. Suddenly, their joyful dance was interrupted when a man with the face of a jackal mysteriously appeared and dragged the boy away.

In an instant, the enchanted field of exceptional beauty became a scene of torment and despair. The sun disappeared beneath a dark gray cloud; the flowers shriveled; and the stench of decaying plant life consumed the air. In a state of panic and amid a haze of darkness, Stella fell to the ground. She struggled and gasped for air.

As she slowly gained consciousness, Stella heard faintly, from a distance, the chimes of a doorbell. In a daze, she jumped out of the Jacuzzi; rushed out of the bathroom, through the bedroom, down the stairs into the foyer, and to the front door; and opened it without hesitation.

"Yo … yo … you're naked," stammered an astonished voice. "Ma … Ma'am, you … you're naked."

"Oh my god!" Stella yelped in horror as she came to realize that she was stark naked and dripping wet from head to toe.

Jolted by a mixture of shock, embarrassment, and shame all bundled in one, Stella jumped back from the entrance and slammed the door. Like the wind in a storm, she raced up the stairs to her bedroom.

Minutes later, Stella reappeared at the front door. This time, she was fully dressed in a white terry robe draped loosely around her slender body and a towel wrapped around her head like a turban.

Before opening the door, under her breath, Stella swore. "If it was not for the want of cool air, I would not be showing my face at this door."

She was absolutely, devastatingly embarrassed. She took a deep breath, slowly wrapped her hand around the handle of the door, and stood motionless for a brief moment as she gathered her composure. Then, with a tight, firm grip, she reluctantly pressed the handle and pulled the door toward her.

There, on the other side, stood a handsome, distinguished young man leaning against one of the two large Roman columns at the entrance. He had a smug look on his face. Unlike Stella, he seemed to have recovered from the shock of her nudity, quite unraveled.

Determined not to display any emotion, Stella stared directly at the young man and was blindsided by a slight familiarity, as if something within her recognized him from somewhere. Her attention was diverted from the previous events, as she thought, *where on earth have I seen this man before?*

Stella stood speechless, looking at the young man as she tried to jog her memory.

It was not a good time to play the waiting game, as Stella soon realized.

The young man instantly flashed his pictured ID and asked, "Where is your central air unit, ma'am?"

Stella was still standing with her eyes fixed on him and her lips beginning to move when the young man said, "Oh, never mind; there it is," and walked away.

On reaching the unit, he removed a screwdriver from his tool bag and immediately went to work.

Where on earth have I seen him before? Stella continued to ask herself.

In his peripheral vision, the young man could see Stella, still standing at the doorway, looking directly at him. "What now?" he murmured under his breath. He wondered what other surprises this weird woman had in store for him. He turned his head, looked directly at Stella, and saluted.

Stella chuckled at his brashness. "How should I call you?" she asked in a raised voice.

"Victor is my name, but call me Vic," he answered without interrupting his work.

"Vic, how long will it take to get this thing going?"

"I don't know, ma'am. I must first find the problem."

"Okay," Stella responded as she calmly closed the door and walked inside.

Stella's mind reverted to the dream, and as she replayed it over and over, she was overcome by a sense of panic. *What was the meaning of it all?* she wondered. She made every attempt to push aside her premonition that the dream meant something ominous, but she could not.

Stella walked up the stairs to the bathroom. She released her bathwater and retreated to her bedroom, where she changed into a red satin kimono.

The bedroom was elegantly designed. The walls and ceilings were painted eggshell white with an 18 karat gold foil crown molding bordering the perimeters of the entire ceiling. The silk window treatment and bedroom linen were pastel peach, accented with a touch of green. A king-size canopy bed made of mahogany wood was positioned against the wall overlooking a huge marbled fireplace. The mantel over the fireplace mimicked the 18 karat crown molding. On the mantel, a portrait of a woman with a slight resemblance to Stella was hung in a golden frame similar to the molding. The rest of the furniture, including her eighteenth-century armoire, was made from mahogany.

Adjoining the bedroom was a sitting area that led to a balcony overlooking the west side of Stella's estate. From the balcony, Stella had a plain view of the pond and a beautiful flower garden, which always seemed to be in bloom.

Upon leaving the bedroom, Stella descended the stairs to the kitchen, where she grabbed an ice-cold Carib beer from the large stainless steel refrigerator. Still deeply focused on the dream, she sat at the breakfast table, opened the beer, and raised it to her lips. At that instant, there was an abrupt tap on the kitchen door. Stella jumped, causing the bottle to fly out of her hand. With a quick reflex, she caught the bottle, but not before half of its content was emptied onto the marble floor. When Stella eventually looked toward the door, Vic was standing outside trying to get her attention.

"Come in," she said. "It's unlocked."

Vic slightly pushed open the door, popped his head in, and informed Stella he was going to CEGSC's warehouse to get parts for the unit and would be back in an hour.

Stella nodded her head slightly, acknowledging Victor's presence without paying attention to what he was actually saying. She even ceased to remember how hot it was as she continued to reflect on the events that had occurred after she'd stepped into the Jacuzzi. She could not erase the dream from her mind.

Victor returned within the hour. Shortly thereafter, he replaced the defective part, reassembled the central air unit, and had it working as if it had just come from the manufacturer.

When Victor tapped on her kitchen door for the second time, Stella was still sitting at the table. This time, she was looking through her mail, which had not been checked in over a week.

Before Stella could answer, Victor walked toward her and handed her a receipt in duplicate, requiring her signature. Stella signed and returned the receipt to Victor. He flipped through the pages, pulled off the yellow copy, gave it to Stella, thanked her for her patience, and walked away.

"Thank you!" Stella shouted absentmindedly as Victor walked through the open door.

As he closed the door behind him, Stella stared blankly, tapping her right index finger on her chin. She was still trying to remember where she had seen him before. Her memory failed, but deep within, she knew that they had met. She just could not remember where, when, how, or under what circumstances.

PART ONE

Stella

The Little Girl Who Lost
All She Ever Loved

Chapter 1

Stella was born in early spring in 1952 in a small midwestern town called Mount Pleasant. The town had a population of fifty-five thousand. Of these residents, two-thirds were natives, and the others were transitory students and their families, residing in Mount Pleasant because of their affiliation (directly or indirectly) with Mount Pleasant University (MPU). MPU was a private university, known globally for its outstanding curriculum in business and agricultural sciences.

In addition to revenue generated through the university, agriculture was the pillar of Mount Pleasant's economy. This, unfortunately, was in the hands of only the wealthiest few. As a result, gainful employment in Mount Pleasant was extremely competitive among locals with lesser means.

Other than farming, limited job opportunities could be found in the industrial and financial institutions. This situation created a problem for transient residents. The locals could not afford to share their limited openings with outsiders. In fact, most of the businesses looked like family picnics. Once one family member obtained employment with a company, a slew of other family members, relatives, and friends followed.

On top of that, the affluent were suspicious of outsiders, whom they feared would threaten the prevailing structure. Such mistrust and limited opportunities in Mount Pleasant led to the creation of a closed and nepotistic society. The rich dominated, outsiders were locked out or pushed out, and diversity stifled. Additionally, upon graduating from MPU, both transient and local graduates left Mount Pleasant to seek employment in other towns, cities, and states. This created a brain drain in Mount Pleasant.

Stella was the daughter of two wealthy landowners, Nelly and Hugo James. They owned one thousand acres of farmland, on which they predominantly grew wheat and grains of different varieties. They employed a workforce of over three hundred during the sowing and harvesting seasons and maintained over a hundred field hands during off-season.

In addition to growing grains, the Jameses had a reasonably large orchard of apples, pears, cherries, plums, and peaches. They also raised livestock for local use.

Hugo established, operated, and maintained a greenhouse with a laboratory in which he experimented and performed grafting of plants and fruits. He also voluntarily ran a two-hour weekly workshop from the greenhouse for the agricultural science division of MPU. With the help of his right-hand man, Scuffey, Hugo controlled all technical and daily operations of the farm.

Nelly managed the administrative and accounting side of the business. She also sought and negotiated contracts with clients and potential clients, both on a local and national level. She was considered a genius by many of her colleagues and those who had the honor of working with her. She prided herself on knowing the needs of potential clients long before contacting them for their business. She was an expert researcher.

Other than a handful of business associates; Nelly's sister, Theresa; their family attorney and best friend, John Godfrey; and their closest neighbors, Lucy and John Honig, hardly anyone made social visits to the James's home. One reason for their social unpopularity, or one might say their seclusion, was location. The farm was situated miles from the main highway. To get there from the city, one had to travel almost eighty-five miles.

Another reason was Nelly's estrangement from her youthful friends and family, who had deserted and ostracized her long before she'd moved to the farm. Nelly's childhood had been blessed with countless friends and family members who'd adored her and pledged their heartfelt love for her. She had been the apple of everyone's eyes—until she had been unexpectedly struck with the disease called poliomyelitis. Nelly's family members and friends had seen the results of the disease on Nelly as having rendered her weak and frail. They believed that the disability it left her with, had stripped from her all of her potential. And thus, in their minds, they categorized her as being infirmed and no longer one of them. They quickly disassociated themselves from her.

To make matters worse, Nelly had also gone beyond the norms of the times and her community and married a black immigrant. To all, this was an abomination. It was an unforgivable betrayal that could not be overlooked. In fact, it was the straw that had finally broken the camel's back. Nelly became a complete outcast in her community, with her family members at the helm.

Until she was three years old, Stella's only contact with children her age was at her doctor's office or at the Winnie Tods playhouse, which she attended once weekly.

Winnie Tods was located about fifty-five miles from the James farm. Four days per month, Stella spent about ninety minutes traveling to and from the playhouse and two hours socializing and playing with the children in attendance.

When Stella was three years old, Nelly gave birth to a baby boy, whom she and Hugo named Eric. Like Stella, he was greatly loved and cared for.

While trying to get their business off the ground, Nelly and Hugo personally cared for Stella. Wherever they went, they took Stella. By the time Eric came along, they were able to employ a nanny, named Mimi, to care for both Stella and Eric. They also employed a housekeeper, Miranda, who cooked and maintained the household.

As their business flourished, Nelly found herself spending longer hours dealing with its expansion and all of the responsibilities that came with it. Yet, in spite of her increasing dedication to the business and her busy schedule, Nelly never lost sight of her obligation to her children. She reserved special bonding times, as her favorite moments were the times spent with her family.

Without failure, the Jameses had dinner together every evening, after which Nelly gave Stella and Eric their evening bath and read them bedtime stories before she and Hugo tucked them in for the night. For Nelly and Hugo, that was a ritual—a time when they both spent uninterrupted, quality time with Stella and Eric.

After putting the children to bed, Nelly and Hugo would work for at least four more hours before retiring for the evening.

Stella welcomed the addition of her little brother to her family and became very attached to Eric. She called him Ricki. She was delighted to help her mother give Ricki his bath, even if her role was only to splash water on his tummy. Stella was fascinated with the birthmark on the left side of Eric's abdomen. She always tried to scrub it off with her soap rag and marveled that she could not.

The birthmark was the image of an eagle in flight. After Nelly explained to Stella that the dirt she wanted to scrub off of Eric's abdomen was a birthmark and could not be removed, Stella started referring to the birthmark as the "Birdy Mark."

As they grew older, Stella and Eric became inseparable. Mimi took them for long walks around the farm, usually with Stella pushing the carriage. One of Stella's favorite stops was at the cows stall and pasture. She loved to look at the cows as they chewed their cud. She could not help but wonder why one bite lasted so long. She wished she could ask them but settled for asking Mimi.

Occasionally, Nelly took Stella and Eric to downtown Mount Pleasant whenever she had limited business obligations to attend to. For the children, that was a delight. While in the city, Nelly made it her duty to treat them to ice cream at Sam's Ice Cream Parlor, which was located across the street from Cosgrove Supermarket, in the middle of the city.

Nelly and the children developed a trusting relationship with the ice cream man, Jerry Malone, who was always delighted to serve them. When they walked into the parlor, he would greet them with the biggest welcoming smile, and he was able to guess what flavor ice cream they wanted even before they decided.

Nelly was fascinated by his enthusiasm to serve her, since few people, if any, were as helpful to her as Jerry was. Nelly trusted Jerry to the point where they began communicating on a first-name basis.

Whenever she entered the parlor, she would greet him with a big, "Hello, Jerry." And Jerry, with his contagious smile that spread from ear to ear, would make the parlor the most comfortable and welcoming place in the city. Nelly even accepted assistance from no other attendants as long as Jerry was available. Stella and Eric also adored Jerry Malone.

Another of Stella and Eric's fascinations was their love for the outdoors. They were sometimes left in the backyard to play for short periods without adult supervision. Those moments were very important to Stella, as she was able to be mummy for just a little while. With hands on her hips, she would demand that Ricki do exactly as she ordered.

"Pick up your truck," she would say. "Don't do that Ricki. Don't go there, Ricki."

Stella felt like a real grown-up ordering Ricki around. At the tender age of five, she wanted to be in authority.

Stella also started full-time school at the age of five, and though she made numerous friends, she could not wait to get home to Ricki at the end of her school day.

Her newly found friends visited Stella at home on the farm and had many pajama parties and sleepovers. Like Stella and Eric, Stella's school friends loved the outdoors. And they loved to explore. But most of all, they adored Eric.

He was chubby with a round face and a beautiful, broad smile that highlighted a dimple on each cheek. Eric had dark, straight hair and beautiful, dark eyes with thick, black, curly lashes—the type girls would die for. Stella's friends loved to pinch his chubby cheeks and have him chase them around the yard. Those chases took Eric farther and farther away from the house.

As Eric grew older and stronger, with increasing curiosity, he continued to venture farther off than his parents would allow. Their concern led to minor restrictions being placed on Eric whenever he went outdoors.

During Stella's absence, Eric spent most of his days with Mimi and Booboo, his brown teddy bear. On occasions, he was left to roam about freely in the backyard, where he chased the chickens and ducks and sometimes rode on the back of Rover, the black-and-brown German shepherd, who was now growing weak with age. During those activities, there was always someone close by. Never was Eric left unsupervised for more than fifteen minutes.

The Jameses chose to send Stella to St. Benedict Private School because of its religiously rooted principles. St. Benedict also had good academic standings, and Nelly and Hugo's best friend, Lucy Honig, was the vice principal and music teacher at St. Benedict.

The Honigs were immigrants from Western Europe. They moved to and settled in Mount Pleasant because of John's job as head of the business division at MPU. After completing his graduate studies in business at a university in Chicago, he accepted a position with Mount Pleasant University. The Honigs moved into the neighborhood only three years before the Jameses.

They had always wanted children but were unsuccessful. They adored the Jameses and treated Stella and Eric as they would have treated their own kids.

When the Jameses decided to send Stella to St. Benedict, Lucy was elated and wasted no time volunteering to drive Stella to and from school each day. After all, she welcomed the companionship for her thirty-five-mile drive. It was an excellent arrangement. The Jameses trusted the Honigs with their lives and knew Stella would be in good hands while under the care of Lucy Honig. They knew also that St. Benedict was an excellent school, and with Lucy as vice principal, Stella would be well cared for.

Every weekday at exactly 3:45 p.m., when Mrs. Honig's Mercedes-Benz rolled into the driveway of the Jameses' home, there on the veranda, overlooking the driveway and the courtyard, stood Eric, waiting. As the car cruised to a complete stop, he would rush to the top of the stairs, where he and Stella would embrace and immediately begin a conversation as they walked hand in hand through the open doorway.

Mrs. Honig was always thrilled by the affection exchanged between the two siblings. Lucy had her own ritual. She would sit in her car and watch until the moment Eric and Stella disappeared through the huge, mahogany front door before driving off.

The most discussed topic at the Honigs' dinner table was their admiration for Stella and Eric, and these conversations were imbued with a sense of pride and joyous elation.

"Eric and Stella are so adorable," Mrs. Honig would often say to Mr. Honig. "Their love for each other is so pure it's contagious. I feel it in my heart every time I drop Stella off."

The show of affection exhibited by Stella and Eric anchored in the heart of Mrs. Honig feelings of joy, love, adoration, and togetherness. She loved them like the children she craved for but could never have.

Autumn had begun, and the leaves on the trees were beginning to change to orange and red. Soon they would all fall to the ground, leaving the now-beautiful vegetation empty and lifeless, with the hope of rebirth and renewal in the not too distant spring.

Stella and Eric would soon be jumping in and out of piles of leaves gathered for mulching. As she watched the leaves gradually change, Stella talked to Mrs. Honig at length about the fun she and Ricki would have once all the leaves were on the ground.

Mid-October approached, and Stella's wishes began to materialize. The trees started to shed their leaves as quickly as the weather changed. Stella was overjoyed. Then one cool Friday afternoon, as Mrs. Honig journeyed to the James farm with Stella sitting in the passenger's seat, as she had done countless times before, they were both overcome by a sixth sense that something dreadful was about to occur.

The afternoon looked gloomy. The blue sky had disappeared, and gray clouds overshadowed the sun. The falling leaves seemed to have lost their motion of flight. Instead of dangling in the cool autumn air like butterflies gliding through the forest, they were stripped from their branches and, like rocks, fell directly to their resting place on the cold, damp earth. Fall had always been one of nature's unforgettable beauties. But on that day, it was plain dread, the scenery lifeless.

Stella was unusually quiet as she looked out the window of Mrs. Honig's car. Mrs. Honig experienced a sense of uneasiness unlike anything she had experienced in the past. She anticipated that Stella did too, so to ease the tension surrounding them, she tried to force a conversation with Stella. "Stell," she said, "it looks rather gloomy this afternoon. Maybe it is going to rain. Do you think you and Eric will be able to play in the leafy piles this weekend?"

Stella did not answer. She just shrugged her shoulders as she continued to look out the window of the moving car.

Mrs. Honig's anxiety was further exacerbated by the growing traffic. For the first time since she'd moved into the area, traffic seemed unusually heavy. Mount Pleasant only experienced such heavy traffic flows during two periods, harvest season and the beginning of fall, when students from area schools and other learning institutions visited the farm as part of their curriculum and for agricultural development and research. That busy period had ended weeks earlier.

Within ten minutes of her drive, more than twenty vehicles had passed, including five police cruisers. Mrs. Honig momentarily lost her calm and pressed hard on the accelerator, but in the interest of not alarming Stella further, she forced herself to relax and continue at a normal speed. Mrs. Honig's uneasiness turned to fear as she pulled off the road onto the James estate. The big, black, heavy wrought iron gate, which was always locked and took almost five minutes to glide open, was ajar. Her blood ran cold through her veins as she turned and looked at Stella.

The look on Stella's face told her that the little girl too seemed taken aback by the sight of the unlocked gate. Without speaking, they both looked blankly at each other and then back at the gate. Mrs. Honig slowly drove through.

Straight ahead in the distance, four police cruisers and two unmarked cars were parked in the driveway. As the pair drew closer, they saw men in police uniform and civilian clothing scattered throughout the courtyard. Mrs. Honig continued to drive slowly toward the place where she dropped off Stella every weekday. Before she'd reached her destination, two policemen, one with a police canine and the other with his hand on his holster, signaled her to stop and get out of the car.

On that gloomy day in October, Stella would find that nothing would again be the same. In an instant, her entire life would change in ways a child seven months into her sixth year on earth could never begin to comprehend.

Chapter 2

In the midst of all the commotion going on around her, Stella's eyes were fixed to the veranda where Eric stood every afternoon awaiting her arrival. On that solemn afternoon, he was not there. Stella panicked. She knew something was wrong. She felt it in the pit of her stomach. It was as if a bolt of electricity had ripped through her tender heart.

Except for one day when Eric was in bed with influenza, he had always waited in that very same spot. The absence of Eric on the veranda and the unsettling feeling churning within her created such great fear that Stella could not wait for the car to come to a complete stop. She opened the door of the slowly moving car and jumped out, leaving the door swinging behind her as she headed toward the veranda. Her heart pounded faster with every step she took.

"Ricki, Ricki!" she yelled, running up the stairs, through the veranda, and into the foyer.

Nelly heard Stella's dreaded call and rushed, with open arms, toward her daughter. She grabbed and cradled Stella all in one swift scoop and lifted her off the ground. Nelly was crying.

Stella's spirit sank deep as she saw the tears running down her mother's cheeks.

"Mommy, Mommy, what's the matter?" she asked. And then she too started to cry. "Where is Ricki? Mommy, where is Ricki?"

Overwhelmed with emotions, Nelly opened her mouth and started to speak, but there was no sound.

Hugo, Mimi, and Miranda all came rushing out of the living room behind Nelly. The sight of their little Stell with tears streaming down her cheeks and her tiny arms wrapped around her mother's neck made them hold on to each other and sob profoundly.

The sobbing continued until Nelly initiated silence with a cough. And then quietly, she led the way back to the living room.

On entering, Stella noticed two men leaning against the mantel of the fireplace, over which hung an autographed portrait of President Franklin Delano Roosevelt, Nelly's hero and motivator, who she ardently admired. She idolized him because of his ability to perform as commander in chief in spite of his polio-stricken body. To Stella, the men seemed to be conversing with each other while looking directly at her.

Nelly and Hugo resumed their position on the sofa. Nelly placed Stella on her lap, wiped away her tears, and kissed her on the forehead. This time, she dug deep within to muster all the strength she could. She had to keep from falling apart as she struggled to explain to her six-year-old daughter what was going on.

As Nelly was about to speak, Mrs. Honig walked into the room. She was shaking. Nelly noticed the condition she was in and asked Mimi to get her a drink as she prepared to tell Stella about an occurrence she could not have anticipated in a million years.

Moving Stella from her lap, Nelly placed her daughter in a standing position facing both her and Hugo. She put her right hand on Stella's left shoulder. Hugo did likewise. Then, looking directly at Stella, with tears streaming down her face, Nelly spoke. "My darling Stell, I am sorry for the confusion. When I got around to calling Lucy, you had already left."

Nelly desperately needed a distraction. She paused as if trying to find something else to say without saying what she needed to. She took a deep breath and then, pointing toward the men standing near the fireplace, she said. "These men are policemen, and they are here to help us."

"Where is Ricki, Mummy? Where is Ricki?" Stella interrupted.

Nelly knew that she could no longer prolong the inevitable. She turned away for an instant to wipe away a tear, and then, turning back to Stella, she said. "Something terrible has happened. Ricki was playing in the backyard earlier this morning, and without warning, he disappeared. We searched all over but could not find him. We will continue to search. Stell, I promise, we will never give up searching until Ricki is found." With her voice lingering on the word *found*, Nelly felt as if she had told the story while holding her breath. She needed air. Nelly moved her hand from Stella's shoulder, got up from the sofa, and quickly walked away. She could no longer bear to look at the pain in her daughter's eyes. She wanted to scream. She wanted to hold Stella and never let go. She was afraid but could not show fear. She had to be strong. She must be strong for Stella.

Hugo placed Stella on his lap and held her tightly, not wanting ever to let her go.

Mrs. Honig followed Nelly into the bathroom. With tears rolling down her cheeks, Nelly covered her mouth to drown her sobs. She could not allow Stella to hear her bawling. Mrs. Honig put her arms around Nelly, and they both cried on each other's shoulders.

For the next few days, policemen and detectives went in and out of the Jameses' home. They combed the surrounding areas but could not locate Eric.

Acquaintances of the Jameses came to express their sorrow and to join in the search. Even people who had never met the family assisted. For days, two helicopters flew over the property while searching an area of over two hundred miles from the farm. Yet Eric could not be found.

A policeman found Booboo, Eric's brown, stuffed teddy bear, which he always carried under his arm. It was lying face down under the large pear tree, about two blocks from the house. Not too far from Booboo, Rover was found staggering. He was drugged. Rover died two days later.

The intense search for Eric continued well into the following month. Every stone was overturned, every lead was followed, and still, they were nowhere closer to finding Eric than when they'd first begun. It was as if he had been swallowed up. But by what?

Through this ordeal, Nelly stood strong. But with each passing day she grew more and more frustrated. Soon, she was consumed with fear. She feared that if Eric were not found very soon, he would be lost forever. She feared that Stella would get sick and Hugo would go mad. Nelly's fear for everyone reached the point that she could no longer cope with the feeling of being afraid without doing something about it.

Against strict orders from Chief of Police Harold Newton, Nelly offered a reward of $100,000 for information leading to the whereabouts and return of Eric. She also established a twenty-four-hour hotline to accommodate incoming calls.

Hundreds of calls were received, including crank calls. Every lead was followed and sightings checked. Still, there was no sign of Eric.

Nelly could not believe what was happening. Her son had disappeared from the face of the earth and she could do nothing about it. For once, rather than being in control, Nelly felt that she was being controlled. She was helpless, and despite her strong faith, she began to think that hope was not enough.

Exactly six weeks from the day Eric disappeared, Nancy Newton, a social worker from Mount Pleasant Social Services, Child Welfare Department, and two police officers, visited the Jameses' home. They requested an urgent meeting with Nelly and Hugo.

Nelly escorted them into the library where, moments later, Hugo was heard yelling at the top of his voice. Concurrently, Nelly screamed, a continuous scream of horror and despair. The yelling and screaming continued for almost five minutes before Miss Newton and the policemen stormed out of the house. They got into their parked vehicle and quickly drove away.

Moments later, Nelly and Hugo emerged from the library to find Stella standing at the doorway with tears rolling down her face. She had heard the screaming and wanted to know what was happening.

Nelly placed her hand around Stella's shoulder and led her to the sofa in the living room—the same place they had sat six weeks earlier when Nelly had reluctantly told her about Eric's disappearance.

Nelly tried desperately to hold back the tears while sounding normal and fearless. That did not work, for even to a six-year-old, it was difficult to pretend that all was well while looking at her with a tearstained face and red, swollen eyes. Stella knew that her mother had been crying. For almost sixty seconds, they sat on the sofa in silence as Nelly tried to control the knot that was forming in her throat.

Finally, she turned to Stella and said, "Honey." Her voice trembled as the tears, which she could no longer subdue, rolled down her cheeks. Nelly wiped away the tears with the back of her hand and coughed to clear her throat. Then slowly, she said to Stella, "The policemen could not find Eric and do not know why he disappeared."

Nelly again paused for a moment, this time to dig deep within her soul to find the words to explain to Stella what no parent could ever dream of saying to a child. She could not and would not lie to her child. Stella had to know the truth. She took a deep breath and then proceeded to pour out her heart to her beloved daughter. "Stell," she said once more. "They think I might have something to do with Eric's disappearance."

With that, she started to cry aloud. But through those muffled sounds, she managed to pledge her undying love and devotion for Stella and Eric.

"Honey, I would never harm you or Ricki. If loving you is a crime, then of that I am guilty. I would rather die than knowingly hurt you." She paused again, wiped away the tears, and continued. "The lady who was here with the policemen said she will send you away to live with another family until they can find Eric. They think you are no longer safe with me and that you may be in danger if we continue to live in the same home."

Before Nelly could finish her statement, Stella screamed. "No, Mommy! No! I love you, Mommy. I will not go. Why, Mommy? Why?"

Stella could not stop crying. She hugged her mother tightly with her face buried beneath her neck.

Nelly's heart sank as she held Stella firmly, and with her tears saturating Stella's hair, she rocked Stella until she was asleep. "I will never give up, Stell." Nelly whispered. "I solemnly swear that I will fight to my death for you and for Eric."

Thoughts of running away with Stella crossed Nelly's mind as she rocked Stella back and forth. She could not do it. She could not bring herself to run away with one child, while not knowing the whereabouts of the other. Her undying love for both her children would not allow it, especially when, deep within, she knew that Eric was alive.

Nelly called her lawyer, John Godfrey, who immediately enlisted Mr. Oxford to look into the legal aspects of Nelly and Hugo's situation.

Mr. Oxford's contention was that since no charges had been brought against Nelly for the disappearance of Eric, Social Services had no grounds on which to remove Stella from the James household.

Unfortunately, he could not have been more wrong.

Determined to make their presence felt, three days after informing the Jameses about the agency's intent to remove Stella from their home, Miss Newton, and the two policemen returned.

Hugo and Nelly saw them from a distance and met them in the courtyard.

From the veranda, Stella saw Miss Newton hand Nelly an envelope, which she immediately opened. Her mother pulled out a white sheet of paper and began to read.

In slow motion, Nelly handed the paper to Hugo. It was a court order.

As Hugo read the order, he felt strongly the urge to attack Miss Newton. But before he could finish reading, Nelly took one step backward, staggered, and fell to the ground.

"Oh my *God*," Hugo stuttered as the paper dropped from his hand.

"Mommy, Mommy," Stella screamed, running from the veranda, down the stairs, and into the courtyard where her mother lay unconscious.

"She's fainted. Give her air," Miss Newton shouted.

Mimi, who saw what had happened through her bedroom window from the far corner of the house on the first floor, rushed outside with a bottle of smelling salts.

Stella stood in a daze as Mimi waved the bottle under Nelly's nostrils. She feared that her mother had died.

Nelly slowly opened her eyes and stared. Then she whispered, "Stella, I love you."

Those were the last words Nelly spoke to her daughter, as Miss Newton took Stella kicking and screaming into the police cruiser while the police officers held Hugo and Nelly at bay.

Nelly fought to get to the police cruiser but was too weak to get past the officers. As she watched the marked police car pull out of the driveway and drive away with her daughter screaming and locked in the backseat like a convicted criminal, Nelly gasped for breath as a darkness she had never before known, engulfed her entire being. The image of helplessness on Stella's face as the car drove away stuck in Nelly's memory like a dagger embedded in a dying heart.

Nelly was in pain. The City of Mount Pleasant had taken away her pride and joy. The small-minded, vindictive bureaucracy had robbed from her the essence of her existence. They had taken away her soul. What else had she to live for?

Nelly dropped to the ground and screamed the wail of death. She remained seated on the cold concrete and watched until the police car drove past the heavy, black gate, and disappeared with Stella inside.

Nelly felt her soul leave her body. She was like a corpse. Only her breathing was left, and even that she could not feel. Nelly was numb and was no longer dying on the inside. She felt as if she was actually experiencing the real thing, mortality.

In her catatonic state, Nelly did not see Hugo lying on the ground, unconscious from the blow he'd received on the back of his head from the butt of one of the policemen's gun.

As Hugo slowly gained consciousness, he realized that Stella was gone. He had not even been given the chance to see the cruiser disappear in the distance, much less to say good-bye to his beloved daughter. Like Nelly, he too felt the presence of mortality, and he hated every moment of it.

Most of Nelly's and Hugo's adult lives had been marked by ridicule and discrimination, but nothing compared to having lost their children. Worse yet, the system they'd entrusted to help them was the very system that had snatched away their daughter during their moment of vulnerability.

Part Two

Nelly

Disabled, Not Dead
A Woman of Substance
and Courage

Chapter 3

*N*elly was the fifth child and third daughter of Jonathan and Susan Roberts, who were well connected and highly respected in Mount Pleasant.

Susan Roberts held controlling shares in Mount Pleasant National Bank, and Jonathan was the bank's president. Needless to say, the Robertses had vested interests in almost every major institution in Mount Pleasant, including the Mount Pleasant University.

Susan was the only child and heiress to the Daniel Bordeu estate. Mr. Bordeu was an entrepreneur who had made vast sums of money in the steel industry during World War I. It was also rumored that a huge portion of his wealth had been gained through bootlegging during the prohibition years. With Susan's inheritance, the Robertses invested in real estate and the stock market, increasing their wealth a hundredfold. This placed the Roberts family in the registry as one of the wealthiest and most influential families in Mount Pleasant and the Midwest.

Susan's influence also extended to the political arena, which allowed her the honor of having the street she lived on named after her.

Susan saw to it that her family lifestyle reflected a status of wealth. She introduced and registered her children in the most exclusive clubs in Mount Pleasant. She surrounded herself and her family with only the affluent. Susan made it clear that no one in her family was allowed to fraternize with the enemy (indigents). Their only point of contact should be as employer to employee. To achieve that, Susan ran her household with an iron fist, leaving no room for embarrassment among her circle of high-ranking friends and acquaintances.

Nelly had two brothers, Tommy and Jonathan Jr. and two sisters, Gina and Theresa. Gina was the Robertses' first child, followed by Tommy, Jonathan Jr., Theresa, and Nelly.

Nelly was as popular as she was beautiful, both inside and out. She had long, thick, brownish-bronze hair that fell to her shoulders. Her eyes were hazel brown with thick, curly lashes. At age sixteen, she stood five feet six inches tall.

From childhood, Nelly had won the hearts not only of her parents but of everyone in her community, where she was universally loved and adored.

Unlike her siblings, Nelly was very inquisitive, outgoing, and friendly. She showed interest in her entire community. Despite her busy schedule and against her mother's wishes, she found time to volunteer at the Catholic Center for the homeless, where she ran the literacy program and helped in the soup kitchen.

Nelly was athletic and participated in numerous sports. She was the captain of her high school cheerleading squad, president of the local 4-H club, and a candidate for the national volleyball team.

In spite of her many activities, Nelly held a grade point average of 4.0 and won a spot on the dean's list.

At age sixteen, Nelly had already developed a strong sense of self. She knew exactly what she wanted and was candid about it. Unlike most of her siblings, whose dreams were to inherit the family business, marry, and have a family, Nelly's dream was to build her very own business from the ground up, with no help from her family.

This did not sit well with Mrs. Roberts, who was sometimes critical of Nelly's candidness and her willingness to challenge authority. Nevertheless, she was extremely proud of Nelly. She saw in Nelly the potential to become an astute business executive, and she nurtured that potential to its maximum. Susan educated, trained, and involved Nelly in the Roberts family's numerous business dealings, hoping that the business Nelly was so eagerly dreaming of starting on her own would one day be an extension of the Roberts empire. Given Nelly's acumen and proper training, Mrs. Roberts envisioned a grand and prosperous future for her daughter.

Sadly, in the eyes of Mrs. Roberts, all those promises of grandeur ended two weeks after Nelly's seventeenth birthday.

Just before cheerleading practice on a hot summer afternoon, Nelly communicated to Barbara, her best friend, that she was not feeling well. She had a high fever. Barbara encouraged Nelly not to attend practice. She refused to listen. Her determination, dedication, and commitment to responsibilities would not allow her to follow this advice. To miss practice, she had to be practically falling on her face.

"Go home," Barbara insisted as Nelly's condition worsened. "Practice will go on with or without you."

Nelly was adamant. She was there for practice, and practice she would. Along with her cheerleading squad, she went through all of the routines and grueling exercises for the entire two hours of practice. When it was all over, she could not walk past the locker room. She was nauseated, ached all over, had a temperature of over 104, and was soaking wet with sweat.

Barbara urgently sought assistance from Coach Alexandria, who drove Nelly home. By the time the girls and their coach got to the Roberts home, Nelly was too weak to get out of the car.

Jonathan Jr. was pulling into the driveway when he saw Coach Alexandria and Barbara struggling to help his sister. He quickly stopped and rushed to assist them. He carried Nelly into the house.

Mrs. Roberts summoned Dr. Raphael to Nelly's bedside. He was concerned about her extremely high fever and ordered an immediate ice bath and oral intake of extra-strength acetaminophen, which he hoped would reduce the pain and contain the fever.

Temporarily, the fever subsided. But Nelly was not getting better. Within twenty-four hours, she had taken a turn for the worse, as the fever had returned and the pain had intensified. Nelly was rushed to Mount Pleasant General Hospital, where, after going through numerous tests, she was diagnosed with having a rare case of poliomyelitis, an infectious disease caused by a virus that affects the central nervous system.

Such devastating news was surely not what Nelly and her family expected. Nelly's life was immediately turned upside down; news of the disease instantaneously affected the lives and attitudes of Nelly's family, friends, and entire community. They were faced with a situation about which they had no knowledge, for which they were not prepared, and that they were too supercilious to handle.

When Nelly recovered from the high fever and debilitating pain, she was left with a severe spinal disorder. At first, Nelly could not walk. But driven by her will to overcome, she went through intense physical therapy.

The days grew longer with each passing moment as Nelly slowly regained the use of her lower limbs. At times the pain of trying to walk coupled with the look of disgust on her mother's face (when she came to visit) were almost too difficult to handle.

Several times, Nelly pondered her situation and asked, *Why me, Lord?* No answers came. But through it all, she knew that she could not give up, not with her whole life ahead of her. And so, she persevered.

At the end of her grueling therapy, Nelly regained the ability to walk. Nevertheless, the disease left her disabled. With every step she took, her upper body swayed from one side to the other. To remedy that situation, Nelly's doctors advised her that for the rest of her natural life, she would need the support of a cane and a wheelchair.

Nelly was grateful for having survived the disease, but she was fully aware that her new disability was not the only negative effect the disease would have on her life. She was not too naive to know that because of it, her entire life and circumstances would change. She had an uphill battle ahead, and since she could not alter the course of destiny, she vowed never to allow her partial physical immobility to impede her life or destroy her dreams. Nelly was determined to live a full and exuberant life in spite of her condition.

Unfortunately, Nelly's optimism for her future was not shared by many. This was especially true of her mother. Susan Roberts was completely devastated. Before Nelly's release from the hospital, Susan openly affirmed her belief that Nelly would have been better off dead than crippled. She saw Nelly not as having a disability, but as being an invalid.

Susan went as far as telling Nelly that she could not bear the thought of having a crippled child "waddling around Mount Pleasant." All her life, Susan had worked tirelessly to ensure that no embarrassment was brought upon the Roberts family in the presence of her esteemed colleagues and friends. She could not afford to have anything or anyone tarnish her so-called image or position of strength. To Susan, having an invalid in her household would do just that. It would make her appear weak. Added to the dilemma of being embarrassed, Susan was afraid to deal with Nelly's disability, over which she had no control. She could not make Nelly walk normally, despite her enormous wealth and her status. This was unacceptable. She felt cheated. All her dreams and aspirations for Nelly, her little girl, were destroyed by the disease.

Susan could not understand how Nelly had contracted the disease. She tried to remember the places they had been in the past month. Where had they eaten? Who had they interacted with? There were no answers.

"This disease does not just attack anyone," Susan contended, forcing herself into believing it was all Nelly's fault. "If Nelly had not challenged me or so often gone against my wishes and walked among the enemies, the disease would not have attacked her."

Susan decided that she had to control her predicament, and the only way to do so was to eliminate its cause. Who could she blame? It had to be Nelly. Therefore, the moment Nelly was released from the hospital, Susan treated her badly. She perpetually referred to her as an invalid. She attempted to render her incapable of functioning as a normal human being and wanted her locked up in her bedroom, away from the rest of the world.

Unknown to Nelly, Susan hired two full-time home care providers to look after her. She also placed strict restrictions on who could be allowed to visit with Nelly. Worst yet, she forbade Nelly from walking in public. "Use your wheelchair whenever you leave this house," she ordered Nelly. "You should not be seen waddling all over Mount Pleasant." Susan thought the wheelchair was more dignified, as to her, Nelly's twisted gait signaled weakness. And weakness was a stigma she couldn't stand being associated with the Roberts family.

Nelly was aghast by her mother's reasoning and unreasonable demands. She hated the wheelchair, and despite the comfort it allowed, it made her feel helpless, confined, and restricted. In the wheelchair, Nelly could not go wherever she pleased because of lack of accessibility. Nelly vehemently protested Susan's every effort to turn her into a caged bird.

Needless to say, Nelly's protests did not deter Susan's efforts to keep her daughter in check. Whenever Nelly walked in the presence of Susan, she quickly ordered Nelly's caregiver to place her into the wheelchair. "Get her into that chair even if you have to wrestle her into it," Susan would say.

Susan's negative attitude toward Nelly trickled down to the rest of the family. Her siblings, with the exception of Theresa, looked at her with disdain. Whenever she walked among them, they ridiculed her. They treated her like a freak of nature.

Nelly learned to ignore her haters, who time and time again verbally expressed their hatred for the way she walked. They also hated her for defying Susan.

Nelly's only ally in the household was Theresa, who supported her unconditionally. Whenever there was a face-off in the household, it was always Nelly and Theresa against everyone else.

Mr. Roberts was not in agreement with Susan's attitude toward Nelly, but he said nothing. He dared not oppose his overbearing wife. His only opposition to Susan was to insist that Nelly never be placed in an institution, and on that he stood firm.

To keep out of Susan's way, Nelly attended church services on a regular basis. After every Mass, she took a few minutes to meet with Father Paul, whose words of encouragement and wisdom helped her through her recovery. Nelly also resumed her volunteer work with the Catholic Center and found comfort among the indigents who Susan wanted her to keep at bay. Additionally, she took to reading her Bible on a daily basis. Those activities helped Nelly regain her focus. And instead of battling daily with Susan, she decided to learn more about her attacker, poliomyelitis.

Nelly extensively researched the disease and asked, by way of letters and phone calls, countless questions of the experts. She even contacted people outside of Mount Pleasant who were living with poliomyelitis, combing the accounts of their firsthand experiences for information about the disease's long-term effects and physical restrictions. She was determined to know everything there was to know about this disease that had sprung itself upon her.

One of the first things she discovered was that people would look at and treat her differently. This she already knew. What she had not anticipated was that it would start in her very household, the place where she was supposed to feel safe, comfortable, and secure. Susan, her beloved mother, followed by her siblings, became her chief antagonists.

With Nelly home from the hospital, Susan canceled all activities scheduled to take place at the Roberts residence. She could not allow her friends and acquaintances to be subjected to her now-crippled daughter waddling around the house.

Susan gave her household staff strict instructions to lock Nelly in her bedroom before letting visitors into the house. All of Nelly's friends were forbidden from visiting.

Nelly protested to everyone who would listen, but her protests fell on deaf ears.

Susan claimed that all of her decisions were in Nelly's best interest and that they were meant to protect Nelly from herself.

Armed with the information she'd gathered, Nelly struggled unsuccessfully to educate her family about the disease. They would not listen. She reminded them that the only thing different about her was the way she walked. Even that was ignored. Nelly encouraged them to read about the disease and to meet with people who were affected by it. She enlisted the help of a middle-aged woman by the name of Julia to talk to Susan and the rest of her family about the disease.

Julia was around Susan's age and was also a victim of poliomyelitis. Nelly thought that Julia might be able to help Susan overcome her phobia since they were of the same generation. Despite her affliction, Julia had established and was successfully operating a school for the disabled in the city of Chicago. Through their correspondence, Julia and Nelly had become friends, and she'd volunteered to travel to Mount Pleasant to meet with Susan.

On the day of Julia's arrival, Susan conveniently had other matters to attend to. She refused to meet with Julia, and nothing Nelly said or did made a difference.

Julia left Mount Pleasant two days after her arrival, and with the exception of Theresa, none of the Roberts family had taken the time to meet with her or hear what she had to say. They had completely ignored her.

The Roberts family never tried to look beyond Nelly's physical disability or learn about the disease. All they saw when they looked at Nelly was an invalid, a girl with a deformity. They forgot who Nelly really was. They overlooked the fact that she was a part of all of them.

Nelly eventually gave up. She accepted her destiny and came to realize that she could never change the attitudes of those who did not wish to be changed. She felt pity for them, as they were either too scared to deal with the reality of her situation or just too narrow-minded to accept anyone who was not like them, even if that person who was "different" was family. They remained blinded by their perception of what Nelly's world ought to be and not what it was.

Thanks to Nelly's strong will, perseverance, and determination, along with her father, Susan and the rest of the Roberts clan were deterred from having Nelly locked up in an institution for the disabled.

Chapter 4

Outside the Robertses' mansion, people who had once looked up to and revered Nelly turned away from her. The invitations to school and community events stopped coming. The phone stopped ringing, and friends deserted her. Even Barbara, her closest friend, stayed away—at first, because Mrs. Roberts demanded that she did and, later, to appease her newfound friends.

Nelly no longer walked like them, so she gained the status of being an outcast. The people in her neighborhood saw her as a cripple, and the welcoming smiles she'd once enjoyed all turned to frowns.

The neighborhood children nicknamed Nelly "the Twister."

When Nelly ventured into public places, she was either ignored or patronized. At times, everyone wanted to help her. Other times, when they saw her coming, they moved to the other side of the road.

Nelly refused to give in to those attitudes. She would not be deterred by ignorance. She had a life, and she swore that no one but she and God would determine its course. She gritted her teeth and faced her adversities. When necessary, she rebuked with disdain those who exhibited a high degree of intolerance toward her.

Defying protests from Susan, who warned Nelly that her schoolmates would tease, ridicule, and shun her, Nelly returned to school.

Unfortunately, it was not long before Nelly realized that Susan was right. She had lost all but a few of her so-called friends, who remained friendly out of pity. Even they whispered behind her back. And later, the whispers turned to laughter and then outright insults.

Nelly pretended not to care.

A few weeks after returning to school, Nelly made a decision to discontinue the use of her wheelchair because of lack of wheelchair access at Mount Pleasant High. This provoked the wrath of numerous students, who claimed that Nelly was being political. They feared that she was trying to shame policy makers into catering to the needs of disabled persons, which in their opinion would "open the gates" to a more diverse student body, all of whom would have diverging demands.

With that in mind, they moved from bullying Nelly verbally and emotionally to physically assaulting her. They were even emboldened to do so in the presence of teachers and school administrators who looked the other way.

Nelly was purposely bumped into, doors were shut and slammed in her face, and students kicked and occasionally hid her cane.

Physically, Nelly was unharmed. But enduring such intense humiliation from individuals who had once worshiped her was devastating. Those who did not participate in bullying Nelly turned and walked away whenever she walked in their direction. Their rejection was psychologically painful, but Nelly carried on. She was not prepared to have anyone dictate her existence. By no means was she about to miss out on life.

The disease could not stop her, Susan could not stop her, and she would be damned if she gave a bunch of scared, ignorant adolescents the power to send her into hiding.

Just as she refused to adhere to her mother's demands and fold under her cruel treatment, Nelly refused to give her schoolmates the satisfaction of dictating how she should live and where she should go to school. She would not quit.

In spite of her hardship, Nelly picked up where she had left off before her bout with the disease. She continued to excel. She graduated with a grade point average of 4.0 and remained on the dean's list and honor roll.

At the end of her senior year, Nelly celebrated her graduation, not in honor of her accomplishments, but to honor her victory over the disease. She went to her commencement accompanied by Theresa and Mr. Roberts.

As Nelly proudly walked across the stage to accept her diploma and awards for her courage and scholastic achievements, she vaguely heard some boos, along with a few voices referring to "the Twister."

With a broad smile on her face, Nelly whispered, "Go ahead and boo. This is only the beginning. My best is yet to come."

Nelly had reached her first milestone, and already, she was thinking about her journey to the next. She knew that going forward would be an uphill struggle, but strengthened by her present success, she was more determined than ever and ready for the climb.

Riding home in the backseat of her father's car, she closed her eyes and tried to envision the future. *How much worse could things get?* She asked herself. *Living with Mother is far worse than anything I have encountered. She did everything short of locking me up and melting the key.*

Nelly thought of her next step, and with a broad smile, she opened her eyes and exclaimed, "University, here I come!"

No one responded, not even Theresa.

On the day following Nelly's graduation from Mount Pleasant High, Susan applauded her and then, in the same breath, warned that it was time to give up the charade of pursuing a dream she could never accomplish. "Give up the idea of going to university," Susan said. "University is for normal people."

Nelly was taken aback. She had given up arguing with Susan and ignored all of her criticisms, but this statement she could not ignore. Nelly quickly made it clear that in spite of her physical condition, she would make no compromises.

"I may walk funny. I may even waddle like a duck. People will tease and ridicule me, but no one will alter my direction. As long as there is breath in my body and a brain in my head, I am moving on. I promise you, Mother, if you try to stop me, you will regret it. And while you're at it, spread the word. Anyone wishing to take away my dreams will have to kill me."

With that, Nelly walked away without giving ear to another word from her mother, who stood with her jaw dropped.

Nelly was stunned to learn that a vast majority of administrators and politicians in her community exhibited ignorance and indifference toward her. Until her physical disability, she had no idea of how much contempt, disregard, and dislike they had for diversity. She knew that her family was prejudiced, and to some degree, she shouldn't have been surprised that they'd turned on her because of the way she walked. What she hadn't known was that the administrators and politicians were just as bad, if not worse, than her family. Unlike the Robertses, these decision makers had the power to impact and shape the lives of many. Unfortunately, their willful disregard and contempt for multiplicity made that impossible, as Nelly would soon find out. Because of their indifferences, many residents of Mount Pleasant were left out or held back from reaching their full potential and achieving their goals. The decision makers even found ways to hold back those who dared to try.

Nelly was ashamed for not having seen things as clearly before. She was saddened by the fact that she had to be placed in a position of vulnerability before she could understand the ills of a fearful and oppressive society.

All of Nelly's beliefs and her trust in the integrity of the school's system and its professionalism had crumbled before her.

"I feel as if I was living in a bubble for the past seventeen years," Nelly told Theresa one day after returning home from a meeting with Mr. Glen, the director of the board of trustees at Mount Pleasant University. "The bubble has now burst, and I am seeing everyone and everything in a different light. These people are so patronizing and ignorant they make me want to spit. They are not going to get away with it, Theresa. No! Not on their miserable lives. They are not going to succeed."

There was fire in Nelly's eyes as she spoke. Theresa knew Nelly was not bluffing, and a whole lot of people were about to find that out too. When pushed, Nelly could be as devious as Susan.

At the meeting, the director had informed Nelly that the members of the board had voted unanimously to withdraw her academic scholarship—a scholarship she had proudly earned by exceeding all required standards during her tenure at Mount Pleasant High.

Her mother's words—*College is for normal people*—had echoed loudly in Nelly's head as the director had told her that the committee had determined that the scholarship was for students who were able to adapt to and cope with college life.

"Nothing has changed," Nelly had stuttered as soon as she'd recovered from her initial shock. "I graduated with honors. My grade point average was 4.0. I am on the dean's list, and I broke every academic record. What part of my academic achievements has changed? Tell me," she pleaded.

There was no reply to her questions. It was as if Nelly had become invisible in the eyes of Mr. Glen. Without looking at her, he'd adjourned the meeting. The decision had been made, and no question asked by Nelly would change it. He and his secretary had gathered their belongings and walked away, leaving Nelly sitting alone in the conference room.

For the next thirty minutes, Nelly had sat with her head cradled between the palms of her hands. She refused to cry.

Later, as Nelly had walked out of the room, she'd stood at the door; looked back; and, as if addressing the committee, said, "I will get that scholarship. Yes, I will."

Knowing that no law firm in Mount Pleasant would take her case against Mount Pleasant University, Nelly, with the help of Theresa, contacted a law firm outside Mount Pleasant. She was assigned a young associate by the name of John Godfrey. He was a Mount Pleasant native.

After completing his undergraduate degree in political science at MPU, he'd left Mount Pleasant to attend a private law school in Chicago, where he'd obtained his law degree and bar admission.

Nelly's case was John Godfrey's very first assignment as a licensed attorney. He had been hired straight from law school and had worked with the firm as a paralegal until passing the bar only three months before meeting Nelly.

John Godfrey was as nervous as a child on his first day of school. He looked like a teenager straight out of high school. He wore thick, black-framed eyeglasses. He had red hair with bangs hanging over the left side of his freckled face. He wore a white, rumpled shirt with a red, awkwardly tied tie and a black, tight suit that appeared to have been bought from a thrift store.

After speaking to Nelly and Theresa at length, John Godfrey felt confident that Nelly had a strong case and moved swiftly to set things in motion. His first move was to write to Mount Pleasant Board of Education, sending copies to Mount Pleasant University and each member of the decision-making committee, informing them of Nelly's intent to sue.

Without hesitation, and in amazement of her determination, the board overturned the decision within days of receiving the letter.

Nelly got more than she had expected. She was granted full tuition for four years, plus room and board. Her books were paid for through a separate scholarship fund.

Nelly was on her way to realizing her dream of becoming an accountant/business administrator. She enrolled at Mount Pleasant University, where she hoped to complete her double major.

With her scholarship, Nelly had no reason to rely on her family for assistance, which she had already forfeited as a result of her disobedience to Susan. She knew that Susan would never spend her money on formal education for someone she saw as an invalid.

With her financial situation resolved, Nelly heaved a sigh of relief. She understood that there was still a long, hard journey ahead but resigned herself to take it one step at a time until her desired destination could be reached.

Chapter 5

There was civility between Nelly and her schoolmates at MPU. However, that was the extent of their relationship. With the exception of one or two international students who befriended Nelly, her schoolmates ignored her. And her only interaction with her schoolmates outside the classroom was for the sole purpose of working on group projects or assignments.

Nelly was completely isolated, and though she had grown accustomed to such isolation, both at home and in high school, she sometimes, late at night, in the privacy of her dormitory, shed a tear. She refused to let her schoolmates know that their actions were killing her on the inside.

"Why give them the satisfaction?" Nelly would say out loud. "They are acting through ignorance. My own relatives are doing it. Why should I expect anything different from strangers?"

Nelly was not the type to drown herself in sorrow or wallow in self-pity, despite her occasional inner turmoil. She was a strong believer in well-directed energy. Grounded in that belief, Nelly used her energy and abundant free time to study and do other school-related projects. She also used some of her free time to study the stock market and make small purchases with the measly allowance she received from her father.

Mr. Roberts fought hard to increase Nelly's allowance but was vehemently opposed by Susan, who controlled the family finances. Susan had practically disinherited Nelly in retaliation for what she called her defiance.

During the second semester of Nelly's sophomore year at MPU, she was standing in line to register for advanced calculus when she realized that her watch was missing. In her haste to get in line before the many students wanting to register for the course, Nelly had forgotten her watch.

She looked over her shoulder and asked the tall, slim, tanned young man standing behind her what time it was.

He looked at Nelly and then looked into the heavens and said, "Ten off nine."

Nelly was not in the mood for theatrics. She gave the young man an exasperated look and was about to ask someone else when he lifted his hand. His watch read ten off nine.

With a surprised look on her face, Nelly asked, "How did you do that?"

"Elementary, my dear," he replied, "elementary!"

"Really," Nelly answered. "Just how elementary was that?"

"I had looked at my watch seconds before you asked," he responded. "I saw you rummaging through your purse and knew you were searching for something, and since you were not wearing a watch, well, what else could it have been?"

"Very observant," Nelly said as she smiled and looked into his eyes.

He had dark, bright, piercing eyes. His face was oval shaped with strongly defined cheekbones. The young man extended his hand toward Nelly. "I'm Hugo."

Shaking his hand, Nelly responded, "I am Nelly. Nice to meet you."

With that, Nelly and Hugo carried on a conversation that lasted through registration and beyond.

Nelly learned that Hugo was a graduate student, finishing the final year of his master's degree in agricultural science. Hugo and Nelly talked about the difficulty of the course and the reasons so many students gathered in the same spot every year to register. It was mandatory for all students seeking degrees in the sciences and business.

Nelly was very interested in hearing about Hugo's program, and he was willing to tell her all about it. He was humorous and very easy to talk to.

After registration, they continued their conversation as they walked to the cafeteria. Hugo wanted to know why Nelly walked the way she did, and he did not hesitate to ask.

Nelly was eager to reply, as he was direct. And unlike others, he was clearly not inquiring out of pity. He genuinely wanted to know. Hugo was also curious why she was not using a wheelchair or cane.

The passion in Nelly's voice as she revealed her need to be free and independent, led Hugo to be in complete agreement with her decision. They spent most of the morning in conversation and did not part before exchanging telephone numbers.

Nelly and Hugo studied calculus together and, over the next four months, became inseparable. During that period, they got to know a great deal about each other.

Nelly learned that Hugo had been born in Aruba, one of the Lesser Antilles islands located in the southern Caribbean. He was the only child of Edward and Lenora James. Edward James was originally from Portugal, and Lenora was from Aruba. She was of African and English descent. She was a mulatto.

At the age of four, Hugo's parents left him in the care of his grandmother and traveled to the United States. At age ten, he joined his parents, who by then had become US citizens. Since his arrival in the States, Hugo had lived with his parents on a small but lucrative farm in Chicago.

After high school, Hugo had received a four-year scholarship to a private university in Chicago, where he'd obtained his bachelor of science. He'd then enrolled in the graduate program at MPU, where he hoped to fulfill his lifelong dream of becoming an agricultural scientist.

Hugo wanted to take the science of hybridization (grafting) of plants to a higher level. His original plans were to return to his parents' farm after graduation, where he would construct a greenhouse for his experiments with plants. Those plans took a different direction after he and Nelly became fully acquainted.

Upon graduation from MPU, Hugo accepted a junior position at the university's agricultural science department. He wanted to be close to Nelly. This move shocked many of his peers and particularly his parents, who were anxiously awaiting his return. He had always made it clear that he had no desire to stay in Mount Pleasant one minute past graduation. He had also openly voiced his dislike for the bigotry and indifference for diversity that existed in Mount Pleasant. His decision sent shockwaves throughout the learning community, when he declared his intention to remain in Mount Pleasant. More unbelievable, was his reason for staying. They were amazed that he would stay because of Nelly.

When asked why, Hugo proudly responded that he had found a lady with character, who dared to dream and was unpretentious, honest, humorous, full of life, and a joy to be around. Nelly had become his best and most trusted friend.

The Robertses were aware of Hugo and Nelly's growing friendship, which they initially regarded as harmless. Later, as the friendship grew, Susan, through her investigation of Hugo, found out that although Hugo looked like a tanned Anglo-Saxon, he was actually an immigrant with African blood. She went ballistic and demanded an immediate end to the friendship.

Once again, Nelly refused to adhere to Susan's demand, and her friendship with Hugo became stronger.

With the information obtained from her investigator, Susan contacted Hugo's parents in Chicago and sought their help in bringing an end to Nelly and Hugo's blossoming relationship. Susan contended that because of Nelly's physical condition, she was incapable of handling any kind of relationship, much less a husband and, eventually, a family of her own.

Like Hugo and Nelly, the Jameses knew that Susan was grandstanding. What she feared more than having a lame child in her family was having a black man marrying one of her children and bringing an interracial child or children into her brood. She could not allow it.

Hugo's parents were not strangers to those attitudes; after all, they had gone through similar experiences. Nevertheless, Lenora was happy to go along with Susan because she too had an agenda. When it came to marriage, Lenora had "high expectations" for Hugo—she expected that he would marry someone from the land of his birth. In fact, she had already handpicked the girl she wanted to be his bride. The thought of Hugo becoming husband to a girl she had not chosen, much less to a disabled girl, was totally unacceptable. She wasted no time informing Hugo that Nelly would be a burden to him. "You will lose your friends and acquaintances," she warned Hugo. "People will shun you as they do Nelly."

Unknown to Hugo, Mrs. James paid a surprise visit to Nelly. During that visit, she warned Nelly that if she did not end the friendship between her and Hugo, nothing good would come of it. She told Nelly that Hugo had befriended her because of his empathy and that their relationship would not last.

Hugo was astounded by his mother's attitude. He had always admired his parents for their open-mindedness and accommodating nature toward all. He later realized that although Susan and Lenora shared a dislike for each other, they had no problem working together to destroy the relationship between their children.

Both women made it quite clear to Nelly and Hugo that they would stop at nothing to put an end to that "unholy relationship."

Hugo fought back by forcefully advising his parents that nothing anyone did would weaken the loving relationship, the respect, and the warm feelings he and Nelly shared.

He was right. As opposition from the James and Roberts families grew—Susan and Lenora did everything possible to sabotage the relationship—the feelings Nelly and Hugo shared blossomed, and they fell madly in love.

After Nelly's graduation, Nelly and Hugo quietly got engaged. They hoped that their parents would see and appreciate how strong their love was for each other and surrender their attempts to pull them apart. This was far from what happened.

When the announcement of the engagement and their intent to marry within one year were made public, both their parents flew off the handle and promised to completely disown them. That was followed by anonymous threats to both Nelly's and Hugo's lives.

Hugo was beaten on numerous occasions by people he did not know. He was also harassed and beaten by members of the Mount Pleasant Police Department.

As for Nelly, she was run off the road on a couple of occasions. They knew that Susan was behind those incidents but could not prove it, and even if they could, the police were part of the harassment and would have done nothing to stop it.

Nelly and Hugo both loved their parents and hoped that they would eventually understand. They wanted very much to get their families' blessing. They tried relentlessly to convince them of their love. Their continued plea for acceptance of the relationship was ignored. Their parents would not budge.

Nelly and Hugo finally gave up fighting, and six months subsequent to the date of their engagement, Nelly and Hugo eloped. Other than the clergy and his wife, Theresa was the only witness and attendee at the wedding.

Chapter 6

nowing that Nelly would never accept employment with the Roberts foundation, Mr. Roberts offered her a position at the Mount Pleasant National Bank upon her graduation from MPU. Nelly turned down the offer, as she would allow no one or nothing to prevent her from making it on her own.

Long before her illness, Nelly had made an oath to achieve, build, and advance, not on the coattails of her parents but by her own sweat and determination. She was not about to break that promise.

She would not be bogged down by the control and baggage that would be attached to her like an albatross should she choose to accept her father's offer. In spite of her condition, her childhood dream was still burning within her, and whether she succeeded or failed, that rested solely upon her. She would not depend on the Robertses for her sustenance.

Nelly found employment as an accounting specialist with the accounting firm JJ & Associates. She obtained the position largely because of her excellent scholastic achievements and partly because of the federal grant offered to first-time employers of "disabled persons."

Nelly saw this as the opportunity of a lifetime. To find employment through the university job fair was truly a blessing. She was fully aware of the discrimination she would face as a new graduate, a woman, and an individual with a disability. Finding that job shielded her from the ordeal of seeking employment in a hostile environment.

Moving forward, Nelly realized that the workforce would not be a cakewalk. But for now, she had managed to elude one form of discrimination, and it was a wonderful feeling.

Nelly's plan was to use the opportunity with JJ & Associates as a stepping-stone to attaining her goals and realizing her dreams. She worked twice as hard as the coworkers in her department, and in her attempt to learn as much as she could, she put in extra hours for which she accepted no compensation. Like a good soldier, she went beyond the call of duty.

Her colleagues and superiors commended her determination; yet, they ridiculed and shunned her because of the way she walked. She went through the vicious cycle of being alone all over again.

Her coworkers' Friday-night celebrations at Danny's Bar and Grill never included her. She was even left out of her manager's annual pool party, to which everyone but her was openly invited.

In addition to being isolated and ridiculed, Nelly was constantly passed over for promotions, despite her exceptional performance appraisals. To exacerbate the situation, Nelly was sometimes required to train those to whom the promotions were granted. She even trained new hires who filled positions for which she was qualified and had been initially interviewed.

Nelly hated the situation and all those who instigated and promoted it. Though tempted, she refused to abandon her dreams in protest of such blatant discrimination. She reminded herself that her future plans didn't include JJ & Associates. Although she was psychologically affected by the actions of her counterparts, she chose to see them as a temporary discomfort with little or no lasting impact on her future other than to strengthen her resolve.

Keep your eyes on the prize, Nelly, she would silently remind herself whenever she felt dejected. She was reconciled to the fact that at JJ & Associates, she was going "nowhere but out." She continued to work even harder as she envisioned the day when she would walk out of JJ & Associates, directly into her *very own company*.

As Nelly got more and more acclimated to the aftermath of the disease, she learned to accept her differences and vehemently strove to celebrate her adversities. Though difficult, it was through those adversities that Nelly grew stronger than she could have ever imagined. She managed her situation by counteracting every negative with a positive and never allowing the attitudes of others to stifle or break her spirit. One phrase she loved and repeated constantly during times of temptation, was "Never let them see you cry, Nelly girl, don't even let them see you sweat."

She continued to be proactive and outspoken on important matters, and although there were many at JJ & Associates who tried desperately to shut her up or turn her into an invalid, Nelly never succumbed to them. She knew who she was, and an invalid, she surely was not.

Like her neighbors, Nelly's coworkers imitated her walk, and when she appeared not to be listening, they referred to her as "the Twister" and then turned around and smiled at her.

Nelly was never fooled by those plastic smiles and could detect their hypocrisy from a mile away. Occasionally, she responded to their remarks by saying aloud, "Forgive them, Lord, for they know not what they are doing."

She held no malice toward them but showed pity, for in her eyes, they were just a group of insignificant, ignorant adults, afraid of what they did not understand and could never experience unless they were walking in her shoes.

JJ & Associates provided for Nelly extensive lessons in how not to run her business. In fact, she wished she could overhaul the entire organization, starting with upper management.

Mr. Lucas, Nelly's manager, and JJ & Associates personnel team were at the forefront of the firm's lack of professionalism and intolerance for others. Many accounts were lost as a result, and despite complaints from clients, no attempts were made to correct or even address the problems that existed.

The mission of JJ & Associates was to provide exceptional service for all. Unfortunately, their biggest problem was that they provided adequate service only for those who looked like, sounded like, and moved like them. Everyone else had to accept mediocrity or was free to find another accounting firm. JJ & Associates had no provision for clients using wheelchairs. Their representatives met with such clients in locations outside the firm. There were no interpreters to deal with or accommodate non-English-speaking clients. To conduct business with JJ & Associates, non-English-speaking clients had to provide their own interpreters.

Being aware of the problems within, Nelly made countless suggestions to her manager, customer service, and the personnel group on ways to improve relations with people of different backgrounds, races, religions, and cultures. When no action was taken, she used the company's suggestion box to convey her messages and suggestions. Still, nothing happened. It was as if JJ & Associates management was paralyzed when it came to decision making on such matters.

Everyone turned a deaf ear in an environment where intolerance was not only accepted but institutionalized. JJ & Associates saw no reason to change. They were expected to, but there was no mandate for them to do so. Except for the loss of a few customers, JJ & Associates got away with blatant discrimination.

Nelly knew that her time to quit had arrived when Mr. Lucas felt bold enough to inform her that she was never considered for promotions because of her physical immobility. "You do not move fast enough," he said. "Our clients need to meet with people who are adequately mobile to handle their accounts."

For the first time in the four years that Nelly had worked for JJ & Associates, she exploded. She had known that her physical disability was the reason she had been passed over for promotions, time and time again, but hadn't had any concrete evidence. As Mr. Lucas's words rang in her ears, Nelly felt as if a speeding bullet, suspended in midair for four years and aimed right at her heart, had eventually reached its target. She demanded an apology and took the matter directly to the personnel director.

Mr. Lucas denied ever having made such a statement, and since those who'd overheard were his avid followers, they supported him 110 percent. The matter was closed and forgotten within hours of her complaint.

In the weeks that followed, Nelly was cited for insubordination, and for the first time since working for JJ & Associates, her performance review went from exceptional to unsatisfactory, and her responsibilities dwindled.

Nelly's decision to resign came six weeks later, after she and Hugo had finalized their ongoing plans to start a small home-based business. They sectioned out the already small living room in their one-bedroom apartment and bought a desk and a typewriter, a file cabinet, and all the basic equipment and supplies needed to start the business. After neatly setting up the office, they had it blessed by Father Paul in anticipation of Nelly's first client.

Nelly was now ready to walk out the door of JJ & Associates but not before making her own lasting personal statement.

After writing her resignation letter, Nelly personally hand delivered a copy to the personnel director and dropped off another copy in the mailbox of James Jefferson Jr., president and CEO of JJ & Associates. It read:

> Dear Sirs:
> During my tenure as an accounting specialist with your firm, I found your management group to be extremely uneducated and insensitive in matters of diversity. Speaking from experience, I feel it necessary to identify some of the firm's most striking inadequacies. It is quite unfortunate that a company whose mission is to "provide exceptional service, second to none, for all of its customers, from all walks of life, in an expanding global economy" has on staff managers who lack the compassion and eloquence to treat others with respect and dignity.
> The hard fact is that the support staff emulates the actions of those from the top. In so doing, they not only

isolate customers but lose both existing and potential customers. In fact, I am aware of at least five large accounts the company lost as a result of such inadequacies.

For this company to survive and grow in an expanding global market, education and training in dealing with diversity must be provided to your entire staff. It will also be of some benefit to make your workforce more reflective of a diverse society. If such actions are ignored, your company will not be able to compete, much less survive.

It is time to be proactive. Do not be the company that only reacts to situations or, worse, does nothing. Such behavior in a global market spells disaster for any company hoping to be relevant. It is time to have your staff and clients treated professionally and with dignity.

It is with these inadequacies in mind that I hereby tender my resignation.

Sincerely,

Nelly James

Within days, Nelly got a personal call from Mr. Jefferson's secretary summoning her to a meeting in Mr. Jefferson's office. She was given only one hour to prepare. Nelly was not expecting a confrontation with the CEO of the firm, but she was not about to retract anything she had written in that letter. In preparation for her meeting, Nelly pulled a copy of the letter from a file in her desk draw, reread it, folded it, and placed it in the right pocket of her trousers.

Mr. Jefferson had come face-to-face with Nelly before, but never had they spoken a word to each other, not even hello.

As Nelly walked into Mr. Jefferson's office, he greeted her with a handshake and invited her to take a seat. Mr. Jefferson was mild mannered and spoke in a calm voice. He expressed his concern about her resignation and the contents of her letter. Nelly remained focused and unshakable as she repeated her concerns. Mr. Jefferson listened attentively, hanging onto her every word.

By his facial expression, it appeared that Mr. Jefferson was impressed by her ability to state her case in the most eloquent manner without pointing fingers at anyone in particular. She came across not as someone trying to get back at the company, but as someone trying to enhance the service JJ & Associates provided. He also found her to be knowledgeable and passionate about what she believed to be right.

They continued a dialogue for about an hour, discussing the current situation brought forth by Nelly and the kind of changes she thought were necessary to improve customer relations. This was not new to Nelly; she had already written all those suggestions, which had never reached the office of the CEO.

By the time the meeting was over, Nelly felt that she was ready to walk out the door of JJ & Associates and never look back. She had done and said what was in her heart.

Nelly did not know it, but Mr. Jefferson had been impressed by her candid and frank demeanor. At the end of the meeting, he again shook her hand and thanked her for seeing him.

Before Nelly was completely out of his office, Mr. Jefferson was on the phone with customer service. He urgently requested the files on all the accounts the company had lost in the past six months. To his horror, the files included large accounts, all with customers of diverse background. One of the clients was a Japanese firm. Another was an organization for the disabled. Mr. Jefferson was flabbergasted. A meeting was immediately scheduled with personnel.

The agenda was to set in motion a training team for the organization. He also met with the managers and supervisors in the customer service department, where the situation was vehemently discussed. At that meeting, some of Nelly's suggestions were put forward.

Mr. Jefferson demanded an explanation as to why Nelly's suggestions were never discussed. The meeting ended with Mr. Jefferson being completely dissatisfied with the answers provided. He was about to implement sweeping changes.

After Nelly's meeting with the CEO, and during her final two weeks with JJ & Associates, the atmosphere in the office went through a dramatic change. Not only was it evident that her coworkers and manager were cordial toward her; there was a complete change in attitudes. The whispers and innuendos were stopped completely.

Based on the conversation she had with Mr. Jefferson, Nelly had anticipated that some changes would be made, but she could not have imagined the speed at which they would be implemented.

Nelly also received a letter from Mr. Jefferson thanking her for her candid, valued opinions. He assured her that major changes would be implemented within the organization and strongly suggested that she stay on to assist with the implementation.

With a smile, Nelly whispered, "Too late, sir. The train has already left the station. That will never happen."

Nelly knew that her now-executive treatment was not merely a heartfelt response to her letter to the CEO. However, it might have been a genuine desire to make things right since management knew that if she brought a lawsuit against them with the information she held, she would be successful. In this, she had no interest. She was just happy to affect some well-needed change within JJ & Associates, the company that had given her, her first start.

On Nelly's last day of employment with JJ & Associates, Mr. Jefferson personally presented her with the company's insignia for her services with the company.

Ironically, as Nelly walked through the doors of JJ & Associates for the last time, Mr. Lucas, her former manager, was being escorted out of the building by security.

He had been fired.

Chapter 7

After leaving JJ & Associates, Nelly started her mission, fueled by her desire to never again be an employee of any company, firm, or organization.

With her office completed and business plan in place, Nelly perused the telephone directory and compiled a list of organizations, which she later researched at the city's library. She was looking for small, newly formed businesses whose accounting department was not yet established.

Equipped with her list, Nelly got to work calling and offering services of accounting, income tax preparation, and business planning to potential clients. She also placed advertisements in local newspapers, promoting her newly formed business to individuals and companies alike. Her goal was to cater to anyone in need of her business administrative and accounting skills.

As requests for her services slowly trickled in, Nelly smiled in anticipation of the future. She knew she had come full circle but realized that this was only the beginning of yet another difficult journey in her life.

One of Nelly's first clients was John Godfrey. He had started a private law practice in Mount Pleasant three years earlier. According to Nelly's research, he had on staff one associate by the name of Robert Oxford, a secretary, and a paralegal. He provided legal services for a very modest clientele.

Nelly was excited that John Godfrey had his own practice. She saw this as an opportunity to reward him for making it possible for her to be awarded her scholarship to Mount Pleasant University. Nelly walked boldly into John Godfrey's office, congratulated him on his venture, and told him she was going to, as she termed it, "reorganize his establishment."

Mr. Godfrey remembered Nelly, as she was not a person one could easily forget.

"Miss Roberts," he said in amazement.

"James," Nelly responded. "Nelly James."

Nelly cut short the pleasantries and went directly to the matter for which she was in John Godfrey's office.

Mr. Godfrey could not understand why Nelly wanted to reorganize his establishment, as she so bluntly stated. Nevertheless, he was quite impressed that she knew as much as she did about his business. After a brief silence, Mr. Godfrey expressed to Nelly that he was doing as well as expected and had no plans to reorganize now or in the near future.

Mr. Godfrey stood to escort Nelly to the door, but before he could make it around his desk, Nelly placed her hands on her hip, looked straight into his eyes and said, "John Godfrey, I am not asking you for a job. All I want is to assist in increasing your client base. For free," she added. "I have no inclination or desire to work for you, or anyone else for that matter."

Without giving him a chance to respond, Nelly turned and walked toward the door. Before going through, she looked back at Mr. Godfrey and said, "I shall be back in one week."

Mr. Godfrey was left with his mouth hanging and his eyes wide open, staring at the open space where Nelly had stood moments earlier.

⌒

One week later, Nelly, as promised, returned to Mr. Godfrey's office with a business plan. She placed it on the desk in front of him and sat watching as he read. He was staring at a business plan that was thoroughly prepared. Nothing had been left out. It was a plan with vision, a plan to not only expand the business but make it extremely profitable. He was speechless as he sat glued to his chair, reading.

"Do you have any concerns?" Nelly asked.

"No," he replied. "I could not have done it better." He got out from behind his desk, and extended his hand to Nelly.

Without discussion, he gave her the green light to proceed. "Jessica, my secretary, will give you anything you need," he told Nelly as she left his office.

For the next eight weeks, Nelly spent a few hours each day reorganizing Mr. Godfrey's business. By the time the assignment was completed, Mr. Godfrey occupied the entire second floor of the building and had brought in three more associates, a paralegal, a secretary, and a receptionist. A new billboard was hung at the front of the building displaying the sign John Godfrey & Associates, General Law Practice. With the addition of the three new lawyers, Mr. Godfrey was able to offer legal services in all areas and still had room to grow.

Nelly's marketing strategy for John Godfrey had included television and newspaper advertisements in Mount Pleasant and other neighboring areas. Nelly had also encouraged Mr. Godfrey to make himself visible by attending public functions and getting more involved in his community and church. "Potential client base in those areas is endless," she'd advised.

By the time Nelly's assignment with Mr. Godfrey was completed, his telephone was ringing off the hook. Prospective clients were calling from everywhere. Nelly also set up an accounting system, which later became the envy of other businesses. For the new system, Nelly hired and trained an accounting clerk.

Nelly charged nothing for all of her efforts. And although Mr. Godfrey offered her a small stipend, she turned it down.

Mr. Godfrey did put some money into the reorganization, but the rewards far outweighed the cost. He praised Nelly for her good deeds and vowed to be always indebted to her. Through this, an unbreakable bond was created between Nelly and John Godfrey.

In the five years that followed, Nelly's home business thrived.

She helped small business owners get their business off the ground. She found and used every loophole in the tax code to get her clients thousands of dollars in tax breaks they would not have received without professional expertise.

Nelly was in the driver's seat. She set her own hours, decided what jobs she wanted, and was free to reject those with which she felt uncomfortable. The best part of this business was that Nelly performed some of her assignments in the comfort of her home while helping others to achieve their dreams.

Through this period of success, Nelly kept abreast of changes in her field. She subscribed to every trade magazine and upgraded her skill set by taking additional courses whenever she had the time.

As their home-based business flourished, Nelly and Hugo started to concentrate seriously on launching the business of their dream. They wanted to purchase a farm, as they were both passionate about becoming partners in the farming industry. They worked diligently, planning, setting goals, reading real estate publications, and networking for information on property for sale in Mount Pleasant and beyond. They drove around during their free time, looking for "For Sale" signs on farms.

Their initial goal was to acquire at least twenty acres of farmland, and for this, they lived frugally, purchasing only necessities. They saved two-thirds of their monthly earnings.

In anticipation of finding their farm, Nelly and Hugo completed loan applications at almost every bank in and around Mount Pleasant. Unfortunately, every response to their loan applications and interviews was a rejection. The banking institutions stated that they had no confidence in the success of the Jameses' new business venture. Even the banks Nelly and Hugo currently did business with expressed skepticism. Some banks bluntly stated that the loan application was denied because Mrs. James' physical condition was not conducive to the success of the proposed venture. Others were more subtle. They contended that the Jameses lacked the collateral necessary to back the loan for which they were applying. The Mount Pleasant National bank also denied their application. In short, the real reasons why the banks refused the loans were obvious if not outright stated. They could not and would not give financial assistance to a black man and a crippled white woman.

Hugo and Nelly were deeply disappointed by the rejections but refused to allow their spirits to be broken. There were a couple of banks that had not responded to their loan applications, and to them, that represented hope. They continued to remain confident that one of those banks would be willing to take a chance on them. Hopefully, as they saw it, no news was good news, and behind every dark cloud was a silver lining.

They envisioned a miracle through hope. They had no intentions of ever relinquishing their dream. They would not give up.

Almost five years to the date after she'd quit her job with JJ & Associates, Nelly went to do her usual biweekly grocery shopping at Cosgrove Supermarket. It was a Saturday. As she stood in line at the checkout counter, she overheard a conversation between two elderly women. They were talking about a couple that was about to face foreclosure on their farm.

"If a payment is not made on their mortgage within the next two weeks, the bank is going to foreclose on the farm," one of the women said.

"Yes, I heard," the other woman replied. "The bank will just walk in and auction everything the Gerbers own."

"It is quite unfortunate that their children have not stepped in and tried to keep that farm in the family."

"The Gerbers are so independent; I doubt they would ask their children for help."

"I wish we could do *something* to help them without their knowing."

"You are sure right. I wish there was something the community could do to help. That farm has been in the Gerber family for four generations."

"It's sure fed a lot of people in Mount Pleasant. Unlike the rich farm owners, the Gerbers provided for us local folks even through the

Depression. It is a shame they were not able to produce a good crop of corn in the past couple of years."

"Be that as it may, it will surely be sad to see the bank take it over and cut it into pieces."

Nelly, who had been listening in closely, decided to join in. "Excuse me," she said. "I could not help overhearing your conversation. Are the Gerbers really going to lose their farm to the bank?"

The women were more than willing to discuss the situation. "Of course," one of the women said. "And the bad thing about it is that Johnny's great-grandfather was the first to own that land—all one thousand acres of it."

"Yes," said the other woman. "That farm has been in the Gerber family for over four generations, and now they're going to lose every bit of it."

"What about their children?" Nelly asked, using the information she already heard to obtain more.

"They got married and moved to another state, and since they are not interested in farming, the Gerbers will not tell them about their mishap."

"This is sad. It is really sad. I wish the Gerbers good luck. I am sure God will work out something good for them."

Nelly wanted to ask for the address of the Gerber farm but could not bring herself to do so. She did not wish to sound too conspicuous. Yet, she knew that what she'd just learned was a godsend—an opportunity she could not overlook. She had to get that farm. And to do so, she needed to move quickly. She had less than two weeks to put a plan into action before the bank made its move.

Nelly paid the cashier and said good-bye to the two women, who were still busy talking about the Gerbers. She walked calmly out of the supermarket, but when she reached the parking lot, her gait became the combination of twisting and hopping she used when attempting to walk quickly. She could not wait to get to her car.

Nelly broke the speed limit on her way home, driving forty miles per hour in a thirty-mile-per-hour zone. She was rushing to share the news with Hugo and to find the Gerbers' telephone number.

Nelly quickly pulled into the driveway of her small apartment and got out of the car, leaving the groceries behind.

"Hugo," she shouted as she hurried into her office. "Take care of the groceries. Still in the car."

Nelly was moving so fast that when she stopped, she smiled to herself and took a moment to reflect. "My," she said softly, "I never knew I could move that swiftly."

She grabbed the telephone directory from the shelf over her desk and looked up the name Gerber. There were only five Gerbers in the directory, one of which was J. Gerber. Nelly dialed. After five rings, a male voice answered. "Hello!"

Nelly paused. She almost lost her nerves. Then she remembered why she was calling. "Mr. Gerber," she said, "my name is Nelly James. How are you, sir? I was speaking to some acquaintances of yours today, sir. They told me what an exceptional farmer you are. As a matter of fact, they told me that you are the best farmer around. You see ... sir, my husband and I are interested in starting a business in farming, and I would appreciate your advice on how to proceed."

Without asking the name of the person who'd referred Nelly to him, Mr. Gerber instantly agreed to meet with Nelly and her husband. During the short conversation Nelly learned that Mr. Gerber was proud of his heritage and would speak about farming to anyone who would listen. They made an appointment to meet after church the following day. Nelly took instructions on how to get to the Gerber farm, and after the two had exchanged a few pleasantries and Nelly had expressed her heartfelt thanks, she hung up the telephone.

Nelly hurried into the kitchen, smiling from ear to ear.

"What's going on?" Hugo asked. He had not seen that wide smile since his wife had landed her first paying client years ago.

Without a word, Nelly grabbed and kissed him passionately on the lips. She then sat him down at the kitchen table and told him about her encounter with the two elderly women at the supermarket. She, however, saved the best for last.

Still smiling from cheek to cheek, Nelly paused for a minute to let everything she'd just revealed sink in. Then at the top of her voice, she screamed, "We have an appointment to see the Gerbers tomorrow!"

Hugo almost fell off the chair. "How in God's name did you manage that?" he asked.

"Tactfully," she said, "and with great care. After all, I did learn from the best—Susan."

For almost the entire night, Nelly and Hugo discussed, over and over, how they would approach the Gerbers. This was the chance they were waiting for, the chance of a lifetime, the chance they could not afford to lose.

They were up and about before the rising of the sun. They had to seek God's guidance before facing the Gerbers. After church, they made the ninety-minute drive to the Gerber farm.

The scenery was spectacular. Miles and miles of land stretched as far as the eyes could see. The rolling hills and valleys were covered with lush vegetation. Every tree, shrub, flower, vegetable, and pasturage was grouped on its own patch as if carefully sculptured and placed there, with each patch taking on a different characteristic.

Closer to the entrance of the Gerber home, groups of large trees with thick, sprawling branches lined both sides of the street, forming an arch over the winding road. The scenery presented not only a farmer's dream but also a paradise for the romantic.

Nelly and Hugo both saw themselves as proud owners of the property as they drove through the huge, black wrought iron gate toward the expansive courtyard that lay in the distance before them.

When they reached the house, Nelly and Hugo stepped out of the car. And with Hugo ahead of Nelly, they both ascended the stairs in the direction of Mr. and Mrs. Gerber, who were waiting in the veranda.

Before they were halfway up, Mr. Gerber admonished. "I thought your husband was joining you."

Experienced in what discrimination feels like, Hugo quickly responded, "Mr. James could not make it, sir. I am here with Miss … Miss Nelly."

"Then wait in the car, *boy*," Mr. Gerber replied rudely.

Nelly started to back down the stairs as Hugo turned to leave.

"No," he whispered. "Go get that farm."

Nelly climbed the stairs slowly but reluctantly, wondering if the farm was worth the venom that had laced Mr. Gerber's tone as he'd disdainfully called her husband *boy*.

Mr. Gerber's voice reverberated in Nelly's head. But before she could think another thought, it was stifled by Susan's, ringing loud and clear: *Don't get mad. Get even.*

Nelly's heart almost skipped a beat. "Thank you, Susan," she whispered under her breath as she prepared herself to become just like her mother, sweet and ruthless. Then abruptly, she looked up at the Gerbers with a broad smile.

Once Hugo had returned to the car, Mr. and Mrs. Gerber, who appeared to be in their mid-seventies, developed an immediate attitude change. They were friendly and accommodating. In fact, after their brief introduction and expressing their regrets for not having the opportunity to meet Mr. James, they carried on as if they had known Nelly for years. Nelly acted likewise, never letting them know how much she detested them for the way they'd spoken to her husband.

The three retreated to the Gerbers' library, where they discussed the farm. From their conversation, Nelly realized that the Gerbers were reluctant to get out of the farming business, although they had a strong desire to retire.

Mr. Gerber explained that the only reason he was still at the farm was because of his love for farming and his failure to find someone suitable to continue the tradition. He wanted the property to remain farmland. He particularly feared that if the land fell into the hands of a developer, it would be parceled out and used for a different purpose.

The Gerbers and Nelly discussed the ins and outs of running the farm, the difficulties the couple had encountered over the years, and the rewards they'd reaped. The Gerbers got so comfortable talking to Nelly that they told her they were about to lose the farm to the bank. Mr. Gerber sadly explained that at their age, dipping into their retirement savings to pay for a farm their children had no desire to keep or maintain made no sense.

"I wish they would carry on the tradition," Mr. Gerber said, his voice thick with deep emotion and his words catching in his throat as he struggled to hold back tears. He hesitated for a moment, looked into the distance, and then continued in a low, husky voice. "Since their interests lie elsewhere, we have no choice but to let it go."

Nelly's heart broke for Mr. Gerber as she detected in his voice the deep passion he held for farming. But thinking like Susan, Nelly seized on the opportunity to discuss a deal with the Gerbers. She expressed great sorrow and sympathy, and then with sheer diplomacy, she offered to purchase the farm, with a promise that she and her husband would restore it to its original glory, if not make it better.

The Gerbers both showed excitement and a degree of surprise. But neither hesitated—they would sell the farm with all of its functioning equipment to the Jameses. Preventing the bank from foreclosing on the farm was not their sole reason for accepting Nelly's offer. They genuinely felt comfortable and enamored with Nelly. They trusted her.

The Gerbers and Nelly sealed the informal deal with handshakes and hugs and agreed to have their lawyers take care of the details of the sale and closing in the coming weeks.

Nelly was excited. She could not wait to get out of the Gerbers' house to share the good news with Hugo. In just a few weeks, they would be the proud owners of a farm with much more acreage than they had hoped for and at a much lower cost than they'd expected.

Hugo and Nelly had yet another sleepless night. They stayed awake discussing their dilemma. They had set in motion an offer to purchase a farm, a large one at that, but they had no financial backings. The investment portfolio they'd built and money they'd saved over the years were in no way comparable to the amount required to purchase the farm.

Who would give them the mortgage? They had little or no time to find the answer.

The following morning, Nelly walked into Mr. Godfrey's office, leaning heavily on her cane. She was about to take him up on the offer he'd made to her years earlier.

Seldom had Mr. Godfrey seen Nelly with her cane. He knew immediately that she was in trouble.

"John," she said as she sat on the black leather sofa in his office overlooking the city, "you are my last resort."

Mr. Godfrey crossed the room and sat beside her.

Nelly took a deep breath and then told him of the business venture she and Hugo had embarked upon. "The trouble is, John, we are unable to secure a loan. Most of our loan applications were rejected."

Before she could finish, Mr. Godfrey offered to cosign on a loan with the bank that was currently holding the mortgage on the farm. "Nelly, I trust you enough to know that you can achieve anything you put your mind to."

With nothing else said, John Godfrey walked back to his desk, flipped through his Rolodex, picked up the telephone, and dialed. Within minutes, he was speaking to the CEO of MST Bank & Trust.

As he hung up the telephone, he repeated the advice Nelly had given him years earlier. "Make yourself visible, attend public functions and seminars, and meet potential clients." He smiled as he explained that he'd met the CEO of MST Bank while following her instructions. "Now we are not just acquaintances," he said. "We are best friends."

Before they knew it, Nelly and Hugo were signing papers for a mortgage in the local MST Bank, the very first bank that had denied their loan application.

Mr. Godfrey also took care of the closing, free of charge. This was his gift to Nelly, his miracle worker.

John Godfrey not only believed in Nelly but knew that she was destined for greatness. Because of her, his law firm had become one of the fastest-growing law firms in Mount Pleasant. He admired everything about Nelly. She had a strong sense of self; she was independent and self-confident; and despite her disability, she pushed herself to the extreme and strove for excellence in all her endeavors.

After Nelly and Hugo took possession of the farm, they worked more than sixteen hours a day, seven days a week. Nelly took care of the administrative part of the business and, though not very good at it, she sometimes tried her hand at farming. Hugo was solely responsible for the farming and technical part of the business.

Except for attending church on Sundays and occasionally having tea with the Honigs and Theresa, Nelly and Hugo had no social life.

In the first year of operation, the farm brought in a very small profit. This made it possible for Hugo to take on additional staff, including someone to assist him with his grafting. With perseverance, hard work, and good weather, the farm brought in record-breaking profits within the first five years. Nelly never missed a mortgage payment. Nor was she ever late.

Mr. Godfrey was extremely proud of Nelly and Hugo's progress. He continued to be their biggest advocate. He gave them unlimited access to his private phone. They could call him anytime, day or night.

PART THREE

Nelly

But for the Love of Her
Children When Hope
Was Not Enough

Chapter 8

For the first time in her life, Nelly was faced with a situation she found impossible to handle. Her ability to find strength to cope with the loss of both her children eluded her. Nelly's determination and will of steel, which had sustained and ensured her survival and success throughout her life, seemed like things of the distant past. It was as if her soul had been sapped from her mortal body. Her heart was broken, and the emptiness she felt within was unbearable.

For ten straight hours after Stella was removed from her home, Nelly cried uncontrollably. And try as they may, no one could comfort her.

Hugo tried rocking her, talking to her, feeding her, and crying with her. Nothing worked. To Nelly, nothing mattered. It was as if she had entered a zone where no one else could enter, and she was not allowed to leave.

With tears in his eyes, Hugo stood helplessly watching his wife, whom he sometimes referred to as Super Woman, fall to pieces. Like Nelly, his world was shattered; nevertheless, he had to force himself to stay strong, as his overwhelming concern for her mental state increased. His main focus was to help Nelly.

Despite the many hardships they'd endured in the past, Hugo had never seen Nelly fall apart. Nelly had always been able to pull herself together with lightning speed, no matter what the circumstance. She was the rock on which the James family stood. To put it mildly, Nelly was the Jameses' Rock of Gibraltar. Hugo could not bear to see that rock crumble.

Hugo persistently consulted with Nelly's physician on her condition. He placed her under constant supervision and relied heavily on moral support from the Honigs and from Theresa, who canceled her singing engagements in Europe to be with Nelly.

In his desperation, Hugo daringly called Susan for advice.

"You created your problems," Susan told him. "Deal with it." Without uttering a single word of sympathy, she hung up the telephone on Hugo.

As time slowly dragged on, Hugo, the Honigs, and Theresa continued desperately to comfort Nelly. Theresa reminded her of the good times they'd had during their childhood years. Nelly appeared unable to comprehend. The Honigs brought over her favorite meal. She would not eat. They encouraged her to remain confident that Stella and Eric would be returned to them. Like Hugo, they were unable to bring her comfort or pull her out of her unresponsive state.

Not knowing where else to turn, Hugo picked up the telephone and dialed John Godfrey. His voice and his entire body shook uncontrollably as he described Nelly's condition. The telephone eventually fell from his hands as he dropped to his knees, and with his hands clasped at the back of his neck and his head placed beneath his elbows, Hugo screamed for divine intervention.

Within minutes, Mr. Godfrey and Mr. Oxford, senior partner and highly acclaimed family law attorney, arrived at the James residence.

On seeing Nelly, Mr. Godfrey became brokenhearted and livid all at the same time. He was deeply troubled by the position the Department of Social Services had taken. He vowed to do everything in his power to have Stella reunited with her parents as soon as possible.

Together, Mr. Godfrey and Mr. Oxford moved swiftly to have the decision to remove Stella from her natural home reversed. They succeeded in getting an emergency hearing, but their petition to reunite Stella with her parents was denied. A trial date was scheduled to hear arguments six weeks to the date from the day Stella had been taken from her home.

Upon Hugo's request, Mr. Oxford begged the court to appoint Mrs. Honig as Stella's guardian while they awaited the trial.

The attorney for DSS argued that the Honigs were not registered foster parents, and that such appointment would leave Stella in danger, as the Honigs and the Jameses are bosom buddies.

The judge ruled in favor of the Department of Social Services.

With Mr. Godfrey and Mr. Robert Oxford working to get Stella home, Nelly gradually regained both her mental and physical strength.

Two days following the court's denial of the Jameses' petition, Mr. Oxford had a letter hand delivered to the director of Mount Pleasant Social Services Department. He requested permission for Nelly and Hugo to visit with Stella.

Mr. Oxford's office was contacted by telephone, the following day. His secretary was advised that Mr. Oxford's request was denied. The DSS contended that it would be disruptive and not in the minor's best interest for Nelly and Hugo to have any contact with Stella before the trial.

Nelly was devastated. The following day, she personally called the department and pleaded with Miss Newton's supervisor to allow her to see Stella for just one hour or at least talk to her over the telephone. Nelly's request was denied.

The supervisor would not tell Nelly where or with whom Stella had been placed. Her only response was, "The minor was placed with a foster parent, and she is doing well."

"You are wrong about me!" Nelly shouted over the telephone as her sorrow turned to rage and utter contempt for the system. "If you do not tell me where my daughter is, I will—"

Before Nelly could complete her statement, the phone went dead. Miss Newton's supervisor had disconnected the call.

Nelly called Mr. Oxford to explain what had transpired between her and the department. She felt somewhat strengthened as she tried to find alternate ways to see or talk to Stella.

Once again, her spirit broke when Mr. Oxford told her that nothing could be done until the trial.

Nelly suggested hiring a private investigator to find out where Stella was. Mr. Oxford advised her against taking such a measure, for fear such an attempt would hurt her chances of ever reuniting with Stella.

Nelly decided to take Mr. Oxford's advice, and during the six weeks that followed, she worked to regain her strength and preserve her sanity. She embarked upon a project that brought her great joy in the presence of sorrow and pain. For a few hours each day, Nelly arranged and rearranged pictures in Eric's and Stella's photo albums. First, she worked on Eric's album, starting from his pictures taken at birth. She labeled and set each picture in order of age and events. All Eric's pictures up to two days prior to his disappearance were neatly positioned.

She did the same with pictures taken of Stella from birth to present. This turned out to be a more difficult task than Nelly had envisioned. Nevertheless, she refused to allow anyone to assist. Her determination to do the photos on her own was her way of grieving for her children while keeping their memories firmly secured in her mind and in her heart.

Throughout the entire project, Nelly reminisced about Stella and Eric and the happy times they'd had together. She replayed every moment she'd spent with them. Her mind filled with images of giving the children their baths together, taking them for long walks, and playing with them in the pasture at the farm. She remembered their first steps taken and their first words uttered.

Nelly recalled the many times she'd stood at the window overlooking the backyard, watching Stella, hands on her hips, pretending to be Eric's mummy.

Through tears and laughter, sadness and joy, Nelly completed four large albums in which her family activities were carefully recorded. She then wrote two identical notes and placed them at the very beginning of Stella's and Eric's first photo albums:

> My darling children:
> Of all my accomplishments in life, none was as great as having you, holding you, loving you, and seeing you blossom into the most wonderful children a mother could ever hope for. You are my greatest treasures. You brought me joy when I faced sadness. You brought me

hope when I was in despair. You made me smile when, in my heart, I felt like crying. You gave me life when I felt like dying. I loved you then. I love you now. I will love you to the very end. No matter what life throws upon us, my love for you will grow eternally.
Love forever,
Mommy

When Nelly completed the albums, she could not hold back her tears as she flipped through the pages. She was overwhelmed by the love she felt within and the emptiness that surrounded it. Some of the photos were saturated, as Nelly's tears fell upon them. She had neither the strength nor the desire to wipe away the tears or remove the photos. She left them as they were.

Nelly had once stood five foot seven and weighed 165 pounds. Within weeks of the disappearance of Eric and the removal of Stella from her home, Nelly lost thirty-five pounds. The loss of her body weight affected not only Nelly's stature but also her already severe limp, making it more pronounced. This resulted in Nelly's complete reliance on her cane and on her wheelchair. By the time Nelly regained her desire for food, she found it extremely difficult to swallow or eat a full meal without gagging and eventually vomiting. Even her favorite foods could not be easily swallowed.

Nelly's physician recommended gradual consumption of light soups before moving onto regular meals. With the help and support of Hugo and Theresa, Nelly eventually overcame the gagging problem. Feeling a bit stronger, Nelly willed herself to attend church after a two-week hiatus. In church, she asked God for strength in dealing with her present situation and thanked Him for the most precious gifts He had bestowed upon her—her children. Nelly also thanked God for Hugo and all those who had stood and continued to stand with them throughout their ordeal.

At the onset of their problems, Hugo had relinquished most of the farm's operations to his assistant while he stayed at home with Nelly. He turned over complete management of the Jameses' major business portfolios to Mr. Godfrey, who was already comanager of the family assets.

As Nelly grew stronger, she forced herself to stay busy. Gradually, she was able to spend at least five hours each day relieving her assistant of administrative duties and tending to small business matters.

At times she felt overwhelmed and drained of strength and spirit, but she plunged ahead. Between tears, prayers, and great memories of her children, she managed to accomplish her tasks.

Other than Hugo, one person Nelly always trusted with her business affairs was Mr. Godfrey. As such, she made permanent his position as manager of all of the Jameses' business portfolios and assets while concentrating on her recovery.

Although he served as the family attorney, Mr. Godfrey was like a brother and business advisor to Nelly. Through him, she learned the dos and don'ts of the business world and its operations. Some of her business contacts had come through him. They informed each other of new business ventures worth investing in.

Mr. Godfrey often credited Nelly as being the driving force behind his successful law practice. He believed without a doubt that Nelly's strength in spirit and her willpower were what inspired him most, and he was counting on those qualities to take her through her trials.

Like Nelly and Hugo, six weeks seemed an eternity for little Stella. Her new home was comfortable. Yet she could not enjoy its comfort. She yearned for her parents. As far as she was concerned, this was not her home, and no place could ever be home as long as she was in the midst of complete strangers.

Her foster parents, Tom and Lillian Potter, had been married for fifteen years. They had two biological children, Jerome and Sebastian, and were foster parents to Joanna and Dunstan. The entire family seemed happy and accommodating. They welcomed Stella and tried their hardest to make her feel at home. The children included her in their activities, and each child fought to make her his or her best friend.

All of their efforts seemed in vain, as nothing they did could take away her pain, anguish, and sorrow. Stella was experiencing an inner void, which her foster family could never fill. All of their collaborative efforts to fill that void only succeeded in isolating her further. The kindness they displayed toward Stella led her to believe the Potters were trying to take the place of her family, and she fully resented that. She would never accept their love, and she surely would not allow them to replace her parents.

In order to preserve her parents place in her life and in her heart, Stella purposely remained distant from the Potters. She refused to be in their company unless she had to, and even then, she was there in body only. She was like a zombie in a strange land. Her heart, mind, and soul were at home with her parents, where she knew they belonged.

At nights, Stella cried herself to sleep. And most often, she lay in bed thinking and wishing she were home.

By the middle of her third week with the Potters, Stella was having nightmares about not returning to her natural home. This resulted in sleepless nights for both Stella and Joanna, the child with whom she shared her bedroom. Whenever the nightmare occurred, Stella would wake up screaming, thus preventing Joanna from having a full night's rest.

Like her mother, Stella was also pining away. Within the first two weeks of living with the Potters, she lost five pounds. By the beginning of the third week, bags had formed under her eyes. And by the fifth week, she was seriously lethargic.

Concerned about Stella's condition, the Potters repeatedly reported the young girl's condition to Miss Newton, who ignored it. To her, Stella's pining was normal and would eventually disappear.

Miss Newton's preoccupation with making Nelly pay for her disability and for her biracial marriage completely blinded her to what mattered most—the welfare of the child. In her attempt to teach Nelly and Hugo a lesson, Miss Newton violated the purpose for which the system was created—to protect the rights and well-being of those incapable of protecting themselves.

Based on her extensive and constant investigation of Nelly and

Hugo, Miss Newton knew that Stella was not in danger of being hurt by either of her parents. Yet she had convinced her superiors to take Stella away from Mr. and Mrs. James.

The only crime committed was that of keeping Stella away from her parents and infringing upon her right as a human being to be free and happy.

Chapter 9

Stella was scheduled for a Lincoln hearing before a family court judge six weeks to the date from when she was taken from her parents' home.

During her stay at the Potters she was given no information about her parents. She knew not whether they were dead or alive. However, two days before the hearing, as instructed by Miss Newton, Mrs. Potter informed Stella that she had to appear before a judge and that her parents were going to be there.

For the first time since she had been placed with the Potters, Stella smiled a happy smile. During the next two days, she ate her meals and spoke to her foster siblings. She even volunteered to go to the supermarket with Mrs. Potter.

The change was immediate. It was as if she had broken out of her shell or been set free from bondage. In just two days, she looked stronger than she had in weeks. Her spirit soared, and for the first time in a long time, she began to feel like herself again.

For Stella, the day of the hearing started early. She got out of bed at the crack of dawn and sat for the next hour staring out the window.

"What are you doing, Stell?" Joanna asked, still drowsy from her sleep. "What time is it?"

With a grin on her face and a chuckle in her voice, Stella replied, "I am looking at the rising sun."

She was fascinated by the glowing stars in the twilit morning sky as the gray clouds rolled away, giving rise to a bright coral-pink sky. In the midst of that miraculous transformation, Stella envisioned hope. "I never knew that the sky looked so pretty at dawn," Stella said to Joanna after a period of silence. "I thought it only looked pretty when the sun goes down."

Joanna was now up and sitting in bed. "Silly! You live on a farm, and you don't know that?"

"I am only six years old," Stella replied with laughter. "I never look at the sky that early in the morning."

Stella washed and was ready for breakfast before seven thirty. She could not wait to see her parents.

After breakfast, Mrs. Potter helped Stella get dressed for her day in court. She wore the red-and-white polka-dot dress the Potters had given her as a welcoming gift the day after she'd arrived. It was coordinated with a pair of white leotards, red shoes, and two bows of white ribbons in her hair. Although she had lost weight, Stella looked exquisite in her red-and-white outfit as she sat on a stool at the kitchen window, waiting for Miss Newton to arrive.

As expected, Miss Newton arrived right on time, 9:00 a.m. to be exact. She hustled Stella into her parked car in the Potters driveway and drove off before Stella could say good-bye to Mrs. Potter.

Back at the Jameses' house, Nelly too was up at the crack of dawn. She and Hugo, accompanied by the Honigs and Theresa attended the 6:30 a.m. Mass officiated by Father Malaccan. As usual, Nelly prayed for strength, and as she left the church that morning, she was overcome by the strangest of sensations.

She felt happy and free, as if a weight had been lifted off her shoulders. Concurrently, she was eclipsed by a sense of sadness. Nelly became overwhelmed by the contradictory emotions and what they might presage.

Later that morning as Nelly, Hugo, and Theresa left the James farm and headed to the courthouse, Nelly told Theresa about the strange feelings she had experienced while leaving church earlier that morning.

"Considering what you have been through, this is normal," Theresa replied.

"No, Theresa," Nelly responded. "There was nothing normal about the way I felt. It was like a premonition. You would have to experience it to know what I'm talking about." Nelly said nothing further about the incident to anyone, not even to Hugo.

The Lincoln hearing was scheduled to begin at 9:30 a.m. in Judge Crampton's courtroom, number 13, followed immediately by the family court trial. The group arrived at the county courthouse an hour early. They were standing at the door of courtroom number 13 awaiting the arrival of their lawyers when Miss Newton walked in with Stella. She was holding onto Stella's hand and moving so quickly through the corridors that it appeared as if she was dragging Stella behind her.

Upon seeing her parents, Stella freed herself from Miss Newton's grasp and rushed into the open arms of her mother. Nelly held her tightly as they both broke down in tears.

"Mommy," Stella whispered hoarsely through her tears, "please don't let them take me away again."

Nelly was so overwhelmed with the joy of seeing her daughter that she did not see Miss Newton storming toward her. Before she could answer Stella, as quick as lightning, Miss Newton snatched Stella away from her arms, causing Nelly to sway backward.

"This is against policy," she grumbled as she rushed Stella past Hugo, who had his arms outstretched, ready to put them around Stella and Nelly.

With no remorse, Miss Newton entered courtroom number 13 and took a seat next to the DSS attorney, while Stella was escorted into the judge's chamber by a female officer of the court.

Based on the events that had transpired within the past months, Hugo should not have been surprised by Miss Newton's action. Nevertheless, he was. He stood wondering what hatred could possess anyone to treat a human being the way Miss Newton treated Nelly.

Mr. Oxford and Mr. Godfrey had walked into the courthouse just in time to witness Miss Newton's appalling treatment of the Jameses. They were already troubled by the system, but this latest act infuriated them. Without saying a word, Mr. Godfrey walked over to Nelly, placed his hand on her shoulder, and led her into courtroom number 13.

After a short interval with Stella, Judge Crampton and Mr. Oxford in the judge's chamber, the bailiff entered. He called the court to order as Judge Crampton, gavel in hand, came into the courtroom and took his seat behind the bench. The judge instructed the bailiff to escort Stella from his chamber to the witness stand, where he asked her three set questions.

First, she was asked if she missed her parents, and whether she wanted to return home. She was then asked if she loved her new home. Finally, the judge asked Stella if she thought her mom and dad were bad people.

Stella answered his questions with reverence and innocence. Then as Judge Crampton was about to have the bailiff remove her from the witness stand, the little girl turned to him with tears in her eyes and pleaded. "Mr. Judge, sir, please do not let that evil lady"—she pointed to Miss Newton—"take me away again. Nobody in the world could make me happier than Mummy and Daddy could. They love me, and I love them."

The judge smiled but quickly slammed his gavel against his desk to bring order to the court as the attendants laughed, scoffed at Miss Newton, and cheered Stella's courage. He then motioned the bailiff to escort Stella from the witness box.

As was customary, Stella was taken from the courthouse to a facility close to the Department of Social Services to await the judge's decision.

Nelly and Hugo had beamed with pride as they'd listened to their daughter's plea to the judge. Like many of the attendants in the courtroom, they'd had tears in their eyes throughout her testimony.

Nelly's pride changed to anger as Stella was escorted out of the courthouse. She was infuriated and about to rise in protest when Mr. Godfrey stopped her. "In order to protect minors from the kind of testimonies that are sometimes heard in these cases," he explained, "it is customary for the court to have the minor removed before other witnesses are called to testify."

"Oh," Nelly responded as she straightened herself in her seat.

The judge instructed the lawyers to give their opening statements.

Mr. Bathalemu, one of the DSS lawyers, stood. He was wearing a black suit and a red tie. He looked very stern and ready for action. With a picture of Eric in his hand, he walked to the middle of the courtroom, and, as if speaking to a jury, he said, simply, "Eric." After a pause, he continued. "Your honor, my learned friend will tell you that this case is all about discrimination, but let us look at the facts. Eric James went missing more than twelve weeks ago, and he was last seen by his mother, Nelly James. Whether she is responsible for physically harming him or not, I will submit to the court that because of her inability to take care of a family, Eric, her only son, is now missing and feared dead. With this in mind, Your Honor, I ask the court to relinquish the Jameses' parental rights to the minor Stella James, for fear that the same fate will befall her."

When Mr. Bathalemu returned to his seat, Mr. Oxford slowly rose, looked over at Nelly, and then turned back to the judge. "Your Honor," he said, "it is quite unfortunate that our taxpayers' money and the court's time are being wasted in this manner. Mrs. James is not on trial for bringing harm to any of her children. In fact, no criminal charges have been brought against her. Contrary to what our government agency would like to insinuate, Eric is still listed as missing, not dead." He paused. "For years, this agency has tried to label my client, Nelly James, an unfit mother because of her inability to walk as straight as the rest of us do. She is different and, therefore, should not be as good as we are. Your Honor, if this is not discrimination, what is? Stella, Nelly's daughter, was taken away from Nelly not because Nelly is an unfit mother. She was not taken away because Nelly committed a crime. Stella James was taken away because Nelly refuses to allow people like us to dictate to her what she should or should not do."

He continued, "Your Honor, Nelly does not walk as perfectly as you or I, but she is a good mother, better than most mothers I know. Your Honor, I will prove to the court that Mrs. James is a good mother and that the claim against her ability as a mother is blatantly discriminatory. I, therefore, ask the court to have Stella James, Nelly's daughter, immediately returned to her parents with no further attempts by the Department of Social Services to remove the minor from her biological home."

After Mr. Oxford's opening statement, witnesses for both sides were called to the stand. Among those testifying for the Department of Social Services were Miss Newton, Susan Roberts, and Lenora James. Mrs. Roberts and Mrs. James testified that choosing to marry and have children had been a predestined curse for Hugo and Nelly from the onset.

Upon cross-examination of Susan Roberts by Mr. Oxford, it was discovered that Miss Newton and Susan had attended high school together. When Nelly was pregnant with Stella, Susan had contacted Miss Newton and expressed her opposition to the marriage and pregnancy. She'd questioned Nelly and Hugo's ability to raise a family and had requested, from an old friend, an investigation into the suitability of Nelly and Hugo to raise children.

Since then, Miss Newton had become actively involved in Nelly's life. Her first attempt to block Nelly from motherhood had been to convince Nelly to place her firstborn, Stella, up for adoption. When this failed, Miss Newton had investigated Nelly and Hugo on an ongoing basis, almost to the point of harassment.

Among those testifying on behalf of Nelly were Mr. Godfrey, Theresa, the Honigs, and the Jameses' immediate household staff.

Overall, the parade of witnesses on the stand took almost three days. By the time the lawyers' summations were heard on the third day, the judge looked like he was ready to bring the trial to an immediate end and he did.

It was nearly a quarter to noon when the lawyers rested their cases. The judge adjourned and informed all parties to stick around, as he would have a verdict before the end of the day. He picked up his gavel and the documents lying on his desk and walked out of the courtroom through the door leading to his chamber.

Nelly and Hugo followed Mr. Oxford and Mr. Godfrey into the conference room adjoining courtroom number 13. Assuming that at least one hour would be set aside for lunch, Mr. Godfrey invited Nelly and Hugo to join them at the restaurant across the street for a bite.

Though she had not eaten, Nelly rejected the offer. She had no intention of leaving the room until the judge's return.

Nelly paced the room from one end to the next.

"Sit down, Nell," Hugo urged. "You are going to bore a hole in the floor."

Nelly was so deep in thought she did not hear a word he said. The two lawyers left and shortly thereafter, Mrs. Honig entered the room carrying two club sandwiches and two cups of coffee on a Styrofoam tray.

"Here," she said, as she handed Hugo the tray. "Mr. Godfrey said to eat something."

Hugo ate half of a sandwich, while Nelly left hers untouched. She hardly noticed the sandwich as she continued to pace back and forth.

Three hours into the recess, the telephone in the meeting room rang. Mr. Oxford answered. It was a court officer informing him that the judge was about to return.

Before Mr. Oxford could finish affirming what he had heard, Nelly rushed through the door, leaning heavily on her cane with every step she took. Despite her condition, she entered courtroom number 13 before Hugo and her lawyers.

The court was called to order as Judge Crampton entered, looking extremely serious. His demeanor was far from polite when he asked the involved parties to stand. He held his gavel with both hands, looked at it, and shook his head. "It is days like these that keep me sitting on this bench," he said. "The underdogs of this world need a modern-day Robin Hood to fight the injustices that some of our agencies inflict upon them just because they have the power to do so. Today, I feel like Robin Hood, ready to do some justice." After a thud on his desk with the gavel, Judge Crampton quietly laid down the gavel and sat in his chair.

He proceeded to read the verdict. "It is ordered that Stella James be immediately returned to her biological parents, Hugo and Nelly James."

He turned toward Miss Newton and the lawyers for the government and, in a scolding manner, he continued. "This whole situation is an abomination and should never have happened. There is no evidence that Mrs. James committed a crime against her son, Eric James, for whom she now grieves. There is also no evidence that Mr. and Mrs. James are unfit parents, unable to care for their daughter. I find the decision to remove the child, Stella James, from her parental home, at a time of grief, both reckless and highly prejudicial."

Judge Crampton paused; took a drink from the cup sitting on his desk; and then, looking toward Miss Newton, he added, "I am also ordering an investigation into the agency's misuse of its power and its policies toward the disabled. This court is now adjourned."

Without another word, Judge Crampton picked up his gavel and walked out of the courtroom into his chamber.

Before the door closed behind the judge, Nelly dropped into her seat and wiped a joyful tear from her eyes. Hugo reached over and hugged her as tears rolled down his cheeks. Mr. Godfrey moved in to hug Nelly but quickly moved back as Theresa and the Honigs rushed over to congratulate them.

Despite Nelly's emotional state, she wasted no time asking for the address where Stella was waiting to be picked up. Mr. Oxford handed her a card on which the address for the facility was written and informed her that he would meet them there.

Chapter 10

*N*elly and Hugo rushed out of the courthouse to their Land Rover in the parking lot. Theresa had driven with them to court but decided to give them a chance to be alone with Stella. She took a ride with the Honigs.

Mr. Oxford had double-parked, blocking the Jameses' Land Rover when he'd arrived at the courthouse earlier that morning, so he hurried to let them out. He backed off to the side as Hugo backed up and pulled out of the parking lot onto Main Street. From Main Street, Hugo made a left turn heading north onto Jarvis Street, the street on which the facility was located. The lawyers drove behind him.

Two street lights ahead, at the intersection of Jarvis and Lapel Avenue, Hugo stopped behind a blue Cutlass sedan as the streetlight turned red. About two minutes later, the light changed to green, and the sedan pulled out. Hugo proceeded behind it. At the middle of the intersection, a large, eighteen-wheeled tractor-trailer traveling east on Lapel Avenue ran the red light and slammed directly into Hugo and Nelly's Land Rover.

Mr. Oxford, who was following close behind, saw the impact and immediately pressed on his brake and swerved to avoid running into the rubble in front of him.

He jumped out of his car, and rushed to the telephone booth at the southwest corner of Jarvis and Lapel. Trembling like a leaf, Mr. Oxford dialed the 911 operator for assistance. Within minutes, an ambulance, fire trucks, and police cruisers were on the scene. A host of other vehicles came to a standstill, both because the traffic was blocked and because motorists wanted to see what was going on.

Hugo was pronounced dead on impact as he had crashed headfirst into the Land Rover's windshield.

Using the Jaws of Life, rescuers spent almost thirty minutes removing Nelly from what remained of the Land Rover that had been reduced to rubble in less than a minute. Nelly was rushed to the hospital, where she would be pronounced dead on arrival. The autopsy later would show that she'd died of internal hemorrhaging caused by injuries to the head and internal organs.

The driver of the tractor-trailer sustained minor injuries. He had just finished working a twenty-four-hour shift and was returning the truck to the base, which was located only two blocks from where the accident occurred. During the investigation that followed, it would be discovered that he had fallen asleep at the wheel.

It had taken some time for Mr. Oxford to pull himself out of the numb revulsion of shock as emergency crews flooded the scene. He could not stop wondering what was worse—having been a witness to such a catastrophic accident or the knowledge that it could have been him lying in the rubble that still lined the intersection. Had he not pulled aside and allowed Hugo to go ahead of him, he would have been dead. The thought of that continued to send chills running through his spine and tears rolling down his cheeks. He had seen his life flash before his very eyes.

When the shock wore off, Mr. Oxford's emotions had shifted from dismay to profound outrage, and right there, in the middle of Jarvis Street, he'd vowed to avenge the deaths of Nelly and Hugo James: for, having witnessed the horrific aftermath, he knew without being told that neither had survived. "As God is my witness," he swore, "I will make the system pay for the devastation brought upon this family."

Now, with his mind cleared, Mr. Oxford realized that he needed to make some quick decisions for Stella's sake. He headed back to the courthouse to seek an immediate conference with Judge Crampton. He was determined to see to it that Stella would not remain under the control of the Department of Social Services and Miss Newton for one more minute. He was lucky to catch the judge just as he was about to leave his chamber.

"I heard," Judge Crampton said, as Mr. Oxford walked in. Not only had he heard the crash from his chamber, but Miss Newton had already approached him with a request to have Stella returned to the Potters.

Mr. Oxford explained his concern for Stella's well-being. He asked that the judge appoint a psychologist to be present when Stella heard of her parents' death and during her mourning period.

The request for the psychologist was immediately granted. However, the judge ordered that Stella be taken back to her foster parents pending a new hearing to determine, for her, a suitable and permanent place of residence. That hearing was set to take place two weeks from the date of her parents' passing.

Mr. Oxford pleaded with Judge Crampton to give temporary custody of Stella to the Honigs. The judge refused.

Having to tell Stella, a six-year-old, that both her parents were dead soon after she had lost her only sibling was unimaginable.

Mrs. Honig volunteered to break the news to Stella. She tried to be as calm as she knew Nelly would have been, but by the time she was finished explaining to Stella what had happened, everyone in the room was in tears. Even Patricia Sybolis, the court-appointed psychologist, was crying.

No one was able to get Stella to calm down. Her overwhelming show of emotion was not just for the loss of her parents; she was also mourning the loss of her happy and familiar home.

Minutes after Stella received the heart-wrenching news, Miss Newton entered the room, and without a word of sympathy, she attempted to take Stella away.

Stella held onto Mrs. Honig and would not let go. Miss Newton tugged at Stella's arms in her attempt to pry the little girl loose. This became a struggle of will, and although Miss Newton was bigger and stronger, she was unable to pull Stella away. Instead, she, Stella, and Mrs. Honig all landed on the floor.

Miss Newton's malicious and insensitive behavior drove Mr. Oxford into a rage. He picked up Miss Newton by her upper arm and practically dragged her out of the room and closed the door behind her. "This woman has no conscience," he snapped. "She is an insufferable lunatic."

With gentle persuasion by Mrs. Honig and Theresa and a promise that she would soon return to the farm, Stella calmed down and left the room with Patricia Sybolis.

Arrangements for the Jameses' interment were made by Mr. Godfrey, Mrs. Honig, and Theresa. Three days after their death, they were given a small funeral attended by a few friends from Nelly and Hugo's church, business acquaintances, and other relatives. They were buried in a mausoleum constructed on the farm exclusively for the James family.

Stella attended the funeral with her foster parents, but her demeanor was somewhat anesthetized. She moved like a zombie and seemed out of touch with her surrounding. She did not cry one tear as she sat staring into space.

During the week following the deaths of Hugo and Nelly James, life seemed almost unbearable for Stella. When not in a daze, she tried talking to the Potter children about Ricki and her parents. They changed the subject every time, as they had been instructed not to discuss that topic. Only her psychologist was allowed to talk to Stella about her loss, and even then, not much was said. The psychologist's main objective was to erase from Stella's mind the memories of her family.

Stella had been told that her parents were in heaven, but she could not understand what she had done to send them there or why no one would talk to her about it. To cope with her loss, Stella again became reclusive and void of emotions. She talked to no one, except to answer questions. Night after night, while everyone was asleep, she lay awake for hours, staring at the ceiling before crying herself to sleep. Soon, the sparkle in Stella's eyes had been completely extinguished as she grieved in silence.

Her psychologist suggested that returning to school would help alleviate the pain. This failed miserably, as Stella was placed in an environment where she knew no one. And making new friends wasn't on Stella's radar. She was quiet and withdrawn, and the other children knew not how to approach her even if they wanted to.

By the middle of her second week of mourning, Stella had the first of many dreams about her mother and father. In that dream, Nelly and Hugo comforted her, telling her that she had done nothing wrong and encouraging her to be strong. When Stella woke the following morning, the first thing she remembered was the smile on her mother's face.

"She is happy," Stella whispered. "Mommy is happy." Then for the first time since the death of her parents, Stella smiled.

Gradually she emerged from her solemn state, but the sparkle in her eyes remained a distant memory.

Chapter 11

After the funeral, Mr. Godfrey was in his office looking at a newly compiled list of the Jameses' financial portfolio when Mr. Oxford walked in.

"John," he said, "I need to talk to you."

Mr. Oxford was unable to get past the despicable actions the Mount Pleasant DSS had taken against the Jameses. Now, more than ever, he was determined to follow through on his vow to avenge their deaths. Mr. Godfrey lifted his gaze toward Mr. Oxford, who, with no wavering or uncertainty in his voice, made known to Mr. Godfrey his intent to bring a lawsuit against the Mount Pleasant Department of Social Services. Mr. Godfrey was taken aback at the revelation but remained silent as he kept his eyes fixed on Mr. Oxford.

"I hope that I have your blessing," Mr. Oxford said to Mr. Godfrey. "Someone has to take responsibility for what was done to Stella. No child should have to suffer because of the system's inability to deal with diversity." His voice trembled. "Nothing but prejudice was shown toward the Jameses. Nelly died because of her inability to walk like us, and Hugo, because of his race. John, some may say that the people in the agency were not driving the tractor-trailer that killed Nelly and Hugo, but they created the situation that placed them in that location at the time of their deaths. For that, they are g-guilty." Tears were streaming down Mr. Oxford's cheeks as he spoke, and through the tears, he confessed his own personal ills regarding discrimination.

"John," he said, "I'm embarrassed to admit that I was against interracial marriage. Fortunately for me, I met Nelly and Hugo, and all that changed. After seeing firsthand the love that existed between them, I was rehabilitated. They had a love seldom seen among my people. It was a love that, at first, I could not understand. But I eventually realized that their love for each other and for their children was their greatest strength, which, in the end, became their greatest nemesis. They died because of it."

Mr. Oxford further revealed that his interaction with Nelly and Hugo during the last month of their lives had enhanced his ability to respect the differences in others. "For this," he said, "I am a better man."

"I understand, my friend. I truly understand," Mr. Godfrey murmured, shaking his head from side to side. "No one knows better than I do." He was remembering Nelly's dying words as he sat beside her in the ambulance on her way to the hospital.

"Tell Stell ... and Er ... E-Eric I l-love them," she had gasped. "Pl ... Please take c-care of them for ... for me," she had instructed him just before taking her last breath.

Mr. Godfrey sat quietly, staring into space, as if he were hearing Nelly's instructions all over again and communicating with the unseen.

With tears still running down his cheeks, Mr. Oxford waited for Mr. Godfrey's answer.

After an extended period of silence, Mr. Godfrey looked at Mr. Oxford and gave his consent, with a strong warning. "If your intent to sue the DSS is solely for Stella's financial security or for your atonement, forget it. Stella is financially secure, and there are other ways for you to seek absolution. I have known Nelly for a very long time," Mr. Godfrey continued. "I have never met anyone as capable as she was, God bless her soul. If by suing the system you are able to prevent at least one family from enduring a portion of what Nelly and Hugo endured, then so be it. You have my blessing. For that reason, Nelly and Hugo would have also approved."

"This goes way beyond money," Mr. Oxford replied. "Short of dismantling the entire agency, this is the only way I can get those bureaucrats to acknowledge what they did to an innocent child and to be accountable for their actions. If it is the last thing I do, *Stella will receive justice.*"

⟜

Eight days after Nelly and Hugo were laid to rest, their Last Will and Testaments were read in the main conference room of Godfrey, Oxford, Smith, Jeremiah, & Associates. In attendance were Stella, her court-appointed psychologist, and Miss Newton, along with Mr. and Mrs. Honig, Theresa, Mr. Scuffey, Nelly's parents, Hugo's parents, all of the Roberts siblings, and the Jameses' employees.

While awaiting the arrival of the attorneys, Theresa overheard Hugo's mother telling her husband that if Nelly and Hugo had listened to reason, they would still be alive.

Theresa was dumbfounded by the statement and flew into a rage. She stopped short of physically throwing Mrs. James out of the room. For Stella's sake, she restrained herself from causing a commotion. Instead, she rebuked Mrs. James in a firm but low, steady voice. "Lady," she said, "you are completely out of order. You have tormented my sister, disowned and disinherited your son, and made their lives a living hell. Now that they are dead, please give them the chance to have the peace and respect they deserve."

Mrs. James showed no remorse. Nor did she indicate in any way that she was grieving the loss of her son. Instead, with a repugnant look, she scoffed at Theresa, and said, "Lady, mind your own business." Then she walked away.

The will was specific. Mr. Godfrey and Theresa were named coexecutor and executrix. Mr. Honig was named executor in the event that Theresa was unable to fulfill the obligations placed upon her. As expected, Stella and Eric were sole beneficiaries of the James estate in the event of the death of both parents. Theresa received a cash inheritance and a sealed envelope. The Honigs received a sealed envelope, on which was written, "To be opened only in the event of the deaths of Nelly and Hugo James." They were also willed some of the Jameses' personal possessions.

Nelly and Hugo left no stone unturned. The Jameses and the Robertses were each willed one dollar. Nelly's siblings, with the exception of Theresa, each received one dollar.

Mr. Scuffey and the permanent farmworkers were given lifelong employment and a stipend. The household staff also received cash.

Hugo's and Nelly's parents were in awe as Mr. Godfrey read the will. They were amazed by their children's accomplishments and the wealth they had amassed during their lifetimes. It was hard to imagine that through their adversities, Nelly and Hugo had been able to persevere and become wealthier than both of their sets of parents put together.

Mr. Godfrey was still reading the will when Mrs. Honig opened her sealed envelope. She immediately recognized Nelly's handwriting. And together, she and Mr. Honig read its contents. They were pleasantly amazed. Nelly and Hugo had entrusted to them the care of Stella and Eric, in the event of their deaths. Mr. and Mrs. Honig embraced each other as tears gushed down their cheeks. Nelly and Hugo, their beloved friends, had blessed them with something they could never have—children. They were overflowing with mixed emotions as they joyously cried over their inheritance and sadly mourned the death of their dearest friends.

Theresa simultaneously opened her envelope, and as she read the letter inside, she could not help remembering why she so dearly loved her sister.

"Nelly," she whispered, as a tear rolled down her cheek, "why did you have to be so wise? Why did you have to die?"

Nelly's letter to Theresa explained why the children should be with the Honigs. "You are so right, Sis. You are so very right," Theresa whispered softly as the continuous tears rolled off her cheeks and onto the handwritten letter on her lap.

The reading of the will in its entirety ended at approximately one thirty, with Mr. Godfrey stipulating the uncontested clause.

By two thirty, Mrs. Roberts was in her attorney's office, and Mrs. James was on the telephone instructing their attorneys to file for joint custody of Stella, the grandchild they did not want and had never taken the time to know.

PART FOUR

Stella

Alone in the World Yet Loved and Protected by a Legacy of the Past

Chapter 12

At the custody hearing, Theresa told the court how deeply suspicious she was of Susan and Lenora's sudden interest in Stella. She accused them of being interested in the wealth Nelly and Hugo had left behind and not in the granddaughter they now claimed to love.

To substantiate her charge, Theresa testified that at the time of Stella's birth, with assistance from Miss Newton, Susan and Lenora attempted to have Stella placed for adoption. They even sanctioned a couple to become the adoptive parents.

In their adoption petition to the hospital, they alleged that Nelly was an invalid who was unable to care for herself and most definitely could not care for an infant. Their petition was turned down, but in the years that followed, they had continued their quest to render Hugo and Nelly childless.

The motivation for their persistence was simple—Susan Roberts could not stomach being grandmother to biracial children, and Lenora could not get over what she termed her son's betrayal.

Theresa went on to explain that Hugo's parents had never taken the time to know Nelly, and although the Roberts family knew her, they had never looked past her disability. They had seen her through colored glasses and had allowed her circumstance to dictate their actions. They had concentrated on her physical condition and, in so doing, had failed to see her strengths and learn from her the virtue of sacrifice, the power of believing, and the value of self-worth.

Susan's and Lenora's losses were greater than those of Nelly's, Theresa added, and although time had passed, they had learned nothing. Their pursuit for custody of Stella was not an effort to right the wrong that they had done. Their goal was to reap the harvest of something they were never a part of, had never understood, and never would understand. All they saw in Stella was her wealth, and that was not hard to discern. Even Stella, a six-year-old child, was able to recognize that. They had paid her no attention during the funeral. But after the reading of the will, they had surrounded her like bees on nectar, pretending to be concerned about her well-being.

Theresa clarified to the court that she was the only relative who had not been estranged from Nelly. She added that her interaction with the children had not been nearly as frequent as that of the Honigs. Her career as an opera singer would make it impossible for Stella to be adopted by her, as Nelly had so eloquently stated in her letter, which she offered as evidence. As such, Theresa begged the court to honor Nelly's wishes and grant full custody of Stella to the Honigs.

At the end of her testimony, with tears flowing from her eyes, Theresa asked the court to do the right thing for Stella. "This child has suffered enough over the past months, Your Honor. Please let us not prolong her suffering. Place her where she is loved and will be properly cared for. Give her back her happiness."

After hearing testimonies from two more witnesses, the judge adjourned the court with a promise to carefully weigh all the evidence and render a decision within the week.

At the beginning of the third day following the hearing, all parties involved were summoned back to court. With no tedious explanation, Judge Crampton rendered full custody of Stella, with first right of adoption, to the Honigs. He instructed Stella's attorney, Mr. Oxford, to remain her legal guardian in all matters concerning her finances, until she reached the age of majority.

He ordered the Department Social Services to have Stella brought to the Honig residence no later than twelve thirty the following afternoon. He also ordered the continuation of Stella's therapy with her psychologist for a time period as determined by the psychologist or until she reached eighteen.

Susan, Lenora, and Miss Newton were unhappy with the outcome of the proceedings. They left the courtroom silently and with great dissatisfaction.

Susan and Lenora wasted no time instructing their attorneys to file appeals. They wanted to stop the will from going through probate by any means necessary.

All of their attempts to appeal were denied.

As Stella's legal guardian, Mr. Oxford filed a civil lawsuit against the Mount Pleasant Department of Social Services, its staff, and its management. He sought damages in excess of $10 million.

The suit made headlines on the local news and reached the national circuits soon thereafter. Mr. Oxford relied heavily on the widespread publicity and public opinion to help his case against the department. Nevertheless, he, Mr. Godfrey, and the Honigs were extremely vigilant of the media circus and fought to shelter Stella from the limelight.

After a hard-fought, five-year battle, the lawsuit ended without the case going to trial. It was settled out of court with a stipulation that "the settlement amount awarded to Stella James never be publicly disclosed." Stella was also awarded a huge settlement from the insurance company of the tractor-trailer's owner that had killed Hugo and Nelly. By the time the legal wrangling ended, Stella was millions of dollars richer than she had been before it all started.

Chapter 13

With Stella in the backseat of the car, Patricia Sybolis and Miss Newton pulled into the Honigs' driveway exactly one hour before the deadline set by Judge Crampton.

Coming from foster care, where everyone was cordial toward her, Stella felt somewhat apprehensive. The Honigs had always been good to her, but she had never lived with them and didn't know what to expect. That feeling disappeared as soon as the car came to a complete stop and the door on her side opened.

There to meet her with open arms and tears of joy were Mr. and Mrs. Honig, Theresa, Mr. Godfrey, Mr. Oxford, and Mr. Oxford's daughter, whom she was meeting for the very first time. They all stood in line and hugged and kissed her as she stepped out of the car. Seeing so many familiar faces brought back joy Stella had not felt since the day she'd last hugged her mother in court.

As the outpouring of love continued to flow toward her, Stella realized that she was in the right place, and what used to be her sad smile turned to laughter. She chatted and played with Nancy Oxford, her new eight-year-old friend, as if she'd known her all her life.

Mr. and Mrs. Honig were overjoyed and consumed with gratitude that Stella was finally in the place her parents had chosen for her, a place with unconditional love and affection. They, together with Mr. Oxford, were prepared to do everything necessary to ensure Stella's comfort, happiness, and peace of mind. Mr. Oxford showed his concern for Stella by pulling Nancy out of school to meet and be with her on her first day with the Honigs.

Though mesmerized by all the love and fuss surrounding her and the happiness she felt within, the emptiness in Stella's heart still lingered. The most precious people in her life were gone, and her broken heart could not easily be mended. She understood that her parents were dead and would never return. Nevertheless, she wished that they would reappear just for a moment.

Mrs. Honig could not wait to give Stella a grand tour of her temporary bedroom, which, with the exception of some family photos and childhood mementos, was a replica of her room at the farm. It was a room overflowing with love and memories of a wonderful and joyous past. She worked diligently to put everything in its place, just as Nelly would have.

As she was about to reveal to Stella what she thought was a masterpiece, Patricia Sybolis intervened. She wanted to examine the bedroom before Stella was allowed to enter. "I have to ensure that the bedroom and all living quarters are appropriate for a grieving child," she explained.

Mrs. Honig proudly accompanied her into the bedroom but was amazed by the woman's reaction. Upon entering, Patricia demanded that the entire bedroom be redecorated and certain items be immediately removed. She even wanted the color of the walls changed. She made it clear that under no circumstances would Stella be allowed to enter, much less sleep in, that bedroom until her demands were met.

Upon Mrs. Honig's request for an explanation, Patricia affirmed that her intention was to keep Stella away from anything that would continuously remind her of her past. "These things," she said, pointing to a family photo on the dresser, "will impede Stella's recovery. She will be unable to move forward if she is constantly reminded of what she had and lost. For those reasons," Patricia added, "any and all items that remind Stella of her family must be removed."

Mrs. Honig was disappointed by Patricia's demands but agreed to comply for Stella's sake. She would do anything to ensure Stella's happiness, and if her psychologist thought that distancing her from her past was the way to go, then so be it. She wanted Stella's transition to be smooth and problem-free. She wanted Stella to be Stella again. She moved Stella into another guest bedroom while she awaited completion of her newly renovated bedroom.

Mrs. Honig and Patricia were about to leave the bedroom when Miss Newton entered, uninvited. Without saying a word, Mrs. Honig grabbed her by the upper arm and led her away from the bedroom, through the living room, through the foyer, and out the front door.

Before closing the door, Mrs. Honig issued a warning to Miss Newton. "Ma'am," she said, "your business with this family has ended, and you are now trespassing. Don't ever show your face here again!" With that, she shut the door behind her.

Mr. Oxford, Mr. Honig, and Theresa all cheered.

"I wanted to do that a long time ago!" Mr. Godfrey exclaimed. "I am glad someone finally did."

Miss Newton did not return to the house, but her car horn roared as Patricia left instructions with the Honigs for her next visit with Stella.

"Good riddance to bad rubbish!" Theresa said. "That woman has inflicted enough grief upon my sister. It is time to see her disappear."

Patricia said not a word about the incident, but the apparent smile on her face said it all. She, too, was glad to see Miss Newton go.

Patricia's instructions to completely change Stella's room annoyed Mr. Godfrey and Mr. Oxford. They thought it absurd and overreaching on Patricia's part, so before following her instructions, they tried to have her removed.

Mr. Oxford filed an emergency petition to overturn Judge Crampton's order to keep Patricia on as Stella's psychologist. In the petition, he emphasized the psychologist's overreach and stated that the Honigs were capable of employing an independent psychologist to treat Stella.

The judge ruled that the Department of Social Services must remain a part of Stella's life in some capacity until she reached the age of majority. However, he offered Mr. Oxford the option of continuing with Patricia Sybolis, the psychologist, or having Miss Newton, the caseworker, reinstated.

Mr. Oxford opted for the lesser of the two evils.

Before long, all reminders of Stella's family, including pictures, portraits, and beddings, were packed in boxes headed for Mr. Oxford's basement.

Two weeks later, Stella was moved into her newly renovated bedroom. It was spacious, with a living room; a study area; two beds, one for Stella and the other to accommodate her friends; and a four-piece bathroom.

Stella loved her new bedroom suite but could not understand why all of her favorite items from her parents' home were missing. Even the childhood books Hugo and Nelly had read to her and Eric had been removed.

Patricia was overwhelmingly happy with the new bedroom, as she'd succeeded in having all reminders of Stella's family removed. She was also able to eradicate any and all memories of the Jameses from the rest of the Honig household.

The only connection Stella had to her now defunct family was the familiar face of her nanny, Mimi, who Patricia threatened to dismiss. That threat was put to rest after Patricia's encounter with Mr. Godfrey.

During that encounter, Mr. Godfrey warned Patricia that he knew more people in Mount Pleasant than she did and that if Stella's nanny was dismissed, her career as she knew it was not going to be the same.

Patricia said nothing more about Mimi's dismissal. However, Stella was forbidden from ever setting foot on the farm. In fact, her entire lifestyle was rearranged. It was as if her psychologist wanted to create for her a completely new identity—one in which she had no past and her parents and sibling had never existed.

Patricia mapped out a regimented life for Stella. From Sunday through Saturday, every minute of her every day was strategically planned and filled with activities. She took lessons in piano, swimming, and ballet; went ice-skating, and frequently visited the art gallery and science center. Regular travel out of Mount Pleasant also became part of Stella's extracurricular activities. The only time Stella had to think about her family was during the night, and even then, she was too tired to reminisce.

Her fondest memories of her parents continued to appear in dreams, which she shared with no one. Despite her tender age, Stella sensed their presence and knew they were guiding her. That gave her strength to face each day.

During Stella's first week with the Honigs, Mr. Oxford introduced her to his family, her soon-to-be extended family. He had three children. Raymond, his only son, was twelve years old; Nancy was eight; and India was four.

Surprisingly, Stella felt an immediate connection to the Oxford siblings—a connection she'd never made with other children while in foster care. With the Oxfords, she experienced a feeling of comfort and belonging. It was as if they had always been in her life. From the day she'd met Nancy at the Honigs, the two girls had become best friends and were almost inseparable. In addition, Raymond and India were fascinated with Stella and she with them. Overnight, Stella and the Oxford children were getting along like family.

Mrs. Oxford, too, was an exceptional lady. She treated Stella like her own.

As Stella grew older and began to understand the world around her, she wondered what good her parents had done to leave with her such a rich and wonderful legacy, one of love beyond all measures—love from people to whom she had no biological connection.

Like the Honigs and the Oxfords, Theresa played an integral role in Stella's life. She visited with and spoke to Stella as often as her career permitted. When possible, she booked her concert engagements to accommodate Stella's school plays, birthdays, and some holidays.

As Stella grew older, Theresa noticed how much she mirrored Nelly in both beauty and strength. Despite losing her entire family and having all visibly memories of them taken away, Stella showed animosity toward no one. Like Nelly, she just kept on living and making the best of everything she did.

Theresa yearned to tell Stella all about Nelly. She wanted her to know that she was as strong and as brave as her mother, who loved her unconditionally. She ached, knowing how much she could comfort Stella but was not allowed to. Many times she was tempted to cradle

Stella and tell her everything, but remembering the psychologist's warning, she reluctantly resisted such temptations.

Theresa also acted as an emissary for Stella, protecting her from the numerous attempts made by Susan and Lenora to overturn her adoption. After Theresa's plea in court to award custody of Stella to the Honigs, Susan disinherited her and barred her from setting foot on the Robertses' property.

Theresa stayed away as ordered but continued to be in contact with Mr. Roberts, who had developed a guilty conscience for not protecting Nelly from Susan. As a remedy, he swore never to allow his vindictive wife to get her voracious grasp on Stella's inheritance. Thus, every time Susan set in motion her plans to overturn Stella's adoption, he contacted Theresa. Once contacted, Theresa would alert Mr. Oxford, who would take preemptive measures to ward off Susan's newest attack.

The Honigs loved Stella and were extremely protective of her. Stella returned their love twofold. At first, she found discomfort in calling them Mom and Dad, but as time progressed, that changed. For this, Mr. and Mrs. Honig's love for Stella grew ever stronger.

As Mrs. Honig admired the strength Stella exerted in handling the loss of her parents and sibling, she silently reminisced about her very first encounter with Nelly.

One day, she'd walked into Ladella's Meat Market and found herself in the middle of a gridlock between a customer and a clerk. That customer was Nelly. Apparently, Nelly had refused to move to the back of the line as ordered by the sales clerk. Her refusal had resulted in an overflow of patrons waiting to be served in an already crowded market.

The standoff started after Nelly had waited almost forty-five minutes for her number to be called. When it was finally called and Nelly got to the counter, she was told that she had taken too long and needed to take another number and wait her turn. Nelly was infuriated but calmly demanded that she be served. The clerk refused, so Nelly blocked the line with her cane. No one was able to get to that clerk, except through Nelly.

The clerk was adamant about her decision not to serve Nelly, and so the standoff continued. By the time Mrs. Honig walked in, the entire market was in an uproar. Some patrons were sympathetic toward Nelly, while others were cursing at her.

Nelly stood her ground. She was staring directly at the clerk as she calmly demanded that she talk to the manager. Nelly showed no fear of what might happen next. Neither did she show any emotion when some of the patrons called her names. She seemed oblivious to what was going on around her, yet her action was calculated and purposeful. It was as if she had experienced such attitudes before and was prepared to bring them to an end.

The confusion ended when the store manager arrived. Nelly calmly told her side of the story to the manager, who immediately apologized and demanded that the clerk do likewise. He personally served Nelly and offered her a special customer status, which she rejected.

"I demand to be treated exactly as everyone else," she said, "nothing more, nothing less."

Mrs. Honig, who had pushed her way through the crowd to witness what was happening, stood in awe of Nelly's determination. She was so impressed, that she followed Nelly through the parking lot as she made her way toward her car. It did not take her long to catch up with Nelly.

"Excuse me," she called as she approached Nelly. "I was fascinated by your action in the market." At that, she stretched out her hand toward Nelly and introduced herself. "Lucita Honig," she said in greeting.

"I am Nelly, Nelly James."

The two ladies started a conversation that led them to discover that they shared some commonalities. They were neighbors, and their birth dates were only two days apart. They also discovered that according to the norms of Mount Pleasant, they were both considered outsiders—Lucita because she was not a native of Mount Pleasant and Nelly because she was disabled and married to a black immigrant.

This tumultuous incident resulted in the birth of a lifetime relationship between Nelly, Lucita, and their families. The two women formed a bond that took very little time to solidify. They were like sisters. Their families got together during holidays and birthday celebrations. They vacationed together, if and when the Jameses were able to pull themselves away from their strenuous and busy schedules.

The Honigs were at the hospital for the birth of Eric. They were his godparents. Other than Mimi, they were the only people Nelly trusted enough to take care of the children during their absence.

The Honigs were honored to be the parents of Stella, and every day, Mrs. Honig prayed that she would be as good a mother as Nelly was.

Stella was loved not just because she was Stella or because of the loss of her parents and brother. She was loved because of her mother. Nelly had been a generous, honest, warm, and free-spirited human being. She'd been strong in her convictions but never overbearing. She'd sought fairness and had given it in return. Every life she'd touched had become better for it. For this, the people who surrounded Stella gave to her the love and care they'd received from her mother. Nelly was missed but not forgotten. In the hearts of those who loved and understood her, the presence of Stella kept the memory of Nelly burning ever stronger.

Chapter 14

$\mathcal{S}$ubsequent to her graduation from St. Benedict, Stella attended St. Augustine's Catholic High School. Since St. Augustine was located close to the Oxfords' home, arrangements were made for Stella to live with them during the week.

Stella welcomed the new living arrangement, as she was accustomed to spending time with the Oxford family. In fact, the Oxfords' residence soon became her home away from home. She enjoyed being in the company of her peers. She even started calling Mrs. and Mr. Oxford Mom and Pops.

Stella's new living arrangement allowed flexibility and saved her time. With it came easier access to her new school, her long, tedious daily drive in her chauffeured limousine was eliminated. Living in the city allowed her the opportunity to attend sports and social events on a regular basis. She was also closer to charitable organizations, for which she was quickly developing what would become a lifelong interest.

The only disadvantage to Stella's new living arrangement was her close proximity to Patricia Sybolis. With such proximity, Patricia now had quicker and easier access to Stella. She could now visit Stella on a more regular basis without even scheduling an appointment.

After her sixteenth birthday, Patricia gave Stella leeway to make some decisions with little or no interference. Stella was overjoyed because, in the absence of state-mandated scrutiny, she could participate more actively in activities of her choosing. One such activity was a grassroots organization that fought for rights and better conditions for disabled people.

The Honigs and Mr. Oxford encouraged Stella's participation in such activities as long as her studies were not compromised. Her schoolwork had to take precedence over all else.

For Stella, prioritizing was not difficult. She'd learned that discipline from her mother, and even Patricia could not take it away from her as she did everything else. It was that discipline that kept her maintaining a grade point average of 4.0 and remaining on the dean's list.

Stella was calculating and purposeful. Nothing important she did was done on impulse. Even her decision to become an attorney was deliberate. She was an avid reader, and at an early age, she'd developed a fascination for what was going on in her community and America as a whole. She realized that her wealth and the people by whom she was surrounded sheltered and protected her from the injustices and prejudices of her time. She was by far luckier than Hugo and Nelly ever were. She hoped to one day right some wrongs created by society. And to this end, Stella decided to become an attorney.

On the evening of her sixteenth birthday, during her surprise birthday party, Stella made her wish, blew out her sixteen candles, and calmly told Mr. Oxford what she wished for. "I will be a defender of the underdogs," she said. "I will be an attorney."

Mr. Oxford beamed with joy when she revealed to him her desire. For years, as he'd watched Stella blossom into a young, inquisitive lady, he'd silently wished that some day she would choose the legal profession, but he'd refrained from coercing her. She was not the type to do anything because someone wanted her to. She would listen, but in the final analysis, she would do things her way.

His next big wish for Stella was that she would join the law firm of Godfrey, Oxford, Smith, Jeremiah, & Associates. He encouraged her to utilize the law library at the firm as often as she could. And she took full advantage of that offer.

Stella was happy to finally have Patricia Sybolis out of her life, though, not completely. According to the adoption decree, she was required to visit her psychologist on a regular basis until the age of sixteen. After that, the visits with the psychologist would continue on an as-needed basis (a need she refused to have) until she was eighteen years old.

Stella confided to the Honigs that if she never saw Ms. Sybolis again, it would be too soon.

The end of Stella's so-called therapy brought with it the beginning of her emancipation. She now had freedom to do as she pleased, without Patricia's stamp of approval. She had freedom to tread on forbidden grounds—in other words, to visit her birthplace and rediscover her roots. This she made her first priority.

Soon after her sixteenth birthday, Stella informed the Honigs that she was going to the farm to visit her childhood residence. The Honigs became concerned and tried to discourage her. "Give it more time," they told her.

For Stella, more time was completely out of the question. "Ten years of waiting is long enough," she explained.

It was as if an unknown force was pulling her. She could not wait. She felt a powerful imperative to visit her childhood home.

The Honigs enlisted Mr. Oxford to encourage Stella to delay the visit only for a little while longer. He too failed. They finally gave up. They had all learned that arguing with Stella once her mind was set was futile. They knew that nothing they said or did would change her resolve.

Stella had always given them every reason to trust her judgment. In return, they allowed her the freedom to make important decisions. They could not change now. They could not betray their trust in her. Reluctantly, they reconsidered, and despite their deepest fears and concerns, they bestowed upon her the freedom to do as she desired.

Mrs. Honig accompanied Stella on her initial visit back to the James estate—ten years after Stella had been dragged away, kicking and screaming in the grasp of Miss Newton and two police officers. Mrs. Honig had visited the farm many times since that day; nevertheless, she found this visit extremely emotional.

As she drove through the heavy, black wrought iron gate and up the driveway to the courtyard, memories of years gone by came flooding through her mind. She remembered all the events that had transpired—from the day Eric went missing to the day Nelly and Hugo were killed. With Stella in the passenger's seat, driving through those gates was like déjà vu.

Mrs. Honig tried to hold back her tears but could not. Instead, she was blinded by tears gushing from her eyes. Next to her, Stella sat quietly, beaming with joy that radiated on her face as she looked up at the home she'd once lived in and loved.

It was not a memory of things she had done as a child that awakened the spirit of joy within Stella. In fact, she did not remember any of that past. It was the feelings of love, acceptance, joy, and happiness that engulfed her. She could not understand why. She just knew in her heart that even if she never remembered one single moment of her young life within those walls, the serene and peaceful feelings that resonated within her the moment she looked at that house told a million stories. It was a happy and peaceful home, full of love and joy.

Mrs. Honig parked her car and ascended the stairs with Stella in tow. They entered the house through the large wooden door leading directly from the front veranda.

Except for minor changes made by Theresa, who resided at the house whenever she was in Mount Pleasant, nothing had changed. Even the portrait of Franklin D. Roosevelt still hung over the mantel of the fireplace in the living room.

Stella looked with interest at every part of the house, but she remembered nothing. After exploring the entire house, she left with no memories of her past. Yet the warm and welcoming sensation stirring within left her happier than she'd ever remembered being.

Stella continued to make independent decisions after her initial visit to the house. No longer obligated to include her psychologist in any of those life-changing decisions, she curtailed practically all that Patricia had initially demanded of her. As she did, Stella wondered what all the fuss of keeping her away from her family's estate and everything that reminded her of them had been about. She was about to reverse it all anyway.

One week after her initial visit to the house, Stella went back. This time, she ventured beyond the residence. She visited the farm itself. She didn't know or couldn't remember any of the people who now worked on the farm. Nevertheless, as she made her way around the property, feelings of warmth, joy, and love continued to occupy her heart. Then, like a flash of lightning, she remembered. Those sensations were not new; she'd had them as a little girl. She remembered feeling constantly jovial and safe when she'd lived and played here so many years ago.

Stella tried to remember some physical event that might have caused her to feel that way. She could not. Her hiatus from the farm and the willful attempts by the Mount Pleasant Department of Social Services to eliminate her link to her past had resulted in the loss of some wonderful childhood memories.

In spite of it all, the warm, safe, and loving feelings that Stella had experienced as a child continued to hang on like ghosts within her soul. Stella could neither understand nor explain why she had lost so much in thoughts and memories yet retained so vividly the feelings of love and joy deep within.

Stella continued to reacquaint herself with her childhood home by visiting the farm regularly. During her visits, she spent hours in a shaded area underneath the large sycamore tree overshadowing the pond. There, she sat quietly and listened to the toads and the grasshoppers, and when those sounds could not be heard, she listened to the rattling of the wind beneath the leaves.

That shaded spot soon became her quiet place, where she enjoyed her most serene moments. She told no one about that spot, not even her best friend, Nancy. In that quiet space, Stella felt connected and at peace with her inner spirit. There, she quietly relaxed and envisioned herself as a little girl. In that place, she meditated and became one with nature. It was a place where Stella sat and put her thoughts on paper. It was in this very spot that Stella wrote her first diary. This spot was Stella's most cherished sanctuary, and it was there also that Stella experienced her first premonition.

One hot, sunny afternoon, as she sat meditating with her eyes closed, Stella heard the calm whisper of a voice. "You will find him."

She opened her eyes and looked around. No one was there. For an instant, Stella thought someone was playing tricks on her, but she felt no fear. The voice came for the second time. "You will find him."

Instantly, Stella felt jolted by a light breeze going through her body, and her hair stood on edge. "Ricki," she heard herself whisper, although her lips never moved. Then as quickly as the strange phenomenon had occurred, everything became silent. Not even the rattling of the wind beneath the leaves could be heard.

Stella for so long had been forced to forget about her family. Now, out of nowhere, something or someone was telling her she would find him. Stella knew she had a brother, so there was no question as to whom the voice was referring to. From her dreams and her innermost feelings, she knew that Eric was alive. Now she had been charged with the task of finding him. But how was she to do that? She had just turned sixteen and didn't have a clue how to go about looking for a missing person.

"What could I be thinking?" Stella whispered. And she decided to put the thought out of her mind.

For the next few months, Stella fought with the notion that she was supposed to somehow find her brother. As much as she tried to stifle and put the urge to rest, it continued to linger. Every passing month brought closer a deeper sense of Eric's presence. She felt that he was alive. Her emotions related to her little brother were nothing like the feelings she had for her dearly departed parents, whom she loved unconditionally. She missed them deeply, but she was fully aware that they had passed on; even her dreams supported that fact. For her parents, Stella sensed finality. For her brother, the feeling was temporal, like a void that could be filled in an instant, and she alone had the power to fill it.

To declare her desire to find her brother before her eighteenth birthday was a sure way of inviting Patricia Sybolis back into her life, which would mean losing her independence all over again. Stella could not risk that. She decided to wait until she was of legal age to openly conduct a search for her long-lost brother. She could not and would not give up two years of her independence.

Stella remained silent while she planned how and where to focus her search when the time came. She anticipated that Mount Pleasant Police Department would be both the starting place and her biggest obstacle. She knew the department would never support her initiative. She had to find a way to pique someone's interest; she would have to force a confrontation.

One afternoon, she got as far as the revolving front door of the police department, hoping to request information about her missing brother. As she stretched out her hand to push through the revolving doors, a voice said, "Stop."

Stella looked around. There was no one beside her. She thought of Patricia Sybolis, and then, quickly, she dropped her outstretched hands, turned around, and slowly walked away.

"In due time, Stella," she whispered, "in due time."

PART FIVE

Stella

Eighteen and Free

Chapter 15

On her eighteenth birthday, Stella celebrated both her adulthood and her emancipation. She was completely free from the scrutiny of Patricia Sybolis. It was as if a heavy and unwanted yoke had rolled off her shoulders.

She memorialized the day by taking a special trip to her secret place under the sycamore tree. There, she opened her arms to the heavens and shouted at the top of her voice. "Alleluia, alleluia, I am free! Free at last! I am free at last!" She was elated.

Two weeks later, Stella was summoned to a meeting at the office of the law firm of Godfrey, Oxford, Smith, Jeremiah, & Associates.

On her arrival at the firm on the morning of the meeting, Stella was ushered into conference room one, where she took the seat reserved specifically for her. It was between Mr. Godfrey and Mr. Oxford.

In attendance and already seated were Mr. and Mrs. Honig; Mr. Godfrey and Mr. Oxford; Margaret, the chief accountant who Nelly had hired and trained; and Juliet, Mr. Godfrey's senior secretary.

Mr. Godfrey congratulated Stella on reaching the age of majority and explained to her the reason for her presence. The mood in the room was strictly professional, and by Mr. Godfrey's demeanor, Stella knew that he was ready to proceed with the business at hand.

This was Stella's very first formal meeting, but far from her mind was any great concern for wealth. She was more interested in obtaining information about her past than knowing about her future. She decided to gamble on the slim chance that she might use this meeting to get some answers to the many questions lurking in the corners of her mind. Before another word could be uttered from the lips of Mr. Godfrey, Stella interjected. "I need some answers about my parents before knowing how they provided for my future." She was looking directly at Mr. Godfrey but did not give him a chance to answer.

"What was the real reason surrounding their death? Why was I taken away from them? Why did my grandma hate my parents? Why did my mother's childhood friends abandon and shun her? Why did they have to die?"

Mr. Godfrey was taken by surprise. He had always known that one day Stella would ask those questions, but he had not anticipated that they would be asked in that environment and with such intensity.

He stood with his mouth open, not knowing what to say. He looked around the room as if for immediate assistance but was greeted by the same perplexed look on the faces of those around him.

Because Stella had never before directly asked those questions, the Honigs thought that her long, drawn-out therapy with the psychologist over the years had put those questions to rest. They were wrong. After a brief silence, Mr. Oxford and the Honigs looked at one another and then back at Mr. Godfrey and unanimously nodded their heads in agreement.

It was difficult for Mr. Godfrey to tell the story, as the memories of Nelly stirred within him emotions he'd wished would never again surface—the loss of a best friend, a sister, a partner, and a confidant. As he looked at Stella, the tears began to form in the corners of his eyes. And then he took a deep breath. "Okay, Stella," he said, his voice trembling, "I guess that no time is better than the present."

Before Mr. Godfrey continued, he excused his secretary and the accountant. He then told the tale of his first encounter with Nelly and how she'd succeeded in getting the bureaucrats at Mount Pleasant University to approve her fully paid scholarship to MPU. "When Nelly finished with them they did not know what hit them," he said with a smile.

He told Stella the little he knew about Nelly's bout with poliomyelitis and the effects she'd suffered both physically and socially because of it. He emphasized how Nelly had defied all odds and went on to become a powerful businesswoman and owner of the most successful farm this side of the Mississippi.

Mr. Godfrey did not detail the many ways people perceived Nelly, but he said just enough for Stella to understand the kind of ridicule Nelly had experienced because of her physical condition.

While describing Nelly's personality, Mr. Godfrey paused for a moment and smiled. "She surely had fire in her soul," he said. "Nelly did not know the meaning of failure. For her, there were no boundaries. One of her philosophies was that it was better to try and fail than to fail to try. She certainly did try, and whenever she failed, she turned around and tried again. Nelly loved life, and better yet, she lived it. She exerted passion for all her endeavors, and proved herself to no one. She did whatever was in her heart, and when challenged by those who doubted her abilities, she proved them wrong. Nelly was indeed a force to reckon with. She was fighting when we met, and she died fighting."

After a short but emotional pause, Mr. Godfrey again looked at Stella and said, "Nelly loved you more than life itself. She lived, breathed, and worked for you. The only times I can remember seeing Nelly lose control was when your welfare was challenged."

Stella remained fixated on Mr. Godfrey's every word as she sat silently with tears in her eyes and joy in her heart. She was gleaming with pride for a mother she remembered so little of and loved so deeply. She had always believed that the unconditional love she'd received from the Honigs, the Oxfords, and others who surrounded her, including Mr. Godfrey, was a legacy of her parents' past. Mr. Godfrey's words confirmed what she had always known in her heart—*her parents must have done something good!*

Now, as she sat listening to Mr. Godfrey, hearing the emotion in his voice and seeing his love for Nelly radiating through his actions, Stella's belief in her parents' legacy was strongly reinforced. For an instant, she became so inundated with pride and respect for Nelly that she lost control of her emotions and burst out in sobs.

Mr. Oxford poured her a glass of water; Mrs. Honig rushed over to her chair, placed her arms around her, and whispered, "Honey, it is okay to cry."

The meeting was adjourned for fifteen minutes.

When they reconvened, Mr. Godfrey recommended that they continue with the business at hand. Stella disagreed. She insisted that he continue from where he had left off. Her determination to know won over Mr. Godfrey's reluctance to reminisce.

Mr. Godfrey again excused his secretary and the accountant who had returned once the meeting reconvened. He then turned to Stella and continued the narrative about Nelly.

"After the disappearance of your brother, Eric," he said, "the police alleged that it was foul play and subsequently accused Nelly of being involved, since she was the last person to see him. Nelly was not charged because there was no corpse to support their allegation."

Stella interrupted. "How did Social Services get involved?"

"During Nelly's first pregnancy, both Nelly's and Hugo's mothers insisted that the baby be given up for adoption—that baby was you. They even chose the adoptive parents. When Nelly and Hugo refused, they became infuriated. Mrs. Roberts had initiated contact with Social Services through an old acquaintance, Miss Newton. With Miss Newton involved, Social Services conducted probe upon probe into the lives of Nelly and Hugo but found nothing. They even challenged, in court, Nelly's fitness to care for a child. They lost." Mr. Godfrey paused for a moment, took a drink of water, and then continued.

"In this small town where nothing much is happening, Social Services could not concede defeat. Miss Newton took the loss personally. And with her brother as chief of police and Susan Roberts fueling the attacks, the department never let up.

"Miss Newton became obsessed and conducted periodic checks on Nelly. They were searching for anything that would prove her incapable of caring for you and Eric. Their chance came when Eric disappeared. Assisted by her brother, Chief of Police Newton, Miss Newton quickly obtained a court order to take you away from Nelly. That was how you ended up in foster care."

For the first time since the meeting reconvened, Mr. Godfrey smiled. "Lucky for Nelly, she'd documented all that the department put her through. That won you a handsome settlement."

"How could a government agency get away with such a high degree of harassment?"

Mr. Godfrey smiled again. "My dear Stella," he said, "this is a small town with a closed society. The director of Mount Pleasant's Social Services Department is Mrs. Newton, Miss Newton's sister-in-law and wife of Chief of Police Newton. In such societies where decision makers are relatives and friends, those they do not socialize with do not stand a chance."

Mr. Godfrey became quiet for a moment, and then with a solemn tone he said, "Mount Pleasant was and continues to be a nucleus for discrimination. No one and nothing different is welcome."

With this, his entire demeanor changed. He was no longer telling the story. He was living it. The emotions he'd kept within for twelve years had finally surfaced. His voice grew coarse and forceful; he began to sweat; and, without warning, he pounded on the conference table.

"Damn! Damn!" he shouted.

Everyone in the room was taken by surprise. Then, with tears rolling down his cheeks, he said, "Nelly and Hugo were harassed, not because they were unfit parents. They were harassed to their death because they did not represent what Mount Pleasant natives assumed to be a pure society. They saw Nelly as a cripple and Hugo as a foreigner with a complexion slightly darker than their own. Even more unforgiving was the fact that she married the foreigner, a black man. To them, Nelly broke their societal law and threatened the course of their history."

He shook his head. He lifted his hands and, shaking them to the heavens, shouted, "My people are incapable of seeing beyond their prejudices. Lord, Lord, when will we ever learn?"

Mr. Godfrey pulled a white handkerchief from his jacket pocket, wiped his face, and then slowly replaced the handkerchief. He took a deep breath; shook his head; and, after a brief moment of silence, described, with care and as precisely as he could remember, the events leading to Nelly's and Hugo's deaths.

After the heart-wrenching story, everyone in the room anticipated an emotional outburst by Stella.

This was not to be. Instead, when Mr. Godfrey ended the tale, Stella stood up and walked toward the window overlooking the parking lot. It seemed an eternity, though in reality, she had only stood there for a moment.

Only Stella knew the emotions that were taking root inside her. Her heart was breaking, and deep in the pits of her soul, was an emotional roller coaster of grief for her parents and hatred for the institution that had aided in their demise. At the same time, Stella felt a sense of rebirth. It was as if a light breeze had blown through her, leaving in its path a feeling of strength, relentlessness, and determination.

"I will find him," Stella heard herself whisper. "I will find him, if only to prove my mother's innocence."

Returning to her seat, Stella blinked profusely to hold back the tears that were beginning to form in the corners of her eyes, and then slowly she looked at Mr. Godfrey and said, "Thank you."

Mr. Godfrey, Mr. Oxford, and the Honigs all seemed drained of strength. It was as if they had relived the emotional ordeal of Nelly's and Hugo's deaths all over again. None of them said a word, but in a meeting of the minds, they each wished that this day would bring closure to their memories of twelve years ago.

Mr. Oxford suggested that they adjourn and reschedule the meeting for sometime in the near future. Stella politely asked that they adjourn for an hour or two and continue on that very day.

Since Mr. Godfrey and Mr. Oxford had nothing planned for the rest of the day, they agreed to her request.

Stella and the Honigs left the office and headed for lunch at the home of the Oxfords.

After they left, Mr. Godfrey smiled at Mr. Oxford and said, "I see in Stella the fire and passion I saw in her mother." He was thinking of the day Nelly had walked into his office and offered to reorganize his establishment. "She will surely be a force," he added.

Calmly, Mr. Oxford replied with a nod. "That she will be, my friend. That she will surely be."

After lunch, Stella left the Honigs and Mrs. Oxford conversing and retreated to her bedroom upstairs. She made a phone call to her aunt Theresa at her home in Los Angeles. She wanted the telephone number and address to the Roberts estate.

"Thanks," she said. "I will be careful."

Stella dialed the number she'd obtained from Theresa. A male voice answered.

"Can I please speak to Mrs. Roberts?" Stella asked.

"Hang on," the voice responded, and she was placed on hold. Two minutes later, Mrs. Roberts answered. Stella decided to make the conversation as brief and to the point as she could.

"Hello, Nanny, this is Stella. How are you? I need to see you. Will you be home on Sunday? Okay, Nanny, I shall be there at 2:30 p.m. Bye."

Stella hung up the telephone and returned downstairs to meet the Honigs for their drive back to the law firm of Godfrey, Oxford, Smith, Jeremiah, & Associates.

The afternoon meeting commenced without a hitch and with all the original attendees present. Mr. Godfrey, for the second time, thanked everyone for sticking around and, without hesitation, handed Stella a folder, four bankbooks, and an envelope containing keys for two safety deposit boxes.

He advised Stella that the folder contained a complete list of all her holdings that had been held in trust by the firm until her eighteenth birthday. He also added that as executor and executrix of the James estate, he and Theresa had taken the opportunity to have some of the Jameses' assets transferred to her. However, there were still decisions to be made regarding the transfer of additional assets. "Decisions we thought you should make with the assistance of your attorney," he added.

Also in the folder was a list of all the companies Stella owned outright. That included the farm, which was managed by Mr. Scuffey.

As Stella flipped through the contents of the folder, she noticed that she held a substantial number of shares in Mount Pleasant National Bank and that she was the silent owner of Ladella's Meat Market.

Mr. Godfrey advised Stella that she had a trust fund that could not be accessed until she was twenty-five years old. All of her tuition fees were paid by the Honigs. She also learned that her lavish lifestyle was paid for from a fund set aside by the James estate for just that reason. She also had a private accountant.

Stella was informed that Eric's trust fund was still intact and would be transferred to her at age twenty-five.

"No transfer is to be made from Eric's trust fund," Stella responded. "As a matter of fact, I would like to have the James estate executed as per the instructions of the last will and testament. Eric's share will remain untouched."

Everyone in the room looked at each other and then back at Stella.

"Stella, do you know something we don't?" Mr. Oxford asked.

"No, Pops," she answered. "I only feel something no one else feels. Eric is alive. My mother did not kill him. Neither was she responsible for his disappearance. I will find him."

Silence engulfed the room for almost sixty seconds before Mr. Godfrey spoke. "Stella," he said, "the beneficiaries of your parents' life insurance policies were you and Eric. The money was released on your eighteenth birthday and held in trust." He continued, "All securities in the name of your parents were transferred to you. Are you asking the firm to have everything divided between you and Eric and keep Eric's in trust?"

"Yes, sir," Stella answered.

"Okay, Stella," Mr. Godfrey said. "It will be done." Then looking at the accountant and the secretary, he said, "Ladies, we have some work to do."

Because of the lavish lifestyle Stella was provided, she had known that she was wealthy, but she could never have imagined being a multimillionaire. By the time the meeting ended, she realized that she was the owner of properties in places she didn't even know existed. She was also the sole owner of the only five-star restaurant in Mount Pleasant, The Cabana, one of her favorite places to eat.

The meeting ended after four thirty. The secretary and accountant left in a hurry, but before Mr. Godfrey rose from his chair, Stella stood and walked across the room for a second time. Everyone followed her strides. She appeared to have something on her mind. They were correct. Stella had a request.

Stella was hardly settled back in her chair when she requested that the firm petition Mount Pleasant's Criminal Investigation Department to open the case on Eric.

Her request did not come as a shock. Nevertheless, everyone felt as if he or she had been pushed between a rock and a hard place. Following the death of Stella's parents, Mr. Godfrey, Mr. Oxford, and the Honigs had all filed numerous motions and petitions to have the files opened and the investigation continued. Their efforts had been continuously blocked. The CID had the support of Patricia Sybolis and the Department of Social Services, who swore that reopening the investigation would jeopardize Stella's therapy.

They also agonized over whether opening the case was in Stella's best interest. As they sat in silence, each contemplating his or her response, Stella again spoke. "If you refuse," she warned, "I will find Eric anyway." She looked around the room steadily. "I will do this with or without your help."

They asked Stella to leave the room, and after a brief discussion, they decided to honor her request. They also decided to simultaneously enlist a private investigative firm to look for Eric. In return, Stella had to agree to distance herself from the investigation and concentrate on her education.

She reluctantly obliged.

Chapter 16

The ride home, with Stella and the Honigs in the backseat of the limousine, was very quiet. Stella closed her eyes, giving the Honigs the impression that she was fast asleep. What they did not know was that she was wide-awake, thinking of a way to approach Susan Roberts during her planned visit.

At breakfast the following morning, Stella told Mr. and Mrs. Honig of her impending plans to visit the Robertses after church the following day.

"Why?" they asked in unison.

"I need to know why they hated my mother," Stella replied.

The Honigs thought an attempt to try and change Stella's mind pointless. So, like her aunt Theresa had, they advised her to be careful.

At exactly 2:30 p.m. on Sunday, Stella knocked on the front door of the Robertses' home. Hubert, the butler, opened the door and led Stella into the library, where Mrs. Roberts was awaiting her arrival.

"It is nice to see you again, child," Susan Roberts said from behind her desk. "You look very well."

"Thank you, Nanny," Stella replied as Hubert ushered her to a luxurious armchair, upholstered in soft black leather.

Mrs. Roberts instructed Hubert to bring in tea for two and, in the same breath, advised Stella that Mr. Roberts would not be joining them.

Mrs. Roberts left her position at her desk and took a seat on an identical armchair adjacent to Stella. Although they had spoken in the past, this was the first time since the reading of Nelly and Hugo's will that Stella was again in the presence of Susan Roberts, her grandmother.

Stella remembered her well. Though her movements were now a bit slower and her face somewhat wrinkled with age, the smug and vainglorious look on her face remained part of her distinct features. Her hair had become as white as the fallen snow, and although she did not use it, Stella noticed a cane leaning against her desk.

Stella realized that she hated being in the same room as her grandmother, so she eliminated all pleasantries. All she wanted were answers to her questions. "Thanks for seeing me on such short notice, Nanny," Stella said. "I know that you must be busy, so I will not take up much of your time. I am here to tell you, personally, that we have decided to hire a detective to find Eric."

Staring directly at her grandmother, Stella paused, expecting a reaction. There was none.

Void of any emotion, Mrs. Roberts silently stared right back at Stella.

Stella continued, "I need to know if you were responsible for my brother's disappearance."

Mrs. Roberts jerked her head backward and opened her mouth in astonishment. She was not amazed at the question, as it had been asked of her many times before. She was amazed that Stella, her eighteen-year-old grandchild, would ask her that question.

She saw in Stella Nelly all over again. Since Nelly's estrangement and death, no one had dared to challenge her as vehemently as Stella just had. At her age, she was not prepared to accept such a challenge, not ever again. She would not put up with another Nelly.

Susan Roberts's face hardened, and her voice trembled as she stuttered the name, "N-Nelly." She jumped out of her chair without a limp, and pointing toward the door, she shouted, "Get out of my house."

Stella did not move. Still staring directly at Mrs. Roberts, she calmly said. "Nanny, I know what you and Grandma James did to my parents. I am only giving you a chance to redeem yourself. If you know anything about Eric's disappearance, tell me now, not just to ease your conscience but to avoid prosecution."

Mrs. Roberts walked toward the closed library door, opened it, and held it open. "Get out of my house." She was now speaking in a firm, steady voice. "Get out, or I will have my butler physically throw you out."

Stella got up, and without another word, she held her head high, walked passed her grandmother, and then exited through the door from which she'd first entered.

On her drive home, Stella felt somewhat remorseful for the way she'd dealt with Mrs. Roberts. That lasted only for a moment as she tried to picture the ordeal Mrs. Roberts had put her parents through.

Chapter 17

As expected, the request to have Mount Pleasant Police Department reopen the investigation on Eric's disappearance was denied. Chief Newton asserted that since no new evidence was provided to facilitate the request, it could not be granted.

Annoyed by his decision, Stella decided to approach Chief Newton herself. She called the police department to inquire if Chief Newton was in. On hearing that he was, Stella went to the police department and sneaked into his office after she was told that he could not see her.

The chief was at his desk when Stella entered.

"Hello, Chief Newton," she said boldly as she walked up to his desk with her hand stretched out to greet him. "I am Stella James."

Chief Newton remained seated with his hand resting on his desk. "I know who you are, Miss James, What can I do for you?"

"I would like to know what we have to do in order to have your department resume their search for my missing brother, sir," Stella replied.

Chief Newton looked at Stella, folded his arms, and said, "Miss James, bring me some new evidence, and then we will talk. Now please get out of my office. I have work to do."

Stella turned to leave but stopped abruptly as she was about to exit the door. "Chief Newton," she said, "why are you still carrying a grudge against my mother? Why is this department so corrupt? Are you still on my granny's payroll?"

Chief Newton picked up the telephone and dialed. "Get me Mr. Oxford," he said. "I am about to arrest Stella, his protégé."

Stella quickly turned around and walked out of the chief's office in silence.

Chief Newton later visited the Honigs and warned them that Stella would be arrested if she returned to the police department.

A couple hours after Chief Newton left, Mrs. Honig suffered a mild stroke and was rushed to the hospital. Stella blamed herself for giving Chief Newton cause to scare the Honigs. She swore that she would, from now on, distance herself from the actual investigation as previously promised.

Mr. Oxford was livid. After speaking with Chief Newton regarding the incident, he felt that Chief Newton had no right to visit the Honigs, much less threaten them. "This kind of harassment must stop," Mr. Oxford told Chief Newton when he called to complain.

The detective firm Mr. Oxford hired reported promising leads, which eventually turned cold. Each time a report by the firm's detectives ended in a dead end, Stella's optimism turned to disappointment. But she could do nothing except hope that the next lead would be the one.

After graduating high school, Stella won a scholarship to pursue a double major in anthropology and political science at Columbia University. Before leaving Mount Pleasant, she met with her lawyers and accountant to review her business portfolio. She reiterated her desire to keep her and Eric's inheritances separate, even if the detectives continued to be unsuccessful in their search for Eric. There was no wavering in her decision.

For herself, Stella requested that the interest from her share of the proceeds from her parents' life insurance policy be transferred to her new bank account in New York. She also requested that quarterly reports of her and Eric's portfolios be forwarded to her New York address.

As she prepared to leave Mount Pleasant, her good-byes to her loved ones were full of tears. But she knew it was time to start a new life, her life. She had her own dreams to pursue.

Life in New York was not as scary as Stella had been made to believe it would be. In fact, she loved it. In a letter to the Honigs, Stella wrote:

> New York is nothing like Mount Pleasant. The people in this Metropolitan city are open-minded and welcoming, unlike our Mount Pleasant natives. Here, there is less petty bickering and backstabbing. The people are quite approachable, and they refrain from meddling in other people's affairs.

Stella involved herself in extracurricular activities like the arts. She sought out and supported organizations for disabled people and the poor. She also acquired knowledge on how to start up and operate nonprofit organizations.

After her tenure at Columbia, Stella attended Harvard Law School, and upon graduating and passing the bar, she accepted an associate position with the law firm of Joseph Sylvester & Associates. The law firm was located in Haileysville, a metropolitan city in one of the New England states. Stella wanted to serve a diverse group of people, and since Mount Pleasant did not provide such diversity, she accepted the offer in Haileysville, where there was a melting pot of different groups.

Additionally, Mr. Sylvester, the owner and senior attorney, shared her passion to fight for the underdogs. He even allowed her the opportunity to take in pro bono and contingency cases. He was a retired attorney general whose bottom line was not the almighty dollar. He believed in getting justice for those who were not able to fight for themselves.

Stella was made aware of his passion when she articled with the firm one year prior to passing the bar exam.

Stella dedicated most of her time to representing disabled people and employees who became disabled due to workplace accidents. Since she was the only lawyer in the firm assigned to those cases, she remained extremely busy and won large settlements for her clients. She was so proficient at what she did that the corporations she opposed in court wanted her on their legal teams.

As Stella's interaction with the disabled increased, her lifelong dream of building a retreat for disabled people became more desirable. There was a real need for such a place.

Stella presented her plan to the Honigs, Mr. Oxford, and her accountant. And soon, the retreat was under construction on a twenty-five-acre plot of land adjoining the James farm.

The retreat provided a place where disabled people could live or visit at least once in their lifetimes. It was a place for rest and relaxation, a place where people whose lives had been touched by disability could met with their peers for fun, entertainment, lectures, and other recreational and educational activities. It was a place where the disabled were made to feel at home, with all the amenities of a five-star hotel.

Stella named the retreat Nelly's Cove after her mother. The facility was a masterpiece and the talk of the town. Absolutely nothing was spared.

Susan Roberts and those who'd shunned Nelly after her affliction saw the retreat as a slap in the face but could do nothing about it. Their fight to stop the issuance of its building permits failed.

PART SIX

Stella

Search for Meaning

Chapter 18

The thermostat outside Stella's kitchen window read 101 degrees Fahrenheit. Stella walked into the library and turned on the radio just as Lou Smith, the evening anchor on Radio XVYI, was pleading for caution against the record-breaking heat wave that was sweeping across Haileysville. Lou described the temperature as "deadly and stifling," while urging listeners to consume plenty of liquids and remain indoors. "Unless it is absolutely necessary to venture outside," he pleaded, "please remain indoors."

For the first time since listening to Lou over the airwaves, Stella sensed an air of empathy. His voice trembled as he informed listeners of the many casualties the emergency room at Haileysville General Hospital was handling as a result of the heat. He solemnly added that four senior citizens on the west side were reported dead from heat stroke and dehydration. Lou was void of sarcasm. He sounded genuinely humane.

Stella turned off the radio, reached for the telephone, and started to dial. "Darn," she said aloud. "What am I doing? Jeremy is in Europe."

Slowly, she hung up the telephone, the thought of doing something constructive dangling through her mind.

Stella had two tickets for the Annual International Home Show, which was held at the Haileysville Coliseum. She felt compelled to attend in support of the sponsoring organization, Friends of the Disabled (FTD), but she decided to heed Lou Smith's warning.

With no pressing activity or chores on her agenda, Stella decided to read the court transcript she'd brought home from her office the day before. The transcript was in a large manila envelope which she had placed on her mahogany desk after removing it from her briefcase just about the time her central air unit broke. The envelope was labeled, "Jacob Clyde, Criminal Trial." She was in no hurry to review the transcript because she resented the fact that Mr. Sylvester had it sitting on his desk for almost a month before assigning it to her.

Now, confined indoors because of the heat wave, and with nothing else to do, Stella pulled the transcript out of the envelope, and said aloud, "If I am going to read this, I guess that there is no better time than the present."

Stella walked over to the sofa across from her desk and sat at one end with a pillow tucked between the nape of her neck and the hand rest. She lifted her legs onto the sofa, and without further hesitation, she started to read.

During his criminal trial, Jacob Clyde described his occupation as a traveling salesman with no fixed address. When asked to expand on his reason for not having a fixed address, he explained that his expansive international travels made it impossible to settle in one domain. He described himself as a self-made millionaire and businessman, who was abandoned by his teenage mother when he was only six months old.

As Stella read further into the transcript, she realized that Jacob Clyde had experienced a tough and horrendous life while growing up in the city of Chicago. During his childhood years, Jacob Clyde had been bounced in and out of foster care and sometimes lived on the streets. To further compound his hardship, Jacob Clyde had been repeatedly molested and sodomized by people he trusted.

Stella felt a sense of sorrow for Mr. Clyde, but that sympathetic feeling was short-lived as it changed to disgust with and then hatred toward Mr. Clyde.

According to the evidence presented by witnesses during the trial, Jacob Clyde had avenged his childhood misfortune by consciously and continuously reaping havoc on almost every child he came in contact with.

Many people testified that Jacob Clyde was a pedophile, a rapist, a child pornographer, a trafficker, and a smuggler. He was accused of abducting innocent children. One witness said of him, "In his presence, no child is safe." Another witness testified that he lured innocent children from unsuspecting and vulnerable parents, took lewd pictures, and trafficked or smuggled the pictures and sometimes the children for profit.

Mr. Clyde's cargo was distributed globally, and according to evidence, he'd made a vast fortune from those illicit practices. It was also alleged that Mr. Clyde had abandoned some of his victims in different cities and towns, once he felt they were no longer useful or had become burdensome.

As Stella's review of the transcript continued, the hatred she felt for Jacob Clyde was transferred to the legal system that had sentenced him to fifteen years in prison with the possibility of parole for good behavior in seven years or less. Stella found it inconceivable that the legal system would bestow such leniency upon an individual as mean and masochistic as Mr. Clyde. He was a man who'd made a career out of criminally violating children, infants, and their parents.

Stella had never met Jacob Clyde, but reading about his activities made her blood run cold and her hair stand on end. "The man is an animal," Stella said aloud. "He is the devil himself."

About halfway through the transcript, Stella became nauseated and knew that if she continued, someone would have to clean up not only the sofa on which she lay but also the transcript. Stella placed a marker on the last page she had read, and then slowly she laid the transcript on the floor, rolled over to her side, and closed her eyes. Within minutes, she was asleep.

In her unconsciousness, Stella found herself back in the very enchanted field where she had first met the little boy. On this journey, she seemed somewhat younger. Her surroundings looked as beautiful and smelled as intoxicating as the very first time the dream appeared. This time, however, her attention was focused not on her beautiful surroundings, but on the little boy who appeared to be awaiting her arrival.

Without a word, she and the little boy ran through the field of flowers, chasing butterflies, dancing, twirling, and letting the wind blow through their hair. Stella and her companion eventually sat down to rest, but before she could take a good look at her companion's face, he started to retreat, as if pulled away by some unseen magnetic force. Stella reached for the little boy but felt a wall between them. Now airborne, the little boy continued to move farther and farther away, and as he did, he became smaller and smaller.

With outstretched hands and a sunken spirit, Stella screamed, "Don't go! Don't go! Please don't go."

In an instant, the little boy disappeared before her very eyes and was immediately replaced by the man with the face of a jackal.

Stella jumped from her sleep into a sitting position as she continued to mumble. "Don't go! Don't go."

When she fully regained consciousness, she was trembling, and her clothes were soaking wet. Stella was afraid. "Lord," she whispered, "what on earth is happening to me?"

With zombielike movements, Stella rose from the sofa, walked out of the library, and entered the kitchen, where she poured herself a glass of water. She placed the glass between her lips and drank nonstop until the glass was empty. Then going upstairs to her bedroom, she changed out of her wet kimono and into a comfortable, flowing house gown.

Still overwhelmed by the dream, Stella's heart beat rapidly, her breathing became labored, her palms sweaty, and there was a lump of fear rising in her throat as she replayed the dream over and over in her mind.

"What could it all mean?" she whispered nervously.

Later that night, as Stella lay in bed, she prayed that the dream would not reoccur.

It did. Every time she closed her eyes and drifted off to sleep, she was taken back to the enchanted garden with the little boy and the man with the face of a jackal. Stella eventually forced herself to stay awake; she tossed and turned, hoping that dawn would soon arrive.

Stella felt the need to talk to someone about the recurring dream that left her struggling to find its meaning. Never in her life had she been so tormented by a dream.

In the past, even as a little girl, Stella had dreamed strange but sometimes comforting dreams. She's even had occasional nightmares. But her dream world had never contained anything as profound, strange, vivid, consistent, and intense as this.

Tired from lack of sleep, Stella dragged herself out of bed at four thirty in the morning and retreated to the seating area adjoining her bedroom. There, she draped herself in a blanket and settled into her favorite recliner. She looked into the distance as the dark clouds slowly rolled away, giving rise to the first appearance of light before the rising sun.

As rays of sunlight began to peek through the clouds, a sense of uneasiness came over Stella. "Lord," she whispered, "what significance, if any, could be attached to this dream?"

She could think of nothing. She had been raised to believe that every dream was connected to the dreamer's subconscious. Now, here she was, faced with a dream she could not begin to comprehend. She searched deep within herself for something related to the dream. She found nothing remotely connected to those terrifying images.

"What could I be suppressing?" Stella asked aloud. "What in God's name is going on inside my head?"

It was almost a quarter to eight when Stella reluctantly walked back into her bedroom. The radio was on, and according to the announcer, the temperature outside was already in the upper nineties and rising. Like he had the day before, Lou Smith continued to warn listeners to remain indoors.

Stella dropped her blanket at the edge of the bed and proceeded to the bathroom where she took a quick shower before getting ready for the 9:00 a.m. Mass at St. Michael's Cathedral.

After taking one last glance in the mirror to ensure there were no bags under her eyes, Stella proceeded to go downstairs to the kitchen. She hurriedly drank a glass of orange juice and then left through the kitchen door, ignoring the radio announcer's warning. She was attempting to walk to St. Michael's Cathedral, about four blocks from her house.

Stella was oblivious to the fact that she was the only one on the street. Before she could make it past the first block, Stella realized her foolish mistake and started to turn around. Just then, Gwen Miller, the postmistress who lived down the street from Stella, pulled up in her Chrysler LeBaron coupe and stopped.

"Hi, Stella," she shouted. "Hop in."

Stella opened the door on the passenger's side and stepped in. But before she could make herself comfortable, Gwen proceeded to scold her. "You must be either crazy or suicidal to walk this distance on such a hot day, Stella. Do you not listen to the meteorologist?"

Stella smiled in acknowledgment of Gwen's remarks. She had learned long ago that it was better not to argue with Gwen, who'd ordained herself the community's voice of wisdom.

In church that morning, Stella prayed for God's help in understanding the meaning of her dream, and on her ride home, she told Gwen about the dream.

As always, Gwen had the answer. "It must be your state of mind, Stella. Subconsciously, you are craving for a cool place outside your home. The enchanted garden in your dream represents that cool and comfortable place you are longing for, and the stench represents the lack thereof. That little boy, well, maybe it is the son you are going to have someday. Once the temperature subsides, the dream will vanish. In the meantime, girl, consider yourself lucky and enjoy your beautiful garden."

Stella almost choked on Gwen's simplistic analysis. Gwen was the last person in whom she would normally confide, but because of her desperation and for the lack of another soul, Stella had confided in her. With a listless chuckle, Stella nodded her head in agreement with Gwen and ended the conversation.

As she got out of Gwen's car and closed the door behind her, Stella whispered, "Maybe Gwen does have a point after all." With that, she decided to get as far away as possible from Gwen and from her bed. She was going to Cactus Beach.

When Stella got home, she made herself two scrambled eggs, four slices of bacon, two pancakes with strawberry jam, a glass of freshly squeezed orange juice, and a cup of tea. After completely devouring every crumb from her plate, she changed into her swimsuit, covered by a pair of Bermuda shorts; jumped into her Porsche; and drove to Cactus Beach.

Cactus Beach was a haven for tourists and the affluent. It was located in a nonresidential, secluded area. For lack of public transportation to Cactus Beach, it was seldom used by the less-affluent natives of Haileysville. Their only means of getting to and from the beach was through bus parties organized and arranged by local groups, churches, and schools.

Cactus Beach was a national landmark. It was well maintained, and its natural beauty was preserved by the Haileysville National Park. The beach bordered the shore of a beautiful botanical garden, with lush vegetation. Its white sand covered a radius of two miles. Its turquoise ocean shimmered like silver pellets as the sun and light breeze simultaneously played in its tides, further enhancing its glorious beauty. Overall, the water was shallow, warm, and inviting.

Stella had not been to Cactus Beach in years, but to her, nothing had changed. It looked as breathtakingly beautiful as it had during her last visit. Stella's early arrival at the beach allowed her to secure a shaded area under a large almond tree. She pulled out her beach chair, set up her umbrella, and established her very own cocoon.

Stella swam for a while. She read several articles from the *ABA Journal*. And occasionally, she stopped to admire visitors as they engaged in different activities. Though Stella would have preferred not to think about it, she also spent some time meditating on the dream, in hopes of understanding its meaning.

Later in the day, as Stella lay with her eyes closed, she felt a slight breeze brush across her face. She opened her eyes only to see a strange man kneeling beside her with his face so close she could feel his breath. Stella almost fell off the chair. Before she could admonish him, the man, with an adopted French accent, exclaimed! "I was merely admiring the beauty, which before me lie!"

The serious look on Stella's face was intended to warn him that his invasion of her space was unacceptable, but he missed the warning. Instead, he continued.

"Mademoiselle, a jolie femme like you should not be alone. You should be in the company of a handsome prince, as myself."

Stella was aghast at the man's action and wanted him gone. But instead, he eased himself into a sitting position beside her. Alarmed by his continued disrespect and wanting to get away from this man, Stella swung her feet off the chair with such velocity that she almost knocked him over. This did not deter him so Stella quickly concocted a police husband, and in a stern, cold voice she said, "My husband, Officer Leland, will be back in a moment."

No sooner had the word officer come from Stella's lips than the self-proclaimed French prince scampered to his feet and disappeared into the crowd. Minutes later, amused by her lie and the way her prince had taken his leave, Stella could not stop herself from smiling.

Before leaving the beach, Stella took the opportunity to stop and enjoy the beautiful sunset but was somewhat disappointed that her significant other, Jeremy, who was currently in Europe on business, was absent.

More disappointing was the fact that she had forgotten her camera. In the evening sky, a beautiful array of orange, pink, yellow, red, and gold entwined to form a bed upon which laid a golden halo. And the image would forever linger in Stella's mind. Yet, she knew that a picture would have lasted a lifetime. Stella looked with awe at the setting sun as it slowly diverged from its bed of beautiful colors and sank beneath the horizon. Still fascinated by the splendor of nature's handiwork, Stella packed her belongings and headed toward the parking lot to find her car.

The parking areas were swarming with vehicles of all makes, models, and sizes. There were rented vehicles, vehicles with out-of-state license plates, official vehicles, buses, trucks, and on and on.

Stella realized that she had been so preoccupied with her thoughts when she'd arrived at the beach that she had completely forgotten to pay attention to where she was parking. After searching, with the help of an attendant, for almost fifteen minutes, she located her car. She placed her belongings on the seat, locked the door, and then went to dinner at Cobblers Palace, the oldest and best restaurant on Cactus Beach.

Cobblers Palace was the first restaurant and bar built on Cactus Beach. Other restaurants had since occupied the land space surrounding the beach, but none had been able to surpass the excellence in good food and warm hospitality that Cobblers Palace offered.

Stella had almost forgotten how deliciously tasteful the meals were. Her broiled lobster tail, in vinegar wine and garlic sauce, with white rice and steamed asparagus smothered in melted cheese were out of this world, and her virgin piña colada tasted as good as the very first one she'd had. Stella skipped dessert. She was too full to eat another bite. And with her destination in mind, she paid her bill and headed for home.

Stella got home just in time to have a shower and her regular cup of herbal tea before settling in front of the TV to watch the 11:00 p.m. evening news—a ritual she religiously performed every evening before bedtime.

Stella's soul-searching at the beach had not uncovered the reason for or the meaning of her dream. For the next three nights following her visit to the beach, Stella dreamed nothing about the little boy, the enchanted garden, or the man with the face of a jackal.

Unfortunately, the hiatus did not keep the dream from lingering in Stella's mind as she tried unsuccessfully to decipher its meaning. This increased her need to talk to someone about it. Nevertheless, she was not willing to encounter another Gwen. Nor was she ready to confide the dream to her parents and her guardian, whom she knew would worry about her.

Stella longed for her boyfriend, Jeremy, who was expected back from his European trip the following weekend. All of a sudden, one week seemed like an eternity.

Shortly before her graduation from Harvard Law School, Stella and Jeremy had met at a black-tie event, where she'd accidentally spilled red wine on his white tuxedo. Stella had expected Jeremy to be upset, but instead, he'd joked about it. He had taken one look at her and realized how distraught she was and had moved quickly to put her at ease. With a big grin, he'd said, "Don't be so melancholic. I am not going to melt. But I do expect you to keep the ants away from me."

Stella had given him her telephone number, hoping that he would call with the dry-cleaning bill. He'd warned her that he would only call to invite her on a date.

Stella had been impressed by how cool he was, in addition to his frankness, his candid humor, and wicked smile, but when he turned to leave, she took one look at his buttock and knew that she was in love.

"Wow," she'd whispered. "Thank you, wine."

The call had come, and two days later Stella and Jeremy were on their way to Gino's Bar and Grill for a late-night snack and promises of a loving relationship.

Jeremy was traveling through Europe on assignment for Pride, Purcell, & Sons, Inc., his employer. The organization was interested in purchasing a chain of hotels and restaurants in Europe, and Jeremy was the point man. He was on a fact-finding mission to determine which hotels in what cities would be most lucrative. He had been gone for almost four weeks, and for the first time, Stella was feeling the effect of his absence.

Stella was beginning to feel vulnerable. She had always been able to make her own decisions and thought she knew what to do under all circumstances. She considered herself a self-sufficient, independent, individual capable of taking care of herself.

Once, she had been stalked by a deranged man, and against the advice of Jeremy, her parents, and the police, Stella had invited the man to her home, fed him, and then cajoled him into getting the help he needed.

Now, haunted by a dream, Stella could not help herself. She didn't know what to do. She needed a savior. She needed Jeremy. Her confidence, her strong will, and her treasured independence, all seemed to be cloaked under a magnetized spell, pulling away from her with every passing moment.

Frightened by those out-of-control feelings, Stella needed immediate answers. But she had no idea where to find them.

Chapter 19

*S*tella's week was uneventful. She litigated two cases and spent the rest of her working hours preparing for the civil suit a group of Mr. Clyde's victims were bringing against him. As Stella reviewed page after page of the transcript from the criminal trial, she became extremely conflicted and contemplated withdrawing from the case. She was overwhelmed by the graphic depiction of molestation and inhumane treatment suffered by the victims of Mr. Clyde.

Stella feared that her feelings would compromise the trial. Yet, she knew that she could not withdraw. Her conscience would not allow it, and her deeply rooted conviction that all sexual offenders, pedophiles especially, should be punished to the fullest extent of the law kept her committed to the case. Additionally, Joe Sylvester, who had initially accepted the case on contingency, was bogged down with other matters.

After considering the pros and cons, Stella decided that she had no choice. She was in for the duration.

In his criminal trial, Jacob Clyde had been found guilty of sexually molesting minors, child pornography, extortion, and possession of child pornography with intent to distribute. According to the transcript, his victims ranged from ages two to eleven.

Sylvester, James, & Associates was on record as the law firm working with parents of the victimized children to bring a civil suit against Mr. Clyde. They were suing for pain, suffering, humiliation, and the lifelong scars Mr. Clyde had perpetrated upon their children and themselves.

Stella knew that no amount of money could compensate for the harm done to Mr. Clyde's victims and their families, but she wanted to squeeze every penny she could out of him. She promised herself that she was going to turn Mr. Clyde into a pauper. To accomplish that, she enlisted Jim Talbert, her longtime friend and master private investigator to work on the case with her.

Four days into what Stella considered a normal week of pleasurable sleep—the dream had not reoccurred—Stella went home after a hard day's work hoping that the hiatus would continue. She showered, ate a light meal, and went to bed.

While in bed, she made a few phone calls before settling to look at the evening news. Halfway into the newscast, the telephone rang.

"Hi, love," the voice on the other line said.

Stella was elated to hear Jeremy's voice. "I miss you, Jer!" she exclaimed without a thought.

As independent as she was, this was one time in her life when Stella wished she was surrounded by loved ones.

Jeremy told her about the places he had been and the things he had seen and done. He was excited about the trip and the prospect of creating a new chain of hotels. "Stella," he said, "all indications show that this project is shaping up to be the best of my many creations— bigger than anything I have done."

Jeremy was so excited and, at the same time, fatigued, that the conversation went on between them for almost fifteen minutes before he informed her that he was back in town. "I just walked in," he finally said.

"Welcome home!" Stella exclaimed, hoping that he would immediately come over.

Jeremy's plan had been to drop off his luggage and rush over to Stella's house. Unfortunately, he was too tired to do so. His long flight had left him jet-lagged and somewhat immobile. He was practically fighting to stay awake as they spoke. "I will see you tomorrow," he finally said in a drowsy voice. After blowing Stella a kiss, he hung up the telephone.

Stella rolled over to her side, placed the phone on its cradle, turned off the light, and stared into the darkness. She was trying to picture herself in the arms of Jeremy, but instead, her mind reverted to the Clyde case.

Unfortunately, since Stella had made the decision to litigate the Clyde case, she spent most of her waking hours consumed by it. She had recently found out about Mr. Clyde's registered dummy corporations and vowed to render each and every one of them defunct. Now, lying in bed, Stella was thinking of ways to transfer those corporations back to Clyde's name in order to have them seized. She thought of an idea, got up, wrote it on a notepad, and returned to bed.

"Wait! Wait! Wait! Don't go, don't go!" Stella screamed as she awoke from a deep sleep. She turned on the light and looked at the clock. It was only 3:45 a.m. Stella felt a chill and realized she was soaking wet.

"My God," she whispered, "how long did the nightmare last this time? I thought I had kicked this habit."

In her dream, Stella had again been in the beautiful field of flowers playing with the naked little boy. As before, she could not see his face. They'd played for a while and walked hand in hand without saying a word. Suddenly, the man with the face of a jackal had appeared. He was the ugliest and meanest thing Stella had ever seen. She had stood still and unable to move as the man had reached for the boy. He'd grabbed him and slowly moved away. As he'd moved farther and farther away, Stella had regained her composure and started to shout. "Wait! Wait! Don't go. Don't go."

The boy and the man had become a tiny dot and disappeared.

Stella got out of bed, walked into her closet, and pulled a nightgown from a drawer in the lingerie compartment. She changed out of her wet nightgown before slowly returning to bed, where she lay with her eyes closed as she replayed the dream over and over in her mind. She was trying to decipher its meaning.

Coming from within, Stella heard a voice whisper, *you need to chronicle this.*

She immediately grabbed the pen and notepad that were lying on her nightstand. She wrote the dream verbatim. As she wrote, she tried to recall the physical features of the little boy; all she could remember was the clump of hair hanging over his face to create a shadow. She noted that feature and then turned to replace the notepad and pen when she was suddenly struck by a memory.

"Oh my gosh," she exclaimed. "That e-eagle! Yes, an eagle!" The little boy had on the left side of his abdomen, under his navel, a birthmark in the form of an eagle in flight. Stella jotted down that information and then placed the pen and pad on one side of the bed. She then picked up the telephone and dialed Jeremy's number.

She waited for an answer. The receiver was picked up, but instead of hearing Jeremy's voice on the other end, she heard a tumbling sound. Stella stayed on the phone for about five minutes calling Jeremy's name. She got no answer. She finally yelled, "Jeremy, pick up the damn telephone."

There was still no answer.

She hung up and dialed again. For the next fifteen minutes, Stella continued to dial, each time getting a busy signal. Stella finally gave up as the thought of jumping into her car and driving to Jeremy's house entered her mind.

"Stop," Stella rebuked herself as she was about to get out of bed. "Calm down, girl," she said. "Calm down."

Stella silently lay back in bed for what seemed an eternity, and then slowly, she drifted back to sleep, only to be awakened by her alarm clock at 5:00 a.m.

Stella felt as if she had never gone to bed. She was tired. She slowly stumbled out of bed and drifted sleepily into the shower. She wanted to return to bed but was determined not to miss her early-morning exercise class at the Executive Fitness Club, located on the fourteenth floor of her office building.

Stella spent the rest of her morning in court presenting closing arguments on one of her cases, before meeting Jeremy at the La Fontene for lunch.

Their reunion was met with a passionate hug and a deep kiss, with Jeremy reiterating how much he'd missed her. The hostess led them to a table in a quiet section of the restaurant. As Jeremy looked into Stella's eyes from across the table, he realized that something was not right. "Babe," he asked, "what is the matter? Have you been getting any sleep? You are looking more exhausted than I feel."

"It's a long story, Jeremy. I hope you have some time."

A mother's advice, to not talk with one's mouth full, had long fallen on deaf ears when it came to Stella. Some of her cases were discussed at business lunches, where she'd learned to master the art of speaking with her mouth full. Stella ordered a Greek salad, and Jeremy ordered the hamburger combo.

"I need a good, old-fashioned homemade hamburger to feel like home again," he teased the waitress.

While they waited for their meal, Stella began to tell Jeremy about the dream by which she was haunted.

Jeremy jokingly responded that she would stop having the dream now that he was back. "The dream occurred because you had nothing to occupy your mind while I was gone," he said with a chuckle.

Stella was not amused. "Jeremy, if I needed comedic relief, I would go to the comedy club down the street," she retorted.

Jeremy got the message. He sat quietly and listened as Stella continued to describe the dream. By the time she was finished, they had both completed their lunches. Jeremy did not know what to make of the dream, but like Stella, he felt certain that there was a reason it kept recurring.

Jeremy had a very light afternoon at the office and was able to leave earlier than expected. By three o'clock, accompanied by Cookie (Stella's cook whom she nicknamed Cook), he was in Stella's kitchen preparing her favorite meal.

Stella left her office at about 5:30 p.m., and as she entered her driveway, Cook was pulling out. For a brief instance, she wondered what Cook was up to as she seldom left earlier than six thirty on weekdays.

"Whatever the reason, I am sure it is a good one," she said aloud as she stepped out of her car and went inside.

As was her normal routine, Stella kicked off her shoes and headed upstairs to have a shower.

"Wow!" she exclaimed, as she entered the bathroom.

She was greeted by a festival of candlelight. Candles surrounded her Jacuzzi and stood on the vanity. There were candles everywhere. Stella's bathroom looked like a starlit sky on a dark summer's night and smelled like an English garden. Rose petals and lily of the valley blossoms floated in a bubble bath, coupled with the intoxicating aroma of jasmine oil in the Jacuzzi.

"You have surely outdone yourself, Jeremy," Stella whispered.

"I know," said a voice from behind her.

Not knowing that Jeremy was right at her heels, Stella was slightly startled but did not take long to recover. She spun around and wrapped her arms around him. "Thank you," she whispered. "I needed this."

Jeremy kissed her on the neck. "Like what you see?"

"Perfect," Stella responded, "just perfect."

Jeremy kissed Stella once more and left.

Stella dropped her work attire to the floor and slid into the Jacuzzi. With her eyes closed, she listened to the soft music Jeremy had turned on before leaving the bathroom. She sniffed the air to distinguish each individual scent that was coming from the candles and the flower petals around her.

Stella was about to recognize her fourth scent when Jeremy quietly slid in beside her.

"What took you so long?" she admonished Jeremy with a smile.

"Waiting for you to get comfortable," Jeremy responded.

They both laughed, and in silence, Jeremy kissed Stella on the cheek and then slowly ran his index finger down her shoulder. With that, Stella turned toward Jeremy, and they both scooped water into their palms and began to massage each other's bodies. Every stroke was carefully orchestrated, as if they were competing to see who could give the other the most pleasure. They both won, as every stroke created a moan of ecstasy, which eventually led to their most intimate kiss since Jeremy's return.

Neither of them could hold back the passion burning within. And there, in the Jacuzzi, Stella and Jeremy made the most ravishing yet passionate love either of them had ever experienced. Their bodies glided back and forth as one beneath the bubbles and flower petals in the jasmine-scented water. And in perfect synchronicity, they simultaneously moaned as their bodies exploded and grew limp with passion. They released their embrace and looked directly into each other's eyes, acknowledging their love as if for the first time.

"Marry me," Jeremy whispered. "Please marry me."

Without a pause, Stella responded. "Yes, Jeremy. Yes. I will marry you."

They embraced once more and remained in that position. About fifteen minutes later, they emerged from the Jacuzzi hand in hand, put out the candles, and proceeded to the bedroom.

Before Stella could get into her housecoat, Jeremy, who was by then dressed in a black tuxedo and white shirt, presented her with a black, backless, flowing gown, accented with a touch of silvery brocade at the bustline. He insisted that she try it on, and as she stepped in front of the mirror to admire its beauty, he placed around her neck an exquisite 10 karat diamond necklace.

Stella stood speechless as she admired the beauty of the strand adorning her neck and the long flowing gown that fit as if it was specially made for her.

Knowing that Stella's silence was momentary, Jeremy seized the opportunity to waltz her through the bedroom door, and still holding her hand, he led her down the stairs to the formal dining room.

She was presented with yet another surprise. The dining room table was elegantly set for two. It was adorned with her Royal Albert Old Country Roses china and Waterford crystal, with a centerpiece of thirty-six yellow roses bordered by two five-tier candelabras on either side.

Stella smiled as she remembered Cook pulling out of the driveway as she was pulling in.

"Now I know why Cook left in such a hurry. Did you give her the afternoon off?"

"Just an hour," Jeremy replied, "after she helped me with all this."

"Wonderful!" Stella said, "Just wonderful! This room never looked as beautiful as it does this very moment."

Jeremy cunningly smiled, knowing a finale was still to come. He pulled out the chair at the head of the table and invited Stella to have a seat. He took a seat beside her and then, with a slight clap of his hands, summoned Lloyd, the headwaiter from La Fontene. Lloyd, dressed in a black tux, carried a bottle of champagne and pushed a cart with a tureen and ladle on it. Stella was speechless.

For the first course, they were served a lightly seasoned pumpkin soup, Stella's favorite, followed by a garden salad. For the main course, two covered silver platters were placed before them. On each platter lay a steamed lobster covered in garlic butter, with a bed of wild rice between both claws and oven-roasted asparagus smothered in cheese sauce on the side.

Stella ate the asparagus and wild rice before getting to her favorite seafood. After dipping into the rice a second time, she noticed a glitter of light on her fork. Curious, she looked closer into the platter, and there, caught in a claw of her lobster was a diamond ring. For a moment, she thought it was an illusion. She blinked, wiped her eyes with the back of her thumbs, and took a second look. It was real; she was staring at a 5 karat, princess-cut diamond ring.

Stella choked up, and tears rolled down her cheeks. She had not realized how much emotion she had simmering within her. For the first time since her nightmare had begun, Stella realized that she needed reassurance that she was not alone. Jeremy, through his actions over the past few hours, had given her just that. Through sobs and tears, Stella proclaimed her love for Jeremy and vowed to eat her way to the ring.

As promised, Stella ate the lobster, starting with the tail. Then eating claw by claw, she worked her way toward the ring, unlatched it, and handed it to Jeremy.

Smiling from ear to ear, Jeremy took the ring; went down on one knee; and, for the second time in one day, asked Stella to marry him.

"I surely will marry you!" Stella exclaimed as she looked lovingly into his hazel eyes.

"I guess we are official now," she teased as Jeremy placed the ring on her finger.

After dinner, Jeremy and Stella retired upstairs to the bedroom, where they enjoyed one of Stella's favorite movies, *Adam's Rib*. At the end of the movie, Stella curled up in Jeremy's arms, and although she had hoped to talk to him about her reoccurring dreams, all that seemed to have disappeared. She was not about to have anything destroy her marvelous evening with her now fiancé.

They again made passionate love, and then fell peacefully asleep in each other's arms.

As Stella drifted off to sleep, she could think of nothing except how beautiful and safe it was to be in the arms of the one she loved.

Jeremy was awakened by a kick from Stella as she punched, kicked, moaned, and screamed.

"Don't go! Don't go! Don't go!"

In desperation, Jeremy shook Stella until she was awake, and then, pulling her tightly into his arms, he held her until she regained full consciousness. Stella reached for her pad and pen and started to write.

Except for the fact that, this time, she'd put up a fight against the man with the face of a jackal, everything in her dream had happened exactly as it had before. She had been back in the enchanted garden with the little boy whose face she could not see. There was the birthmark of the eagle in flight on the left side of his abdomen, under his navel. And the man with the face of a jackal had come and taken him away.

When Stella finished writing, she nervously placed the pad and pen on the night table.

Jeremy looked on in disbelief. And when she was finished, he asked, "Was this the same dream?"

Stella nodded. "It happened again," she whispered.

Jeremy held out his arms. Pulling her closer, he rocked her for a while. Then kissing her on the forehead, he said "Let's talk about it in the morning."

For the first time, he understood the seriousness of Stella's dream and wished he had not teased her when she'd first told him about it. He looked at the clock on the night table. It was almost four in the morning. He continued to hold Stella until he was certain she had fallen asleep. Then slowly, he pulled away and lay beside her, trying to understand the confusion she felt within.

Chapter 20

Stella had a 9:00 a.m. meeting at her office with Jim Talbert. Surprisingly, when she got to the office building at 8:30 a.m., Jim was already there. He'd signed in twenty minutes before her.

As Stella stepped into the elevator she wondered why, for the first time in three years, Jim was early for his appointment.

"He must have fallen out of bed this morning," she said with a chuckle.

When Stella stepped out of the elevator, the door to the conference room was ajar.

"Hello, Jim," she called, peeking through the partially opened door. "Why do we need all this space?"

"Morning, boss," she heard Jim reply in a disembodied, muffled voice, but when she entered the conference room, Jim was nowhere in sight. Instead, she was greeted by several boxes lying on the large conference room table.

"Wow" she exclaimed, as she looked around the boxes. "Jim, where are you?"

"Here I am," Jim answered, with a less muffled voice than before. He was sitting at the far end of the table, eating doughnuts, which she assumed he had purchased at the corner café on his way to the office.

Stella walked toward Jim, placed her briefcase on the floor, pulled up a chair, and sat beside him. "Now I know why you chose this room," Stella said. "What's up with all these boxes?"

"Evidence, boss, evidence the federal court never saw during Clyde's criminal trial."

Stella became wide-eyed, and curious. She was ready to delve into those boxes, but instead, she took a deep breath, reached for Jim's doughnuts, and leaned back on her chair for a brief chitchat over coffee and doughnuts before getting down to business. Over the years, Stella and Jim had developed a ritual; they never discussed business without first having some small talk about nothing in particular and everything in general.

After their fifteen minutes of small talk, Stella and Jim got to work unpacking and going through each of the boxes. With his penknife, Jim pried open the first box and slowly removed its contents. He placed them neatly on the table. They were all journals.

Stella browsed through each journal individually. Some contained materials of a personal nature. They told where Mr. Clyde went from time to time, what he did, and who he met with. There were numerous romantic escapades in those journals. Stella quickly decided that the personal journals were not a priority, though they may be of some value later. She instructed Jim to return them to the box and label the box "Last Resort."

Some journals included ledger accounts of payments made to and received from clients. As Stella flipped through those pages, she smiled and asked Jim to open the other boxes. She was amazed at the type and amount of information Jim had uncovered.

The other boxes contained identification cards and passports with numerous aliases and signatures. There were hundreds of canceled checks and a list of serial numbers for bank accounts in Switzerland, the Dominican Republic, and in other Caribbean islands. Also included in some of the boxes were negatives from photos, movie reels, and videotapes. There was information going all the way back to the day Mr. Clyde started his illegal activities.

"If nothing else, Clyde kept good records," Stella whispered. Then, pondering deeply, she turned to Jim and asked, "With all that traveling, when did Mr. Clyde find time to compile all this information? He must have had an accomplice."

"He did," Jim answered. "Jasper is his name. He turned state's evidence and walked away a free man."

"Bastards," Stella murmured. "They all should be buried alive."

Jim was excited as he saw the expression he'd come to know as "I've got you!" cross Stella's face. He had been doing investigative work for Stella for the past three years and had learned to read her expressions well.

After browsing through all the boxes, Stella sat quietly for a few seconds without saying a word. Then abruptly, she turned to Jim and asked "How in the world did you obtain all that information when investigators from the police department and the Feds could not?" She was beginning to think that the mob was involved.

Jim replied, "Connections, boss, connections. Called in favors and payoffs too. You see, boss, Clyde is supposedly doing fifteen years behind bars. His friends do not care anymore, especially now that you have his assets frozen. They are no longer getting paid for their silence. No sirree, the big bucks are no longer rolling, so the canaries are singing."

Jim picked up his hat and motioned to Stella that he was leaving.

"Thank you, Jim," she said. "Good work." She gave him a high five and a peck on the cheek and watched him as he walked out the door of the conference room.

As he closed the door behind him, she muttered, "Good old Jim. He always comes through for—"

Before she could complete her statement, the door opened and Jim peeked in. "Oh, by the way, boss, your Mr. Clyde was into more than child pornography. I have reasons to believe that he was also selling babies on the black market. I will call you after I meet with my contact later."

Stella hurried to the door. "Jim, be care … ful."

She was too late. By the time she got to the door, the elevator had closed with Jim inside. Stella slowly shut the door and went back inside.

With all of the evidence separated and like items piled together on the conference table, Stella methodically labeled them and then logged them into a special book. On the photo negatives, she wrote, "To be cleaned on Monday." Then together with the special book, she locked everything she had in her office safe.

Stella moved the empty boxes into one corner, and after making sure that everything was secured, she took her briefcase, double-locked the conference room, and headed for the elevator.

Downstairs, Stella signed the log at the front desk, said good-bye to Kevin the security guard, and exited the large, glass double doors at the front of the building.

As Stella drove home from the office, she could not get Jim's last statement out of her mind. *Your Mr. Clyde was into more than child pornography. I have reasons to believe that he was also selling babies on the black market.*

"This man is indeed Lucifer," Stella said aloud. "Where on earth did he draw the line? How many people did he hurt?"

Chapter 21

It was midafternoon when Stella got home from the office. Jeremy was waiting on the patio with lunch ready to be served.

"Hi there," she called to Jeremy as she walked in. "I did not realize how late it was."

"I'll someday adapt to waiting," Jeremy responded. "In any case, I got quite a bit done myself. I'm still working on my report for Friday's presentation."

Stella reached into the refrigerator, grabbed a couple of beers, and walked onto the patio. She bent over and kissed Jeremy on the lips as she handed him a beer. "I guess this has been a working day for both of us," she whispered.

Jeremy stopped typing, opened his beer, and took a sip.

Stella told Jeremy about Jim's suspicion that Mr. Clyde might have also sold babies on the black market. Before Jeremy could respond, she went on and on about how much she despised Mr. Clyde for all of his atrocious acts.

Jeremy was not surprised by Jim's revelation. However, he was concerned about Stella's state of mind. He reckoned that she was becoming so personally attached to the case that she was on the verge of undermining her ability to be objective.

Jeremy continued to attentively listen to Stella's endless ranting about the case. He took another sip of his beer, placed the bottle on the table, and then reclined backward. He folded his hands behind his head and sought eye contact with Stella.

Stella immediately recognized the look and stopped. "What?" she asked defiantly.

Jeremy got out of the chair, placed his hands in his pockets, and paced around the table without uttering a word. He was thinking of how to say what was on his mind without offending her.

Stella stood staring at him.

He then stopped, looked back at her, and asked, "What do you intend to do about the nightmare that is keeping you awake at night?"

The question took Stella by surprise. She had been so mesmerized by the multitude of documents Jim had uncovered that she had not thought of the dream all day. "Nothing," she responded. "I am too busy preparing the case to think about nightmares. Maybe, if I leave it alone, it will go away as quickly as it appeared."

"I don't think so! I strongly urge you to forget about the case for a while and consider talking to a psychologist. According to most psychologists, dreams could result from past occurrences, which an individual might be subconsciously suppressing. It is called repressed memory. Maybe you experienced something so horrendous that your conscious mind will not allow you to remember it."

Jeremy paused for a moment and continued, "I must say that for you to honestly believe that the nightmare will go away as fast as it appeared shows more than just that you have repressed memories; I think that you are in total denial."

At that, Stella laughed uncontrollably. And then, with a jerk of the head and disdain on her face, Stella looked at Jeremy as if she was about to spit.

Jeremy was not a stranger to Stella's outbursts. In the past, he had always given in. This time, he was not about to. The look on his face immediately alerted Stella to that fact.

He was stern yet nurturing, like a parent ready to discipline a child. Stella seldom saw that side of Jeremy, and since she was not in the mood for a confrontation, she calmly retreated, but not before accusing him of insinuating that she was crazy.

With her index finger pointed and shaking at Jeremy, Stella forcefully informed him that under no circumstances would she have her brain be probed by a shrink. She could not stomach the thought of sitting on the sofa in the office of a psychologist, emptying her innermost thoughts to her. She wanted nothing to do with that. "Absolutely not," she said as she turned and directed her teary gaze into space. "Never again," she whispered. "There must be another way."

"If you want this nightmare to end, you must confront what is causing it."

Stella heard echoes in the wind as tears rolled down her cheeks. There was no indication that she was hearing a word as Jeremy continued his argument.

After a few stoic moments, Stella abruptly broke her silence, "Okay, Jeremy," she said. "Maybe you are right. Maybe I need to look into my past for answers, but not through a shrink. I will find the answers in my own way."

"Tha ... that's a step in the right direction," Jeremy stammered.

For the next hour, Stella and Jeremy discussed ways to research her past. After careful consideration, they both decided to start with the boxes that were stored in Stella's basement.

"If the answer is not found here, I'll fly to Mount Pleasant. Maybe I can find the answers there."

Jeremy was ecstatic about her decision. He was madly in love with Stella, and could not bear to see her struggle through her nightmares.

Stella was ready to begin the search, but she had no intention of putting the Clyde case on hold. As she prepared herself to delve into her past, the words that Jim had spoken once again flashed through her mind. *Your Mr. Clyde was into more than child pornography. I have reasons to believe that he was also selling babies on the black market.*

Stella led Jeremy to her storage room in the basement, where he found himself staring at a mountain of boxes.

"What are all these?"

"My life," Stella answered. "There lies my past, all locked up in boxes. Dig in and help me discover the hidden skeletons."

Stella and Jeremy worked for hours, searching through the boxes, not knowing what they were looking for. They took the rest of the weekend to look for anything that would help to unravel Stella's dream.

Neatly packed away in those boxes were mementos, photos, books, memoirs, letters, trinkets, and all that Stella held dear from as far back as she could remember. Diaries of her studies and travels abroad were also part of the contents stashed in those boxes.

Whenever Stella felt like remembering the two years she had studied in Switzerland or the countries she had traveled, all she did was enter her basement storage and look through a few boxes. Each box was clearly labeled. Some of them also contained postcards and letters Stella had received from relatives and friends.

Jeremy expressed his amazement at how much of Stella's past she had stored away and how organized everything was. "If there's anything in these boxes that can remind Stella of her past, it would not be hard to find," he whispered.

Stella smiled at her ability to save without hoarding. She started laughing as she went through one of the boxes marked "Friends."

"Find anything, Stell?"

"Yes. Fond memories."

Jeremy smiled at Stella and continued looking. He was hoping to find anything that remotely resembled a symbol of Stella's dream.

They found pictures of friends and acquaintances she had met along the way. She even found gifts and souvenirs she had received and bought. There were pictures of birthday celebrations from Stella's seventh birthday and beyond.

By the time Stella and Jeremy finished going through the boxes, it was late Sunday afternoon. They were so exhausted they could not restock the boxes. They left the restocking for Eduardo, the gardener, to complete the following day.

Stella turned off the light and closed the storage room door, and together, she and Jeremy silently ascended the stairs out of the basement. They entered the kitchen, where Stella poured herself a glass of cold water from a jug in the refrigerator. She slowly sipped the water as she stared out the kitchen window, over the sink, into space. She was looking at nothing. The frustration of not finding a clue in any of those boxes was beginning to take its toll.

Jeremy pretended not to notice, but he shared her pain. He had never seen Stella as helpless as she now appeared.

After they had met, Stella had introduced him to her adopted parents, Mr. and Mrs. Honig, and her guardian, Robert Oxford. He'd also met her extended family, Mrs. Oxford and her three children and Theresa. Stella had told him about her search for a missing brother, but at no time had she explained why Eric was missing. She had also told him that her biological parents had died in an automobile accident, but she'd never spoke extensively about them.

Jeremy had never inquired beyond what she'd told him. He knew that if Stella wanted him to know more about them, nothing would stand in her way of telling him. He conceded that she would confide in him whenever she was ready.

As he stood silently watching Stella gaze into space, Jeremy thought of something that, until now, hadn't seemed peculiar. During their search of the boxes in the basement, Jeremy had seen no record of Stella prior to her seventh birthday.

"At what age were you adopted, Stell?" Jeremy asked without thinking.

"What does it matter to you?" Stella replied.

"There was no record of your existence preceding your seventh birthday Stell."

"My earlier existence is stashed in the basement of my guardian's home in Mount Pleasant."

It turned out that Stella's silence, up until now, had been occupied by thoughts of how to access those records without having to take time off the Clyde case to travel to Mount Pleasant.

With hopes of finding the reason for her dream, Jeremy was prepared to travel to the end of the world with Stella. He was going nowhere. Stella had decided to have the records sent to her.

Stella walked over to the kitchen table, picked up the telephone, and dialed.

"Hi, Pops," she said after a few moments of silence. "How are you?" After inquiring about the rest of the family and Mount Pleasant's weather, Stella casually said, "Oh, by the way, Pops, can you please send me some of the records from my earlier childhood?"

Stella heard a thud as if something fell.

After a few seconds of silence, Mr. Oxford said, "Sorry, Stell, I lost the phone for a moment. By the way, did you ask me for your childhood records?"

"Yes, Pops, I did." Before Mr. Oxford could respond, Stella tactfully added, "I was looking at some family photos that you took sometime ago and thought that it was time I look further into my past."

Mr. Oxford congratulated Stella for finally deciding to take that step. He had been trying to get her to go through those boxes since her eighteenth birthday, but up until now, she'd showed no interest.

Stella made arrangements with Mr. Oxford to have the boxes containing photographs, letters, and home movies delivered to her home in Haileysville. She then thanked him and hung up the telephone.

Stella breathed a sigh of relief as she lifted her hand from the receiver. "That was a close one," she murmured. "I hate telling lies to Pops, but I can't have him fussing over me. I cannot deal with another Jeremy."

After taking a long shower and eating a light dinner that Cook had prepared earlier, Stella and Jeremy took a walk on the grounds of her estate. The night air felt fresh and tranquil as the beautiful fragrance from the lilac and roses enveloped the grounds. The squeaking, yelping, and chirping of insects played a sweet melody, and the light of the full moon glowed radiantly, giving new life to every dimension as far off as the eyes could see.

Captivated by the splendor of the night, Stella and Jeremy walked hand in hand, not uttering a sound. As they walked past the gazebo, like a meeting of the minds, they came to a complete stop. Simultaneously, the melody stopped, and all they could hear was the beating of their hearts.

They turned and looked into each other's eyes. Still, without a word, they clutched each other in the middle of the field, under the clear open sky and made passionate love by the light of the beautiful moon. Every care, every worry, every person on earth was swept away by the love they shared. Nothing seemed to matter as they lay happily in each other's arms, looking into the heavens.

"I wish time could stand still," Stella finally whispered.

"So do I," replied Jeremy. "So do I."

That night, Stella was again awakened by the dream. This time, she'd found herself more determined to get the boy away from the man with the face of a jackal. She'd put up a fight that had landed Jeremy on the floor. Jeremy quickly pulled himself back onto the bed and looked at Stella as she punched, kicked, and yelled.

"No. No. No," she cried out. "Don't go. Don't go."

To subdue Stella, Jeremy tightly embraced her while calling her by name.

When Stella finally woke, she reached for her pen and pad and wrote vigorously.

On arriving at her office the following Monday, Stella urgently summoned Wendy, her secretary, into her office. She handed her the special book in which the evidence from Jim was logged. She also handed her the negatives, with strict instructions. "Have them developed as soon as possible. And, please, guard them with your life."

Before Wendy could respond, Stella was out of her office and entering Mr. Sylvester's office. She tapped lightly on the already open door and walked right in. Mr. Sylvester was about to pick up his ringing telephone, but the intense look on Stella's face caused him to pull his hand away.

"What's wrong, Miss James?" he inquired.

Not wanting to cause needless alarm, Stella smiled and assured him that all was well.

Stella's initial intention had been to tell him about Jim's revelation concerning Mr. Clyde, but she decided against it. Instead, Stella advised Mr. Sylvester that she was removing herself from all of her other cases in order to concentrate on the Clyde case. She provided him with a schedule of all her reassigned cases, none of which he had to handle.

As always, Mr. Sylvester trusted Stella unconditionally and had no qualms about her decision. All he asked was that Stella, like all the other attorneys in the firm, continue to give progress reports during their weekly meetings.

When Stella left Mr. Sylvester's office, she was in fighting mode. What she did not know was that this fight would be the fight of her life. It was the fight that would end all fights, the fight that would bring her face-to-face with her demons.

PART SEVEN

Stella

Her Past Revealed

Chapter 22

Four days subsequent to requesting the boxes from Mr. Oxford, Stella decided to sleep in after experiencing another sleepless night. In the middle of her nap, she was awakened by the chimes of her doorbell, which sent her into a stupor. She jumped, wondering what was happening. *Who could be at the door so early in the morning?* She looked at the clock radio on her night table. It was 9:45 a.m.

Carmen, Stella's housekeeper, and Cook both got in about ten each morning, and they both had keys for the house. The doorbell chimed for the second time. This time, she was completely alert. She walked over to the intercom and turned it on.

"Who is it?"

"Delivery," a gruff, husky voice replied.

Stella pulled on her housecoat and rushed downstairs.

Standing at the door, was a postal service carrier. He was standing close to a cart on which six large boxes were loaded.

Stella stood motionless as she stared at the boxes. She could not escape the frightening thought that one of those boxes might very well be Pandora's box. She panicked at the thought. Her heart pounded, her palms were sweaty, and chills ran through her veins.

"Please sign here," she heard in the distance.

Stella jumped, only to realize that the deliveryman was holding before her a green card, with a pen pointed to a rectangular box in which she needed to place her signature.

"Oh, y-y-yes," she stuttered. She nervously took the pen, signed the form, and instructed the carrier to wheel the boxes into the garage.

Stella locked the door and slowly walked back through the foyer and up the stairs to her bedroom. Void of any thought, Stella stood at the bedroom window overlooking the grounds for almost ten minutes before going into the bathroom, where she took a long, hot shower.

By the time Stella came out of the shower, Carmen was downstairs getting her cleaning utensils together. Stella made three phone calls.

First, she called Mr. Oxford to thank him for promptly sending the boxes. Then she called her office to see if anything pressing was on her agenda for the afternoon. Wendy informed her that her three o'clock appointment with Jim was canceled and that the photos were back from the lab.

"Please lock them up," she told Wendy. "I will see you tomorrow."

Stella's third call was to let Jeremy know that the boxes she requested from Mount Pleasant had arrived.

Jeremy wanted to be there when the boxes were opened, but he was busy making last-minute preparations for his big presentation. "Please do not open the boxes until I get there."

"Okay." Stella answered without paying him much attention. She hung up the telephone and went downstairs.

Stella recalled seeing Eduardo on the grounds while she was standing at the window earlier.

"Eduardo. Eduardo," she called as she opened the front door. "Eduardo, where are you?"

Eduardo came running across the lawn. "Yes, ma'am," he shouted, wondering what he had done this time. In the two years since working as Stella's gardener, the only time she'd called him with such urgency was when he had come in drunk and drove the lawn mower through her rose garden.

"Eduardo, please take the boxes from the garage and put them in the library right away."

Eduardo was not drinking, so he knew that the request had to be executed immediately. Without wiping the mud off his boots, Eduardo carried the boxes into the library one at a time.

As Eduardo was leaving the library after dropping off the last box, Carmen saw the trail of mud on the floor and flew into a rage. She picked up a broom and chased him into the garden. She was screaming at the top of her voice. "I'll break your legs, Eduardo. I will break your legs."

Stella heard the commotion and rushed to the door. It was a sight she had not seen before. She knew that Carmen was capable of losing her temper from time to time, but seeing her chase Eduardo all over the grounds was funny.

For a while Stella, forgot everything that was going on in her life and laughed herself to tears.

The boxes were placed in a straight line in front of Stella's desk, making it very easy to choose exactly what contents she wished to look at. Without hesitation, she went straight for the box labeled home movies.

Stella viewed those reels for almost two hours. The first reel showcased a couple and a baby girl. Although Stella did not recognize them, she knew the couple was her parents and she was the little girl.

The second movie showcased the little girl; the couple; Mimi, who Stella recognized; and a little boy. Tears rolled down Stella's cheeks as she looked on. It was difficult to fathom the reality that the people in these movies were blood relatives she had not seen since the age of six—people she would never again see and could not remember. The only consolation Stella had as she viewed those movies was her deep-rooted feeling that, someday, her brother would be found.

As she continued to look at the movies, Stella became emotional, to the point of wanting to turn off the projector. She could not. Since she had no idea what she was looking for, she was forced to examine anything and everything that might provide a possible clue to deciphering her dream. She prayed that her search for answers would not be futile.

As Stella continued her search through the boxes, she smiled at the irony of it all. As a child, she had been protected from the contents of those boxes. Now, as an adult, she was forced to look inside the very same boxes for clues that may preserve her sanity.

She had dreaded going through these boxes for a long time, and she still did. But she was relieved that she was finally able to. Stella skipped the second box, which contained movie reels of events prior to her birth. There were numerous home movies of the family when Stella and Eric were babies.

As Stella continued to browse through the movies, she felt deep within her the love that had once surrounded her. "God," she whispered, "I was loved. My parents really loved me. I was surely a very happy child."

Jeremy drove into the driveway just as Stella was about to open the third box. She was still teary-eyed when he walked into the library, and he was surprised that she had started the search without him.

"This is just too emotional," Stella said without looking up. "I know my parents loved me. But seeing all these family movies reinforces my belief in the power of the love they had for Eric and me."

Jeremy felt her sadness and tried to distract her for just a moment. "Did you eat?"

"Yes, Cook made me lunch."

Unable to divert her attention, Jeremy excused himself for a moment and ran upstairs to change. He returned minutes later, wearing a black polo shirt and a pair of blue jeans.

Sitting on the floor beside Stella, Jeremy took a photo album from the newly opened box and began his search.

Each photograph in all the albums was labeled with an event and the date of the event. When Stella opened one of the last two albums, she smiled broadly as she looked at the caption written at the front: "Property of Eric James, born July 5, 1955, to the proud parents of Nelly and Hugo James." Under the caption was a tearstained note addressed to "My darling children."

After reading the note, Stella could not stop the tears from rolling down her cheeks. Yet she proceeded to turn the pages, each of which told a story. On the first page were Nelly and Hugo. The pages that followed showed Nelly in each stage of her pregnancy. Following were pictures of Nelly and the newborn baby boy at the hospital and at home. There were pictures of the baby boy at each stage of his life. Then there were pictures of him and Stella together.

As Stella continued, through tears, she could not help but wonder where her mother had found the time and strength to arrange those pictures. "She must have been a genius," Stella whispered as she wiped away the tears and struggled to keep more from coming.

Halfway through the album, there was a picture of Nelly bathing the little boy in a blue bathtub. The expression on his face indicated that he was crying.

"He was afraid of water." Stella chuckled.

As she started to turn the page, something caught her attention. She stopped and took a closer look.

"Oh my God. It's Ricki! It's Ricki!" Stella exclaimed, pointing to a picture in the album. Now, she was sobbing uncontrollably.

Jeremy dropped the album he was perusing and quickly leaned over to see what Stella was pointing at. There, at the tip of her index finger, was the picture of a naked little boy being given a bath by a woman. The picture was printed on three-by-five-inch, glossy Kodak paper.

Jeremy moved Stella's finger and looked closely at the picture. He was amazed at its clarity. On the left abdomen of the boy's naked body was a birthmark in the shape of an eagle in flight. The eagle was exactly as Stella had described it from her dream.

Jeremy removed the album from Stella's grasp and took a second look at the picture. Then with tears of joy, he placed his arms around her and whispered. "It is all right, Stell. It is all right now."

Without uttering another word, Stella placed her head on Jeremy's shoulder and continued to sob.

That night, Stella again dreamed of the enchanted garden with its beautiful assortment of flowers and intoxicating fragrances. As before, she found herself playing with the little naked boy, but the man with the face of a jackal appeared at a distance, fighting ferociously to reach them. He was held back by the overpowering image of a woman who blocked his every move toward Stella and the little boy. Protected by the woman, she and the little boy played until the dream slowly faded.

For the first time since the inception of the dream, Stella was able to continue her night's sleep long after the dream ended. She did not wake in a panic.

The following morning, Stella woke at the break of dawn. She chronicled her dream on the notepad, which had now become her dream log. She then handed it to Jeremy, who, after browsing through it, smiled and breathed a sigh of relief.

"Honey, I think your nightmares are over."

Stella inhaled deeply, opened both arms, and exhaled. "I am feeling wide-awake and energized," she said. "I am stronger than I have been in weeks."

Stella and Jeremy left for work earlier than usual. Jeremy was scheduled to deliver his presentation, and Stella, with a burst of energy, was ready to take on the world.

On her way to the office, she looked at her watch as she drove past her church. It was only 6:45 a.m., and a small number of cars were beginning to enter the parking lot for the 7:00 a.m. daily Mass. She turned her car around and followed the cars into the parking lot.

On her way in, she greeted Mr. McManus, the church's deacon. Then she went to the front and took a seat in the first pew from the altar.

The morning mass was officiated by Father Charo, Haileysville's best-loved priest. The first reading was from the Gospel of Matthew 17:20: "If you have faith like a grain of mustard seed, ye shall say unto this mountain, remove hence to yonder place; and it shall remove; and nothing shall be impossible unto you."

After Mass, Father Charo took Stella's hand, and looking straight into her eyes, he said, "My child, God does not always come when you call him, but he comes in time. Have faith, and everything will fall into place. He knows your heart."

Stella could not understand why she had been singled out on this very morning, but as she drove to work, the words kept ringing in her ears. *He comes in time. Have faith. He comes in time.*

"He comes in time for what?" Stella whispered. "Okay, time to find Eric."

Stella walked into her office building at exactly 8:15 a.m., and as usual, she greeted the security guard in the lobby as she headed toward the elevator. Since she was the first to get in, she turned on the lights, put her briefcase on her desk, picked up the telephone, and dialed long distance.

"Good morning, Pops! How are you? Thanks again for the boxes." Stella spoke to Mr. Oxford for a while before telling him that she wanted to resume the search for Eric.

"He is alive, Pops. I know that he is, and I am going to find him."

Mr. Oxford was not enthusiastic about going down that path again, though he stopped short of asking Stella to give it up. He knew she would never give up on something she truly believed in. He called it a "disease of the heart."

After offering to do whatever he could to assist in the search, Mr. Oxford ended the conversation by expressing his love for Stella and wishing her luck this time around.

As he returned the telephone to its cradle, the happy sound of Stella's voice echoed all around him. His heart sank. He feared for Stella as he envisioned her happiness turning into sorrow once again.

He dropped slowly into his chair, and looking into the heavens, he called, "Lord, give her a miracle."

Now that Stella had taken care of personal matters, she was ready once again to fully concentrate on the Clyde case. She was about to call Wendy into her office when Wendy walked in. "Oh, good morning, Wendy. We have a heck of a day ahead of us. I hope you are as energized as I am."

"Good morning, Miss James. I am ready when you are."

"Wonderful, Wendy. Then let's get started."

They moved to Stella's back office, where Wendy had already laid out, in order, all that Stella needed to start on the Clyde's case. Even the projector was set up. And with that, they went right to work.

The receipts were first on the agenda. They were from credit cards, airlines, hotels, and restaurants. Some were dated as far back as 1945.

"My goodness," said Stella, "this man is a real veteran. He must be the granddaddy of child pornography."

"He is also well traveled," Wendy added.

Just as Stella and Wendy were about to look at the photographs, Mr.

Sylvester joined them. He took a seat next to Stella, and together, they separated the pictures into four categories—offensive, more offensive, most offensive, and rejects.

They then turned their attention to the movie. Wendy lowered the screen, turned on the projector, and dimmed the light. About halfway through, Stella asked Wendy to stop the projector and rewind the movie. This happened at least three times. She wanted to be sure that she was not hallucinating. She was not.

On the screen before her stood a little boy, stark naked. He was crying. He appeared to be about three years old. As Stella examined the picture more closely, she noticed on the left side of his abdomen, under his navel, the image of an eagle in flight. It was the same image that had appeared in her dreams and the very same image she had seen in Eric's album the day before. Stella almost fell off her chair as she got up to run to the ladies' room. She was sick to her stomach.

Stella returned a few minutes later, looking as if she had seen a ghost. Her companions assumed that the contents of the film had made her sick. They could not have imagined what she had just discovered. For the time being, it would stay that way. She wanted to be sure. She had to speak to Mr. Oxford.

Stella thanked Wendy and Mr. Sylvester for their assistance. She advised them that she was not feeling well and would be gone from the office for the rest of the day.

They understood.

Immediately after they walked out of Stella's office, Stella, for the second time, picked up the telephone and dialed long distance. "Pops," she said, trying to maintain a calm, steady tone, "I desperately need your help. Can you get here tomorrow?"

It was a request Mr. Oxford seldom got from Stella, whom he regarded as his daughter. He loved her as much as he did his biological children. In fact, he had never gotten such a request from Stella. Without her even having to explain, Mr. Oxford knew whatever she needed, it was urgent.

One hour later, he called Stella to inform her that he and Mrs. Oxford would be landing at Haileysville airport that very evening.

Stella placed the movie reel and two pictures from the pile labeled "most offensive" into her briefcase, and then she left the office in a hurry.

Mr. Sylvester was somewhat taken aback by Stella's hurried exit. Nevertheless, he trusted Stella enough not to ask why. Recently, he had noticed her preoccupation with something other than work but had refrained from asking questions. Her performance as an astute attorney was not a concern, and he knew that Stella would let him know what was going on if and when there was a need to do so.

Stella reached her front door without knowing exactly how she got there. She was numb. On entering the house, she rushed to the library, retrieved Eric's album, and frantically flipped through the pages to find the picture in which the lady was bathing the little boy. With the picture in hand, Stella removed the movie reel from her briefcase and inserted it into the projector in her library.

She rewound it and paused on the naked boy with the eagle on his lower left abdomen. She compared it to the photograph from the album. The little boy projected on the screen and the one in the photograph were one and the same. It was Eric.

Stella sat trembling hysterically, not knowing what to do or say. She tried to cry, but the tears would not flow. Then slowly, an image of Mr. Clyde flashed before her eyes. And in a husky voice, she heard herself repeating over and over again, "My brother was your victim. My mother was your victim. My father was your victim. I am your victim."

Stella felt as if her head was exploding with thoughts of evil, while at the same time her stomach had been trampled upon. And for once in her life, she knew she was capable of murder. If Mr. Clyde had entered the room at that very moment, she would have killed him.

Tears began to run down her cheeks as she swore in a loud voice. "Mr. Clyde, I will personally destroy you."

Stella wiped away the tears, walked to her desk, picked up the telephone, and dialed Jim Talbert's number. No one answered. As she hung up, the telephone rang. It was Jeremy.

With excitement in his voice, Jeremy told Stella how successful his presentation had been but stopped short of inviting her to the celebration.

She was sounding melancholic. "What's wrong?" he inquired. Before she could answer, he said, "Never mind. I'll be there shortly."

Jeremy had called Stella's office and learned that she'd left early. He did not need a response from her to know that something was wrong.

When Jeremy arrived at Stella's house, she was still sitting on the sofa in the library, staring at the image of the naked little boy.

"What's going on?" Jeremy asked as he walked toward Stella.

She pointed to the screen.

"Who shot this disgusting film?"

"The devil did it," she murmured. "The devil himself did it."

Jeremy stood looking at Stella as she incoherently repeated, "The devil did it. The devil did it."

"What on earth are you talking about, Stella?" Jeremy asked, clearly confused.

Stella looked up, and as her eyes caught Jeremy's, she realized that it was finally time to tell him about her blood relatives.

By the time Stella finished telling her story as she knew it, Jeremy was pacing across the library floor, wishing to get his hands on Mr. Clyde. He was so infuriated that he punched a hole through a wall in the library, leaving his right knuckle bruised and in pain. "That SOB should not be alive. If I get my hands on him, he will be dead."

"Take a number," Stella responded solemnly.

Jeremy walked toward the projector, removed the movie reel, and sat beside Stella in silence.

Mr. and Mrs. Oxford arrived in an airport limousine at around nine thirty that evening. Stella saw them and rushed to the door to greet them.

"Take the bags inside," she instructed Eduardo, whom she had asked to work late in case she needed something.

Stella hugged Mr. and Mrs. Oxford and then started to cry.

Though exhausted, the Oxfords insisted that Stella tell them what was going on. She tried to put it off until the following day. They would not wait. They wanted immediate answers. They sat silently in the library and listened attentively as Stella told the story.

Stella started with the very first time she had seen the little naked boy in her dream and told them everything that had happened since, ending with the moment she had seen the movie reel. She showed them Eric's album and then the photos and movie reel she had brought home from the office. Mrs. Oxford was in tears throughout. Mr. Oxford sat motionless, hanging on Stella's every word. He feared that if he moved, he would miss something.

When Stella finished speaking, silence fell over the entire room; all eyes were fixed on her. No one spoke, not even Jeremy.

Mr. Oxford wanted to speak, but he didn't know what to say. He got out of the armchair and slowly walked toward the window. He was thinking of what a father would say to a child who had gone through Stella's experiences. He could think of nothing. All he knew was that he loved Stella as his own. He could not stop her from hurting. He wanted her pain to go away. As he remained at the window, his eyes closed, he forced back a tear. Then, without uttering a word, he walked back toward Stella and wrapped his arms around her. "I love you, Stell," he said. "I love you."

Cook had prepared dinner and set the table in the formal dining room before leaving. No one was able to eat. They all sat at the table in silence.

The following morning, Stella lay in bed, agonizing over whether she should continue to work on the Clyde case or relinquish it to Mr. Sylvester. There was no conflict of interest since she owed no legal duty to Mr. Clyde. Nevertheless, she was unsure of her ability to remain emotionally stable while dealing with the situation. She doubted whether she could legally go after Clyde when, in her heart, she wanted him murdered.

After breakfast, Stella discussed her dilemma with the Oxfords, who encouraged her to stay on the case. They explained that by doing so, she might be privy to information that could aid her search for Eric. Stella seldom backed down from a fight.

And even though she was hurting, the Oxfords knew that now, when so much was at stake, was not the time to start doing so. They had to push her along. "Stella," Mr. Oxford instructed, "life does not always deal us the hand we deserve, and no one knows like you how true that is. You have gone down that path before, and you dealt with the hand that was given you and won. Don't give up now. Through this, you may even find the miracle you have been hoping for—the information you need to bring closure to Eric's disappearance."

Stella thought long and hard about what the Oxfords had said. And by the end of the day, her only question was whether Mr. Oxford would work on the case with her.

He willingly agreed.

Chapter 23

Stella, Mr. Oxford, Jim Talbert, and Wendy worked relentlessly on the Clyde case. They filed briefs, wrote motions, interviewed potential witnesses, and gathered information about Mr. Clyde's illegal activities thirty years prior. With information that revealed his criminal activities went far beyond child pornography, it became easier to obtain incriminating evidence from his colleagues who knew of or were party to those activities.

Many of Mr. Clyde's acquaintances seemed eager to testify against him in exchange for prosecutorial immunity. Even Jim's hunch that Mr. Clyde was involved in black market activities was confirmed by one of Mr. Clyde's accomplices.

Jim's thorough investigation and the new evidence he'd uncovered also led Haileysville CID to bring additional charges against Mr. Clyde. Among those charges were kidnapping, false imprisonment, money laundering, and a host of others.

Stella's interview with some of the witnesses made her shiver as she thought of the fate her brother and other innocent children had suffered while in the hands of Mr. Clyde. It was revealed that he was notorious for holding his victims in rat-infested motels while waiting to escape or make a trade. In tears, one of his accomplices confessed that Mr. Clyde muzzled and sometimes drugged his victims in order to keep them quiet or make them cooperate.

Once, after listening to the graphic details of how Mr. Clyde muzzled a six-year-old boy for hours while taking lewd photos of him, Stella communicated to Mr. Oxford her urge to place a contract on Mr. Clyde's life.

Knowing Stella the way he did, Mr. Oxford quickly advised her to stay calm and use her skills as an attorney to avenge Clyde's victims. "You will have your day in court. Use it wisely," he warned.

Stella struggled with the inescapable emotional pain she felt, and the only way she could break free was through bringing about Mr. Clyde's total demise.

The heightened interest by the Haileysville CID, together with newly uncovered evidence against Mr. Clyde, led Mount Pleasant CID and the FBI to open the case on the missing James boy, Eric.

To Stella's surprise, she received an urgent call from Mount Pleasant CID, requesting her presence at the interrogation of a man alleged to be Mr. Clyde's accomplice.

Stella refused. She was skeptical as to their reasons for wanting her there. A second call from the new chief of police changed her mind—he told her that the request had come from the alleged suspect himself.

Stella's conversation with the new chief left her believing that her compliance might lead to a positive step toward finding Eric. She agreed to make an appearance, and on that very evening, she and Jeremy boarded the last flight to Mount Pleasant, with connection via Chicago.

After their two-hour layover at O'Hare International Airport and a thirty-minute flight to Mount Pleasant, they landed at Mount Pleasant airport at exactly 6:30 a.m. Stella insisted on having their limousine take them directly to the Mount Pleasant CID, instead of to their hotel to check in.

They sat on a bench at the front desk for almost an hour before Chief of Police Casenov walked in.

The new chief of police was a tall, slender, cleanly shaved middle-aged man who seemed eager to get things going. He introduced himself and, without hesitation, led them into his office. Mr. Casenov sympathized with Stella for the death of her parents and then, in the same breath, advised her that her presence at the interrogation was unprecedented. "You are here only because the suspect requested it as a show of respect for Mrs. James. We obliged because of your past ordeal. I felt that we at least owed you that."

It was difficult for Stella to believe that someone her mother knew would hold no regard for human suffering.

"Who ever it is, it is too late for his show of respect," Stella replied. "I am here only to find out where my brother is."

Mr. Casenov led Stella and Jeremy into the interrogation room adjoining his office.

On entering, Stella stood spellbound. She looked as if she had seen a ghost. Her jaw dropped, and her mouth hung wide open. She was stunned.

The alleged suspect was Jerry Malone, the city's most liked and trusted ice cream man. He was standing at the table in shackles, his gaze toward the entrance as if he was waiting for Stella's arrival.

Jerry was one of the few people Stella remembered from childhood. He was the nice, friendly man in Sam's Ice Cream Parlor, where she went for ice cream whenever she was in town.

Her ice cream rituals had started with Nelly and had continued long after Nelly was gone. Going to Sam's Ice Cream Parlor was the only family pleasure Stella's psychologist had allowed her to continue to enjoy.

The Honigs had taken her to Sam's regularly, and she and the Oxford siblings and their friends had frequented the establishment throughout their high school years. By then, Jerry was the manager of Sam's, and his popularity with his patrons had soared.

Stella stood almost paralyzed as Jeremy physically moved her from the doorway into a chair.

The attending officer assisted Jerry Malone into a chair opposite Stella, and with a tape recorder placed before him, Jerry Malone started his confession. "I ... I needed the money," he stuttered sheepishly. "Mr. Clyde and I met in a bar the first time he came into town. A ... a ... at least I thought it was the first time. He knew everything about me. He knew my name. He knew where I lived. He even knew that my girlfriend was pregnant and that I was taking money from Sam's to help pay for her abortion. He ... he knew everything. He asked me to let him know of any children who came into the store looking kinda … lost. He was also looking for vulnerable mothers with toddlers or pregnant teenagers." Jerry paused, cleared his throat and continued without looking directly at Stella. "He told me that if I did not do exactly as he said, he would make sure I lost my job and be thrown in jail. Miss … Miss Stella," Jerry looked into Stella's eyes for the first time, "I … I had no choice."

Stella had by now fully recovered from her initial shock. Part of Stella felt sorry for Jerry Malone. But she was appalled by the fact that he had never come forward, even after the death of her parents. "Get on with it," she snapped.

Jerry bent his head as he continued. "One day, he came by to check up on me, and he saw the misses … Miss … Miss Nelly, that is. She was there with Miss Stella and Eric. Mr. Clyde got all excited by the way Miss Nelly moved. He said he'd just scored his first jackpot in Mount Pleasant. Mr. Clyde followed Miss Nelly to her farm. Then for a month, he continued to make regular visits to the farm, watching what everyone did, where they did it, and how it was done. He even followed the workers to see when they came and when they left. He was like the devil, very persistent. I tried to stop him, Miss … Miss … Stella. I really did. But he was kind of possessed. He said the little one would bring him big bucks. After a month of surveillance, Mr. Clyde left."

With tears rolling down his cheeks, Jerry Malone stopped and asked for a drink, and then he continued. "You see, Miss Stella, I did not think he was coming back. But he did. About a week later, he came back and did the same thing. And after a few days, he told me he was ready to make his move. I drove him to the farm."

Jerry coughed as he choked on his saliva. He took another drink. He then repeated his previous statement. "He told me he was ready to make a move. Miss Stella, I swear I did … did not want to do it, but he made … made me."

Jerry started to cough uncontrollably. After five minutes and a glass of water, the cough subsided and Jerry continued. "I stayed in the car while Mr. Clyde went over to the yard through an opening in the fence. It was quick. First he drugged the dog, took the teddy bear the boy was playing with, and then backed out of the yard. The boy followed him with his hand outstretched as if trying to reach for his teddy bear. Then it happened. As soon as the boy reached the pear tree, Mr. Clyde dropped the teddy bear, grabbed the boy, and rushed to the car. I ... I sped away."

Stella sat in horror as Jerry Malone described the actual abduction of her brother. She wanted to rip out his heart. It took all the strength she had in her body to restrain herself.

"Where did Clyde take him?" she asked painfully.

He shook his head. "I ... I don't know, Miss Stella. I dropped him off at the freeway where he had a car waiting. He gave me five hundred dollars, took the boy, and drove off in the waiting car."

"You son of a bastard," Stella shouted as she charged toward Jerry Malone. Before anyone could stop her, she was hanging over the table with her hands firmly placed around Jerry Malone's neck.

It took Jeremy, the attending officer, and the chief of police to pry Stella's hands off of Jerry's throat.

Jerry gasped for air as he smiled sheepishly in an attempt to mask the baffled look on his face.

Stella was extremely disappointed as she and Jeremy walked down the steps of Mount Pleasant CID. She was afraid that she had come full circle and landed right back where she'd started. She still had no clue as to Eric's whereabouts and no direction to follow.

"I am glad about one thing," she confided to Jeremy. "I now know how and why Eric was abducted, and soon the whole world will know."

With Jeremy by her side, Stella entered the waiting limousine in silence, entertaining, for the very first time, the idea of permanently relinquishing her search for Eric.

As prearranged, the limousine drove Stella and Jeremy to the Honigs, where they spent the rest of the morning and early part of the afternoon.

Stella and Jeremy also stopped off at Nelly's Cove, where they enjoyed afternoon tea with the patrons before heading back to Mount Pleasant Airport for their trip home.

Chapter 24

Stella's first impulse on returning to Haileysville from Mount Pleasant was to visit Mr. Clyde at the federal penitentiary.

With the incident at Mount Pleasant CID still fresh in his mind, Jeremy talked her out of it. Like Mr. Oxford, he advised Stella to allow the legal system to work for her. "Seek your revenge in court, Stella. This is not the time to do anything that will jeopardize your case against Clyde. For once, let the justice system work for your parents. God knows they earned it!"

This was one fight Stella had no intention of losing, and as much as she wanted to physically hurt Mr. Clyde, she knew that Jeremy was right. She had enough evidence to turn Clyde into a pauper, and with her help, the Feds also had enough information to keep him behind bars for the rest of his natural life.

Still, Stella remained mindful of the fact that Mr. Clyde was as cunning as a fox. He was also extremely resourceful. He would stop at nothing to escape the law, civil or otherwise. After all, he had lived a life of crime for more than three decades before being caught, and even at that, most of his crimes had not been uncovered until recently.

Be that as it may, Stella knew she had many things in her favor. Her law partner was good, and also advising her was the best in his field, Mr. Oxford. With all his expert lawyers, Mr. Clyde was in for a battle.

"Good luck, Jacob Clyde!" She smiled in anticipation of her day in court.

Encouraged by Jeremy and the Oxfords, who were now also convinced that Eric was alive, Stella intensified the search for her missing brother. Jim and other detective agencies in different parts of the United States and Canada were working around the clock, looking for Eric. No one could find him. Like before, every lead took them back to square one.

For Stella, this was extremely frustrating. She could not understand why, with such a vast amount of evidence, leads, and resources, Eric could not be found. The only comfort the searches brought was that many of their new leads resulted in the return of children who, in some form or other, had suffered under the hands of Mr. Clyde.

"At least something good is coming out of this," Mr. Oxford told Stella. "Many parents are reuniting with their long-lost children."

Mr. Oxford saw the result as being extremely positive. Yet, with every child reported found, his heart grew heavy with an eerie felling that would not go away.

At breakfast one morning, burdened by the strange and eerie feeling, Mr. Oxford excused himself from the table and walked over to a window. As he stood there gazing into the distance, amid the white pillars of the gazebo, he saw a lone hummingbird. It quickly fluttered its wings, flew back and forth, and then came back again. It seemed to have lost its way.

Suddenly, Mr. Oxford realized that what he was experiencing was a sense of loss and helplessness—something he had experienced before. He tried to remember when this overwhelming feeling had previously weighed on him and to unravel why he was experiencing it again.

"My *God*!" he exclaimed as the memory of the day Nelly and Hugo died came rushing through his mind. It was the very first time he'd met Stella—the day he'd tried to help her but had been unable to do so. He fought to hold back the tears as the events of that day flooded his mind.

Without saying a word to anyone, he rang for a taxi, pulled one of Eric's baby pictures from Eric's photo album, and placed the photo in his wallet. Before the taxi arrived, he grabbed his brown suede jacket that was hanging on the back of a chair in the living room and rushed out the front door.

Two hours later Mr. Oxford was sitting at a table across from Mr. Clyde in Haileysville Federal Penitentiary.

Mr. Oxford was perplexed by Mr. Clyde's appearance. He had imagined him as a big, strong, overbearing, fierce-looking man. Instead, he was met by a man who stood five foot two. He was stocky and had a round belly. His hairline had receded to the middle of his head, and his ears protruded like rabbit ears. Mr. Oxford could not help thinking how much like Santa Claus Mr. Clyde would look if only he had gray hair on his head; had a long, white beard; and wore a red suit.

"Well, Mr. Clyde," Mr. Oxford said as they stared at each other from across the table. "For a little man, you have really done a lot of damage."

Mr. Clyde leaned back on his chair, crossed his legs, and clapped his hands three times. "Mr. Oxford," he said, "the infamous, Robert Oxford. At last we meet. During my travels, I heard quite a lot about you. Unfortunately, we never had the opportunity to meet. How do you do?"

Mr. Oxford found the man sitting across from him to be quite repugnant. He also thought of Mr. Clyde as slick and shameless. Mr. Oxford pulled Eric's baby picture from his wallet and handed it to Mr. Clyde.

He looked at the picture for a split second before handing it back. "Handsome kid," he said with a taunting smile.

Mr. Oxford gave him back the picture. "Look here, Clyde. I am only going to ask you once. Take a good look at this photograph and tell me who you sold this boy to."

Mr. Clyde's smile grew wider as he looked at Mr. Oxford without looking at the photograph. He leaned as close to Mr. Oxford as he could and whispered. "The kid was a little brat who got exactly what he deserved." He pulled himself back, straightened up in his chair, and then added, "I can't very well say where in the world I dropped him."

Mr. Oxford could not have hated anyone more than he hated Mr. Clyde at that very moment. He wanted to strangle him, but he kept his composure. "Mr. Clyde," he said, "your mother must have really done

184

you wrong. But whatever harm she inflicted upon you will be nothing compared to what is in store for you. So help me God, I will personally see to it that you burn in hell."

Mr. Oxford could not wait to get away from Mr. Clyde. He called the guard to let him out and hurried to the taxi waiting for him at the gate.

On his way back to Stella's place, Mr. Oxford thought of how much Mr. Clyde looked like Santa Claus and, yet, was the epitome of the devil. "Looks can surely, deceive," he said out loud.

Mr. Oxford told no one about his visit to the Haileysville Federal Penitentiary—not even his wife.

Despite his visit to the penitentiary, the feeling of helplessness persisted. And as Mr. Oxford watched Stella from across the dining table that evening, he wished he had encouraged her to turn the Clyde case over to Mr. Sylvester. *What have I done to my dear Stella? What have I done to her?* he quietly asked himself.

After dinner, Jeremy suggested that everyone picnic at Cactus Beach before the Oxfords left for Mount Pleasant the following Monday. Though they were expected back in Haileysville for the trial, Jeremy felt that things would be too hectic to even think of Cactus Beach at that time.

The Oxfords declined the invitation. With all that was going on, they felt it inappropriate to have a beach party. Jeremy saw things differently. He was convinced that a picnic at the beach would be the best distraction for Stella. "This will help take Stella's mind off things for a while," he told them. "It will allow her a chance to relax."

He eventually convinced the Oxfords and Stella that there was no better time to have that picnic.

Though not happy with Jeremy's suggestion, Stella went along because the Oxfords had given in. She also felt guilty that their entire stay in Haileysville had been centered on her.

When Cook came to remove the dinnerware, Stella informed her that a picnic lunch for a party of four was needed for early Sunday morning. The group planned to attend the 9:00 a.m. Mass, get to the beach by 11:45 a.m., and leave by 2:30 p.m. to avoid the large crowd that gathered at the beach by late afternoon.

The entire household was off to a very late start on the morning of the picnic. It was as if the house had been overcome by a cloud of sleeping gas. Stella, Jeremy, and Mr. and Mrs. Oxford had all overslept. This rare and mysterious occurrence resulted in a two-hour delay. Instead of attending the 9:00 a.m. Mass, they attended Mass at 11:00 a.m.

They arrived in church and took their seats in the fourth pew from the altar only seconds before Mass began. Mass was officiated by Father Maligan, the oldest priests in the parish. Because of his age, he had become somewhat slow in his delivery. Yet, his Mass remained more spirited and heavily attended than Masses performed by any other priest in the parish.

While listening to the sermon, Stella dozed off. And in that short span of time, she heard clearly a voice saying, "Your search is over. You are free!"

Stella opened her eyes and looked around. To her delight, no one seemed to have noticed that she had dozed off. She straightened herself in her seat and frowned at the thought that her mind might be playing tricks on her.

After Mass the foursome quickly changed and headed to Cactus Beach in Jeremy's jeep, which Cook had packed in preparation for the picnic.

The outing turned out to be something they all needed, but it was particularly good for Stella. She was more relaxed than she had been in weeks. She played volleyball, and for the first time in a long time, Stella talked to Jeremy and the Oxfords about things other than her search for Eric and the case against Mr. Clyde. In fact, not once did she mention either of those subjects. Instead, she discussed her plans for the future, Mr. Oxford's plans for retirement, and his need for some well-deserved rest.

Stella even discussed wedding plans with Jeremy and tried to catch up on his progress at work. It was as if she was back to her normal self, even better.

"Stell, I think we need to do this more often!" Jeremy applauded.

Mr. Oxford chimed in, "I concur." He was very happy, because now he was comfortable with his decision to leave for Mount Pleasant the following day. Prior to the picnic, he had been fraught with concern about leaving Stella while she was still in a state of frustration.

By the time the crowd started trickling onto the beach at about three thirty, Stella and Jeremy had already set a wedding date. Mrs. Oxford was making plans for the wedding, and Mr. Oxford had made a firm commitment to fully retire sometime within the next twelve months.

Stella and her companions were having such a wonderful time they did not notice how crowded the beach had become. When they eventually looked around and saw the number of people who had moved in, Jeremy's mouth swung open in wonder. They all laughed at his reaction and decided that it was time to leave.

They cleared their picnic area and then Stella and Jeremy carried their things to the jeep while the Oxfords went to the water for a final swim.

After locking their belongings in the jeep, Stella and Jeremy walked hand in hand toward the ocean to join the Oxfords. As they approached the area where the Oxfords were swimming, they ran into Victor, the air-conditioning technician from CEGSC. He was standing face-to-face with Stella.

With a mischievous smile on his face, he said, "Hello, ma'am."

Stella immediately remembered the incident at her front door that hot, blistering summer afternoon. It was the first time she had seen Victor since that day, and feeling a bit embarrassed, she quickly lowered her gaze. As her line of sight shifted from his face to the ground, she noticed that Victor was wearing a bright yellow-and-black, bikini-style bathing trunk. And there, on the left side of his abdomen, under his navel, Stella saw it.

It was an eagle in flight. Stella released her grip on Jeremy's hand and dashed forward to grab Victor. With her hands outstretched, her lips parted, and her eyes bulging out of their sockets, Stella's knees buckled, and she fell to the ground. She was unconscious.

Jeremy bent over Stella and screamed. "Please, someone, call an ambulance."

Victor rushed to the nearest telephone booth and dialed 911.

By the time the paramedics arrived, Stella was blabbering incoherently—or so Jeremy and the Oxfords thought.

"The eagle is on Victor's abdomen. I met him before. He fixed my air conditioner. He is my brother. He is Eric. I found him. I found Eric."

Jeremy and the Oxfords tried to keep Stella calm. They feared she was having a mental breakdown. The paramedics examined Stella and found her to be in no immediate danger, but according to protocol, she had to be taken to the hospital to be examined by a physician.

Stella vehemently protested. She insisted that she had fainted due to an immediate lack of oxygen to the brain. She saw no reason to be taken by ambulance to the hospital for just a bruised elbow. She promised to make an appointment to see Dr. Drummond, her physician, the following day.

"Miss James will do it her way," Jeremy told the paramedics as he helped Stella to her feet.

After the paramedics left and Stella regained her balance and clarity of mind, she articulated to her companions what she had been saying while she was lying on the ground. She told them who Victor was, where she had first met him, and what she had seen on his abdomen just before she'd fainted.

Jeremy and Stella combed the beach in search of Victor, while the Oxfords enjoyed a banana split and a chocolate fudge sundae at Cobblers Palace.

They left Cactus Beach two hours later without a trace of Victor.

On their way home Stella was silent. She closed her eyes and allowed her mind to drift from the eagle on Victor's abdomen to the eagle on the abdomen of the little boy in her dream to the eagle on the image of Eric in his photo album and then to the same eagle on Clyde's movie reel. "They were all the same. They were in the same spot. They were all in flight. This could not be a mistake," Stella murmured under her breath.

She then tried to remember everything that had happened on the day she'd first met Victor. It was the very day her dream had started. That could not be a coincidence. Stella opened her eyes and said aloud, "Victor has to be Eric."

No one answered. The others did not know what to say.

Stella was convinced she had found Eric, and not even outspoken Jeremy could bring himself to tell her that the "eagle" on Victor's abdomen might be artificial.

The Oxfords agreed that the eagle might be a tattoo but could not find the words to communicate that to Stella. In silence, they looked at each other and smiled helplessly. They squeezed hands, not in a romantic way, but in a way that demonstrated their strong support for Stella. In a meeting of the minds, they hoped together for a happy ending to a laborious search.

That night, as Stella lay in bed, she experienced a sense of freedom and tranquility. It was as if a heavy load was being slowly removed from her chest as she became more and more convinced that she had found Eric. There was no panic and no doubts. She was in perfect peace.

Stella had a sleepless but restful night as she lay in bed planning her strategy for the day ahead. She was certain there would be no trouble locating Victor. After all, she knew where he worked, and even if he no longer worked with CEGSC, her search would now be limited to Haileysville and its surrounding areas. Best of all, she knew his name.

Stella could hardly wait for the break of dawn.

Chapter 25

The Oxfords cancelled their departure until Stella had the chance to find and talk to Victor. They were overwhelmingly concerned that Victor was not Eric. Worse yet, they feared that Stella could not handle another disappointment.

The incident with Jerry Malone at the Mount Pleasant CID had left Stella unraveled. Now, this latest incident at the beach had increased the chances of Stella becoming completely undone. Should this happen, neither of the Oxfords knew what they would do. Their only certainty was that they had to be there for Stella. Their love for her would allow nothing less.

Mr. Oxford sat up in bed, reached for his glasses and then dialed long distance. He was calling Nancy. The phone rang for a while before she answered. He instructed her to attend the meeting for which he was scheduled to return to Mount Pleasant.

Nancy was curious about his reason for the delay, but Mr. Oxford offered no explanation. All he said was, "We will talk upon my return."

Stella was out of bed before dawn. She took a quick shower, got into a red designer jogging suit, and headed downstairs to the library. Though she'd had a sleepless night, she was wide-awake and focused. Her plan was to first locate Victor. Aside from that, she had not the foggiest idea how she would approach him with the news that he was her brother. "First things first," she said aloud as she looked through her files for the folder labeled "Utilities."

She was looking for the yellow customer receipt Victor had signed and handed to her after repairing her central air-conditioning unit. When Stella located the folder it was only 5:00 a.m. She had to wait until 8:00 a.m. to talk to a customer service representative at CEGSC. The office hours were from 8:00 a.m. to 6:00 p.m.

Stella sat for half an hour examining the receipt. It showed a work order number, the date and time of the repairs, the parts used, and the name of the technician who'd completed the job. At the bottom left of the form was Stella's signature. It was followed on the right by the signature of Victor Chance.

"Victor Chance," Stella said aloud. "Victor Chance, what will you say when I tell you that you are my brother?"

Stella's heart began to thump. For the first time since beginning her search, she was terrified. Her fear was not that Victor would turn out to be someone other than Eric; she feared that she would not know what to say to him.

Stella placed the folder on the desk and rushed out of the library. She entered the kitchen and helped herself to a cup of freshly brewed coffee.

The sun was rising, and through the open window over the kitchen sink, Stella could see a beautiful day dawning. The bright morning stars were fading, the birds were chirping, and she could hear the croaking of frogs and the chirping of grasshoppers in the distance.

Stella walked out onto the patio and took a deep breath. The morning air was cool and fresh. She placed her cup of coffee on the patio table, and slowly but decisively, she walked out of her backyard gate onto the grounds of the estate.

Ninety minutes later, Stella returned with her hair dripping wet. She felt refreshed from her morning exercise. She had jogged a couple of miles and, in the nude, swam a few lapses across the pond. She had no fear of being seen. She did not care. She felt as free as a bird.

Stella washed and dried her hair, got into her office attire, and then rushed downstairs to have breakfast with the Oxfords. Their flight was scheduled to depart at eleven thirty that morning, and Stella had hoped to spend some time with them before their departure.

Stella could not stop smiling after Mrs. Oxford had informed her that they were not leaving until she spoke to Victor. She was extremely appreciative of their support but felt guilty that she had once again kept them from their duties.

During breakfast, the Oxfords and Stella discussed how well business at the farm was going and her decision to expand the retreat. In the middle of that conversation Stella glanced at her watch. It was 8:30 a.m. She politely excused herself from the breakfast table and retreated to the library.

Stella nervously sat at her desk, opened the folder, took a deep breath, and dialed the telephone number listed on the yellow receipt from CEGSC.

"Good morning. How may I help you?" Stella heard a voice say.

Her heart skipped a beat. She paused for a moment, and then answered. "Good morning. This is Stella James." Her voice shook as she tried to pull her thoughts together. "My account number is 55532824." She looked at the receipt in the folder on the desk in front of her and continued. "I had my central air unit repaired sometime ago, but for some reason, it seems to be spewing smoke." Stella paused. "I would like to have someone take a look at it. Oh, by the way," she paused again. "Please send that young man, uh, Victor Chance. I was very delighted with his work the last time. He was polite and seemed quite knowledgeable."

Stella crossed her fingers and waited for an answer.

"Did you say within the next twenty-four hours, ma'am? Sure, that's fine. Thank you."

Stella hung up the telephone and slid forward on her chair. "I did it! I surely did!"

Stella was so excited she did not see Mr. Oxford standing at the doorway of the library. She almost dropped to the floor when she finally looked up.

Stella motioned for Mr. Oxford to enter as she once again picked up the telephone and dialed. She informed Wendy that she would be working at home for the rest of the day.

After placing the telephone in its cradle, Stella tried talking to Mr. Oxford. She could not. A lump formed in her throat, and tears rolled down her cheeks. She walked toward Mr. Oxford and placed her arms around him. "P-pops," she stuttered, "he will be here within twenty-four hours."

"I heard, Stell. I heard," Mr. Oxford replied. He, too, placed his arms around her. In his heart, he shed a tear. He was afraid of the outcome.

Chapter 26

For the second consecutive night, Stella was sleepless. Like a child on Christmas morning waiting for Santa to arrive, Stella lay in bed listening to hear the doorbell. She had been told that Mr. Chance would be at her house within twenty-four hours. And nothing, not even sleep, could keep her from hearing those chimes.

By dawn, she was out of bed getting ready to start the new day. Just as she'd finished applying makeup to mask the bags under her eyes, the doorbell rang. She scrambled to put away her makeup while taking a last look in the mirror. The clock hanging on the wall in front of the mirror read 8:15 a.m.

Stella hurried out of the bathroom. Minutes later, she stood fully dressed in a silk Armani skirt suit, nervously opening the front door. Victor was about to ring the doorbell for a second time when the door opened. He quickly put his hand to his side and stood at ease.

Stella thanked him for coming and invited him inside. He hesitated for a moment and then entered. He looked extremely uneasy as Stella led him through her foyer. He could not understand why he had been invited into her house when the central air-conditioning unit was outside.

Stella, too, was apprehensive. She was so nervous that the palms of her hands were sweating. She knew that her voice was next to go. She had to calm down.

On entering the library, Stella turned to ask Victor to have a seat. He had stopped at the door of the library and would not enter.

"Miss James," he finally said, "why am I here? Is there really a problem with your air conditioner? I hope you understand that you are not CEGSC's only customer. I have a schedule to keep."

As nervous as she was, Stella realized that she was working with limited time and an unwilling participant. She decided to be blunt. "Mr. Chance." She took a deep breath, paused, and then continued. "My central air unit is not broken. My reason for bringing you here under false pretense is somewhat selfish. For years I …" Stella stopped. She decided that the story could be told later.

"Mr. Chance, is the eagle on your left abdomen a tattoo or a birthmark?"

Victor looked at Stella in disbelief. He had been asked that question a thousand times before, but never had he been summoned to someone's home to be interrogated about it. "How do you know about the eagle? And what is it to you?"

"Mr. Chance, what I am about to tell you rests solely upon that eagle. I must know whether or not the eagle is a birthmark."

The surprise in Victor's expression deepened; he could not imagine why it was so important for Stella to know whether or not the eagle was an authentic birthmark. He hesitated for a while, and then as he had done a thousand times before, he responded, "I was born with it."

Stella did not know whether to hug Victor or tell him her story. She dropped into the armchair and stared at Victor as tears rolled down her cheeks. Without a doubt, she knew she had found her brother.

Victor stood looking at Stella, not knowing whether to run or stay. Then suddenly, he heard a voice behind him.

"Sorry, my boy …"

Victor jumped and landed in the arms of Mr. Oxford, who he had not seen or heard enter the room. Mr. Oxford quickly introduced himself and apologized for the deception under which Victor had been brought to Stella's house.

"Your employer would never have given me your address, Mr. Chance," Stella said, adding her own apology. "This was the only way I could have gotten you here."

Victor's demeanor slowly changed from suspicious to curious. He crossed to the other side of the library and sat on the sofa.

Stella rose from the armchair and took a seat at the other end of the sofa. She warned Victor that what she was about to say would sound crazy, but it was true.

Mr. Oxford looked over at Victor and nodded as if to assure him of Stella's sincerity.

Stella formally introduced herself.

"I know who you are," Victor responded. "It is impossible to miss you. You are in every newspaper in town. In fact, the world is depending on you to bring down the so-called notorious Mr. Clyde."

Stella ignored his statement, but she could not help thinking of its irony. She wondered what he would do when he found out that he, too, had been Mr. Clyde's victim. It pained her to think that she would eventually have to do the inevitable—tell Victor who Mr. Clyde really was. For now, she waited. There was something equally important to divulge.

Stella told Victor that, for years, her family had searched far and wide to find her brother, whose name was Eric. Victor listened attentively, wishing she would get to the point. To him, Stella was not making much sense, and he could not see what finding her brother had to do with him.

Stella stopped for a moment. She looked at Victor with a broad grin on her face, and then with no warning, she exclaimed. "Eric! Your name is Eric! You are my brother!"

Victor's jaw dropped, his head jerked, and his eyes popped open all at the same time, and then he froze.

Mr. Oxford immediately interjected. "Mr. Chance, what Miss James is trying to say is that she thinks you might be her brother. Please give us the opportunity to explain."

After taking a drink of water, Victor agreed to stay and listen.

First, Mr. Oxford introduced himself and revealed to Victor that he was not Stella's biological father. He added unequivocally that despite that fact, he loved Stella unconditionally and would destroy anyone who tried to take advantage of her. He then proceeded to ask Victor to tell him about himself.

Victor bluntly refused. Instead, he insisted on knowing why Stella thought he was her brother and why Mr. Oxford felt it necessary to threaten him.

Mr. Oxford grew silent. He noticed something very familiar about Victor. He had seen it in Nelly the very first time they'd met. He had seen it in Stella throughout her life with him and the Honigs. Now, there it was, staring him straight in the face. Victor exhibited the same stubborn, uncompromising force of will that Nelly and Stella so strongly possessed.

Together, Stella and Mr. Oxford told Victor the story of Eric's disappearance; the death of the Jameses; and the long, laborious, and unending searches they'd conducted over the years.

Victor listened in silence, absorbing every word. By the time Stella and Mr. Oxford had finished telling the story, both Victor and Stella were in tears. Stella's tears were tears of joy because she knew she had found her brother.

For Victor, it was different. Nothing Stella and Mr. Oxford said sounded familiar. In fact, he could remember nothing prior to his fifth birthday. He had been adopted, and over the years, he had tried unsuccessfully to locate his biological parents. To him, this new revelation seemed as close an answer to his prayer that someday he would be reunited with his biological parents as he had come. He had no idea that the strangers in whose presence he sat were actually telling him the truth. Yet he felt a connection to Stella. It was a connection he had never felt before, and to him, that was a good place to start.

Chapter 27

On the morning of his eighteenth birthday, Victor had overheard an argument between his parents, Elizabeth and Alan Chance, and a stranger—an argument that had confirmed his long-held suspicion that he was an adopted child.

On numerous previous occasions, Victor had asked his parents if he was adopted. And they had sworn to him that he was not. This time, Victor had confronted them with what he'd heard, and they had reluctantly admitted that he had, in fact, been adopted.

The revelation left Victor feeling somewhat deceived but not at all surprised. In fact, his overwhelming reaction was relief. He had always believed that it was he who had caused the emptiness and lack of passion and love that existed within his household. For that, he'd carried the burden of guilt. Discovering that he was adopted freed him from this self-inflicted guilt.

Victor had grown up in a small, middle-class community on the outskirts of Detroit, Michigan. His parents, Elizabeth and Alan Chance, both worked for a major motor vehicle manufacturing company. The Chance family lived a simple, modest lifestyle. All of their children's needs were met, and even their wants were seldom denied. The Chance children attended the best public schools in their community. Of all the children, Victor was the only one who excelled in school. And for this, he earned a scholarship to MIT.

As a child, Victor had always felt an internal void. He'd grown up with an older sister and two younger brothers in the same household, but they were as different from him as night and day.

Victor had felt like a complete stranger, and try as he may, he could not fit in. His values were unlike those of the entire Chance family. He responded differently to every situation, and it seemed that the Chances were always at odds with each other. The only similarities shared among the family were the family name and their surroundings.

Their motto was tolerance in the name of peace. And they even struggled to adhere to that. There was no friendship among the siblings.

Each of the Chances had a completely different personality. Victor was independent, headstrong, and extremely passionate about what he believed in. As a result of those qualities, countless clashes erupted among the siblings. Such clashes often left Victor feeling alone and misunderstood. Not even his parents seemed to know him.

With age and increasing wisdom, Victor realized that something was definitely missing. Many times he sought answers from Elizabeth and Alan Chance. They complimented him on having an active imagination for seeing things that did not exist. They even assured him that the Chance family was as normal as any other. Thus, when Victor was finally told that he was adopted, his entire being was placed into perspective. There was a logical reason for the lack of warmth that existed within the walls of the Chance home.

After Elizabeth and Alan admitted to Victor that he was adopted, he'd sworn he would find his birth parents and had started his own investigation into their whereabouts. His efforts had proved unsuccessful. The family service agencies he'd contacted in Detroit had no records of his existence. He'd tried to obtain hospital records. There were none. He'd gone to every adoption agency he could think of or locate. They could not help because the only information he had, as provided by his adoptive parents was that his adoption was done through a lawyer whose existence they couldn't determine. Victor had even contacted numerous detective agencies, all of whom had refused the case because there was no information to start with.

The stories told by those who claimed to have known his biological parents were all inconsistent. At times, he was told that his mother had been a single woman who'd lost her life during childbirth. Other times, he was told that he had been given away because his single mother was too poor to care for him. The last he'd heard of his birth parents was that they had died in a boating accident, leaving him with no surviving relatives.

Victor had eventually given up his search, but he'd never abandoned his hope of one day finding his biological parents.

In spite of the many conflicting stories Victor received about his birth parents, many of which were sanctioned by Elizabeth and Alan Chance, the Chances cared for him. And like the other siblings in his household, Victor was brought up to be an upstanding citizen. The Chances did the best they could.

The conversation Victor overheard at the age of eighteen also led him to suspect that Elizabeth and Alan were concealing much more than his adoption. It seemed they had been blackmailed for years.

When Victor had confronted them about what he'd thought he'd heard, they'd dismissed it as being preposterous and admonished him never to bring it up again. Victor remained suspicious that something was going on but decided to leave it alone.

Victor had completed his undergraduate studies with a bachelor of science from MIT, after which he'd taken some time off school. At age twenty-seven, Victor was working to put himself through graduate school. He was in his second year of studies at Princeton University and hoped to obtain a master's degree in engineering.

Victor had landed his summer employment with CEGSC during a fall semester job fair held at his university. For a number of reasons, he'd gladly accepted the company's offer. For one, the pay was good. In addition, there was a chance he could secure a permanent position with the company's engineering department after he graduated.

Prior to Victor's summer employment in Haileysville, he'd worked with a major electronic repairs company in Detroit.

To Victor, landing the summer job in Haileysville had been a blessing. To Stella, it was a miracle, not short of divine intervention.

Chapter 28

With tears streaming down their cheeks, Stella and Victor looked at each other, and through the tears, they started to laugh.

"The very first time I saw you, I thought you looked familiar," Stella told Victor in a raspy, crackling voice.

"You made quite an entrance," Victor replied as he wiped away a tear.

They were like two long-lost friends. They laughed, cried, and even poked fun at each other. To further convince Victor of his identity, Stella invited him to look at their childhood photographs in the albums that were still lying on the floor in one corner of the library.

The look on Victor's face told how fascinated he was with each picture. As he browsed through the albums, he hoped against all hope that he would remember something of his childhood. He even tried to envision growing up in a home surrounded by laughter and unconditional love. He remembered nothing.

Seeing how intensely preoccupied Victor and Stella were with the albums and with each other, Mr. Oxford left the library in silence. He felt no apprehension about leaving Stella alone with Victor. He was convinced that Stella needed no protection.

He had never met little Eric, but something about Victor kept reminding him of Stella and her many traits now and as a child growing up. They were too many similarities between the two to deny that Victor might indeed be Stella's brother.

Mrs. Oxford was flabbergasted when Mr. Oxford stated simply, "Victor Chance might indeed be the son of Nelly and Hugo James." Mr. Oxford had always been the skeptic who would not jump to conclusions without first verifying facts. But there he was, standing before her, making a qualified statement for which he had no basis.

Mrs. Oxford could not believe her husband. This was too quick. She had to find out for herself. She had to be certain that they were not being duped. As much as she trusted her husband, she hoped that he had not reached that conclusion in order to save Stella from an impending emotional slump.

She hurried downstairs to the library, where, to her surprise, Victor and Stella were sitting on the floor looking through the photo albums. They were oblivious to their surroundings. She was amazed at how at home Victor had made himself.

"He is too comfortable," she muttered under her breath. She cleared her throat to alert them of her presence. Then, cautiously, she introduced herself to Victor without shaking his hand, although he offered his. Mrs. Oxford was certain that Victor was up to no good.

However, after speaking to him for some time, her skepticism diminished somewhat. She found no immediate reason to doubt his authenticity. However, she did not rule out the possibility of having a serological test completed to determine possible relationship between Stella and Victor, for the sake of caution.

The Oxfords, Stella, and Victor all spent the rest of the morning getting to know more about each other. Stella had Cook prepare brunch. By the time Victor radioed to let his office know that he was on his way to the next appointment, it was almost noon.

Over the next few days, Stella and Victor spent a great deal of time swapping stories. They shared more in common than they could have imagined. Like Stella, Victor enjoyed the blues, classical music, and the arts. They both devoted a great deal of time to charitable causes and participated in numerous sporting events. They were both avid tennis players, and former captains of their track teams in college. They spoke, almost as if they were speaking about the same experiences. It was strange.

In just a few short days, Victor was beginning to feel closer to Stella than he was to the siblings he'd lived with for as long as he could remember. This scared him. Things were moving too quickly. He had not stopped to consider the ramifications that may occur if it turned out he was not the brother Stella thought she had found. He would be devastated. Even worse, from what he'd learned since meeting Stella, he realized the repercussions for her would be far greater. He could not inflict such pain upon her.

Victor wasted no time communicating his concerns to Stella and the Oxfords. He demanded a paternity test.

Stella was completely aghast by his demand and would hear nothing of the sort. She knew she had found Eric, and nothing could prove otherwise. She vehemently fought the idea with every argument she could think of. She eventually conceded, at Victor's insistence and with Jeremy and Mrs. Oxford's encouragement.

"No serological testing could prove what I already know," she said. "Victor is my brother. He is Eric, and soon, everyone will know it too."

Mr. Oxford called Dr. Samuel Solticix, an old and trusted friend, at Mount Pleasant General Hospital. After a brief but cordial conversation, they made arrangements for a serological test to be administered immediately upon their return to Mount Pleasant. Victor was more than willing to accompany them back to Mount Pleasant for the serological testing, as did Stella. Jeremy decided to tag along for moral support.

Jeremy and the Oxfords were very understanding of Stella and Victor's need to be together. They felt comfortable enough with Victor to trust him.

Since they'd met, Stella and Victor had spent their evenings together. They were almost inseparable. They engaged in long-drawn-out conversations and extended walks around the grounds of Stella's estate. They went riding on Stella's favorite stallions. Stella was experiencing a childlike happiness that she had never experienced before. He never said it, but Victor was experiencing the same.

Stella had always been energetic and pleasant, but finding Eric seemed to have breathed new life into her. She was happy, and she showed it, not only in her actions but also in her words. Her newly found happiness was echoed loudly and clearly over the telephone when she broke the news to the Honigs, the Oxford siblings, and her aunt Theresa. She even called her grandparents.

The Honigs could not stop crying. Through tears, Mrs. Honig exclaimed, "Finally, true joy has returned to Stell! She has found Ricki."

Stella, Jeremy, Victor, and Mr. and Mrs. Oxford flew out of Haileysville Airport on a chartered airplane to Mount Pleasant.

On their arrival at the Oxford household, they were greeted by a lavishly planned family celebration. Although they had never met Eric, the Oxford siblings wanted Victor to feel at home. Present at the party were the Honigs, Mr. Godfrey, his family, and the entire staff of Godfrey, Oxford, Smith, Jeremiah, & Associates. Theresa also flew in from Europe. The celebration lasted until dawn. And to Victor's surprise, no one left until the very end. Even Mr. and Mrs. Oxford, as exhausted as they were, stayed up until dawn.

There were countless questions for Victor. The Honigs, Theresa, and Mr. Godfrey were all perplexed to see how little he had changed. Together, they agreed that his name might have changed, and he had grown into a handsome young man, but his features remained the same.

He was tall and slender but quite muscular. His hair was still straight and black, and his dark eyes shone as brightly as they had when he was a baby. The dimples still appeared on his cheeks when he smiled. His tanned complexion was reminiscent of Hugo's, and his walk was as majestic as that of a prince.

Like Stella, the rest of her family didn't just feel that Victor was Eric; they knew it was him. Nevertheless, out of respect for and to honor Victor's wishes, they agreed that the serological testing should be completed.

Before going to the hospital the following morning, Stella and Victor purchased two bouquets of yellow roses, each containing thirty-six stems. They traveled to the James family cemetery, where they laid the roses on the tomb of Nelly and Hugo.

Since her eighteenth birthday, every year, on the first day in November, Stella visited the family cemetery to lay at her parents' tomb dozens of lit candles amid a sea of flowers. Theresa had told Stella of Hugo's many traditions, and this was one tradition she promised to uphold in honor of her dearly departed parents.

Her visit with Victor on this bright, sunny Saturday morning was, however, different. She was not just honoring her parents. She was bestowing upon them a most precious gift—a gift that had been boldly taken away from them. She was returning to them their son, Eric.

For more than an hour, Stella and Victor sat at the tomb and did not speak a word. It was as if they were communicating through their spirit.

The visit left Victor more emotional than he'd expected it would. Before leaving the gravesite, he stood looking at the tomb, tears running down his face. "Who could have been so heartless as to take from me the love of my parents, the sound of their voices, the feelings of their touch, and the smiles on their faces?" he asked. "Those things I will never know." Then, as if talking to the tomb, he added, "I wish I could remember the times we spent together. I wish I could remember you."

In his sadness, Victor was thankful that he was only a serological test away from finding his true identity. This provided him strength to overcome the absence of love and the emptiness that had once monopolized his existence. He had a warm feeling within. It was a feeling of belonging, and as he silently followed Stella into the parked limousine, he knew that he was finally home.

Victor and Stella rode silently from the cemetery to Mount Pleasant General Hospital. Halfway into the ride, Victor leaned over and squeezed Stella's hand. "Thank you, Stella. Thank you for never abandoning your search. Thank you for taking me to the cemetery." He paused for a moment, sighed, and added, "Now that I know where I came from, my journey into the future will be much more meaningful."

Stella rested her other hand on Victor's and smiled. "The pleasure is all mine, Victor. The pleasure is all mine."

Stella and Victor rode in silence for the duration of the trip.

With her eyes closed and her head on the headrest, Stella was thinking about her next move. She knew without a doubt that she was going to destroy Mr. Clyde. She had the evidence to turn him into a pauper, while at the same time helping to keep him locked up for many lifetimes. What she was not sure of was how to tell Victor that Mr. Clyde—the pedophile, pornographer, extortionist, and baby seller—was also his abductor. In silence, Stella prayed for another miracle. She needed divine intervention.

As the limousine pulled into the parking lot of Mount Pleasant General Hospital, Dr. Solticix was about to step into his car. Stella rushed out of the limousine and ran toward him. "Dr. Solticix," she shouted. "Sorry we are late."

"You surely are, Stella," he responded as he looked at his watch. "You are over thirty minutes late. I guess I'll see you on Monday."

Dr. Solticix opened the driver's door of his car and was about to enter when Stella reached him.

Mr. Oxford had requested the serological testing but had not told Dr. Solticix that the person accompanying Stella might be her missing brother. After breathlessly explaining to Dr. Solticix the reason for the serological test and why she and Victor had been delayed, he was happy to hustle Stella and Victor back to his office.

Dr. Solticix instructed his nurse to draw blood from both Stella and Victor. When she was finished he asked her to pull Hugo and Nelly Jameses' files from the archives and leave them on his desk.

Within minutes, Dr. Solticix, Stella, and Victor were walking through a narrow passageway of the hospital that led to the parking lot. Dr. Solticix expressed well wishes for Stella, adding that he hope the serological test would establish genetic proof that Victor was indeed her brother.

Stella refrained from telling Dr. Solticix that she already knew that Victor was Eric. She just smiled and thanked him for his assistance.

In the limousine, on their way to the Oxfords, Victor asked Stella about the Clyde case. She told him about the mountain of evidence she had gathered. As she spoke, Victor detected in her voice and expression, the malice she felt toward Mr. Clyde. She did nothing to mask her feelings. Victor could not understand why Stella hated Mr. Clyde with such passion. This was one of the hundreds of cases she had litigated. And on top of that, she had evidence that would get her clients justice. *Why then was she taking this case so personally?* Victor silently asked himself. *Was there something more to this case than Stella was saying?* He was about to ask Stella those questions when the limousine pulled into the Oxfords' driveway. He would have to save the questions for another time.

After a well-needed rest at the home of the Oxfords, Stella, Jeremy, and Victor went for a ride. Victor welcomed the opportunity to view the city. The trio visited City Hall. They drove past Sam's Ice Cream Parlor and other interesting landmarks, including the newly constructed stadium in downtown Mount Pleasant.

To Victor, nothing looked familiar.

Stella wanted to end the ride at the farmhouse, the home of their childhood. Victor declined. He wanted to stay away until he knew for sure that he was Eric James.

They returned to the Oxfords just in time to prepare for the dinner party that Nancy, Raymond, and India had planned for the family, including Theresa and the Honigs.

After dinner, they said their good-byes and checked in at the Ramada Renaissance Hotel, located close to Mount Pleasant Airport.

They left Mount Pleasant on their chartered flight early the following morning.

Chapter 29

Stella, Jeremy, and Victor were back in Haileysville by noon. While in the air, Victor had made numerous attempts to ask Stella about the Clyde case. Each time he'd been prepared to broach the subject, Stella had either been sitting with her eyes shut or in deep conversation with Jeremy.

Victor did not know it, but Stella had intentionally been trying to avoid discussing the case with him. Stella anticipated that Victor would ask questions whose answers she was not yet prepared to give. She felt badly enough withholding information from him. Being forced to tell him lies would be far worse.

On arriving in Haileysville, the trio was picked up by a limousine. Each was taken to his or her respective residence. They were all too tired to focus on anything other than resting from their hectic weekend or preparing for work the following day.

The moment Stella walked into her house, she called the Honigs and the Oxfords to inform them of their safe arrival. Following that, she spent the rest of the day relaxing. She even refused to check her answering service.

When Stella entered her office the following morning, she was greeted by Mr. Sylvester. "Good morning, Stella," he said, "I hope you had a restful weekend."

Unless there was a pressing matter, Stella seldom saw Mr. Sylvester first thing in the morning. Still carrying her briefcase, she waited to hear what Mr. Sylvester had to say.

"You are due in court in two days," he continued. "Mr. Clyde's lawyers requested an emergency hearing. It looks like they want a change in venue. They claimed that their client would not be given a fair trial in this district and that they have reasons to believe that Clyde's life is in danger."

"Not on his miserable life," Stella retorted as she forcefully placed the briefcase on her desk. "He will never get away with this."

"I know," Mr. Sylvester answered calmly as he left Stella's office.

The minute Mr. Sylvester walked away, Stella's phone rang. It was Mr. Oxford.

"Hi, Stell. I just got off the phone with my contact in Haileysville. Mr. Clyde's lawyers are attempting to get a change in venue."

"Yes, Pops. I just heard."

"Do you have a plan?"

"Not yet, Pops, but I will, soon."

"We will take care of it, Stell. See you later. I have a flight to catch."

Before Stella could say another word, the telephone went dead.

Mr. Oxford arrived later that night. Cook had already left, so Stella prepared for him a light snack and a warm bath and insisted that he hit the sack early.

Mr. Oxford was too tired to argue. He was in bed and fast asleep by the time Stella stopped by his bedroom to say good night.

Early the following morning, Stella and Mr. Oxford worked on arguments they planned on presenting to rebut Mr. Clyde's request. A contact of Mr. Oxford had also obtained information about Mr. Clyde's reason for the request. It turned out that Mr. Clyde, for some years, had contributed heavily to the reelection campaigns of numerous state officials. By moving the hearing to a venue of his choice, Mr. Clyde hoped to call in favors that would, for him, lead to a more lenient outcome.

Stella knew that exposing a link between political figures and a convicted pedophile could mean threatening or even destroying careers.

This, she told Mr. Oxford, was not an issue. She would stop a change in venue by any means necessary. Under no circumstances was she going to allow Mr. Clyde to manipulate the system. "He had done enough manipulating," she said calmly. "This time, the shoes are on someone else's feet—mine."

Stella got into her office at noon and did not leave until late in the evening. However, before leaving, she called and invited Mr. Oxford to meet her at La Fontene for a late snack.

At the restaurant, they reviewed their strategy for the hearing and agreed that they had covered every aspect of the motion and prepared for every possible contingency. Even their backup plan seemed impenetrable.

As their conversation dwindled, Stella began to show some uneasiness. She anchored her left elbow on the table, cradled her forehead between her thumb and index finger, and moved her head from side to side. She looked as if she had developed a headache.

Mr. Oxford realized that something other than the Clyde case was bothering Stella. "Speak," he demanded sternly.

Stella flinched, and then, with a smile, she looked into his piercing, deep brown eyes. She could not help but notice the lines that now occupied permanent spaces at the corners of Mr. Oxford's eyes and the sides of his mouth. His once firmly defined cheekbones were beginning to lose their youthful curves. The sparse streaks of gray that had once dwindled at his temple were beginning to invade the entire circumference of his head. Even his trademark brown mustache, which he had worn for as long as Stella could remember, was now invaded by patches of gray. It was as if Stella was looking at her guardian for the very first time. She had been so consumed by her present situation that she'd missed the changes that were taking place before her very eyes.

Stella sat in silence as reality struck her. Mr. Oxford was getting on in age, and she had not, until now, thought about a future without him. He was her rock.

Stella's silence was brief, as Mr. Oxford repeated his command. "Speak up, Stella," he demanded. "Something is bothering you, and it is not Clyde."

Stella quickly gathered her thoughts, and before Mr. Oxford could say another word, she told him about her inner turmoil. She was wrestling with when and how to tell Victor that Mr. Clyde was his abductor. Because Mr. Clyde's reputation as a notorious pedophile was public knowledge, Stella feared that disclosing such information to Victor would send him into an emotional tailspin. She did not know how vulnerable or timid Victor was, and Stella wanted to protect her brother.

Mr. Oxford understood Stella's concerns. He knew that her heart was in the right place, but he was unsympathetic to her inaction. "It is a grave mistake to withhold such information from Victor," he told her sternly. "If he learns that this animal was his abductor from a secondary source, the impact will be far greater than you can imagine. You do not want that. As soon as you can do it, sit Victor down, and tell him the story as you know it." Mr. Oxford held her gaze steadily and said gently but firmly, "Tell him the truth! Do it before it is too late."

Stella knew that Mr. Oxford was right. Yet her fear for Victor's sanity had overshadowed her judgment. She wished that this one secret of Mr. Clyde's would remain buried forever.

On their drive home, Stella thought seriously about what Mr. Oxford had said. In her mind, she formulated a list of those most likely to know the secret. Among them were Mr. Clyde, whom she despised; Jerry Malone; and, possibly, Victor's parents. As for the latter, Stella felt confident that since they had kept the secret for all those years, they may be inclined never to divulge it. For a brief moment, she entertained the idea of prolonging the secret, but she was overcome by rationality.

What would I want me to do if I was in his place? She asked herself. She shuddered when the answer hit her. She knew she would want to know. She would investigate what had happened to her, and Victor would too.

Stella glanced over at Mr. Oxford, who was riding in the passenger's seat, and said calmly, "I will tell Victor, Pops. I will tell him tomorrow."

Mr. Oxford nodded without saying a word. He was proud of Stella for deciding to do what was right. He was glad to be around to provide moral support for both Victor and Stella.

By the time Stella pulled into her driveway, she had decided where and how she would break the news to Victor. She made two telephone calls before going to bed. One was to Jeremy. The other was to invite Victor to lunch after court the following day.

"I have something extremely important to tell you," Stella said to Victor over the telephone. "Please meet me at La Fontene. And don't be late."

"Is the serological testing result back?"

"No. What I have to say is far more important than the serological test."

Victor could not imagine what Stella had to say that was more important than the results of his serological test. He could hardly contain himself as his mind began to wonder.

Chapter 30

Mr. Clyde walked into the courtroom accompanied by two US marshals. He was wearing a black tweed suit, a red tie, and a blue shirt. His hands were in shackles.

This was the very first time Stella had laid eyes on him, and she hated the man who stood before her. Chills ran through her veins as Mr. Clyde stared her directly into her eyes and smiled. His stare was mocking, as if to say, "Get me if you can."

Stella felt cold. The hair on her body stood on edge, and for a moment, she was transfixed by his presence. Her heart began to race. Her palms were sweaty, and in the back of her head, a voice screamed, *Destroy him! Destroy him!*

Stella had started to move toward Mr. Clyde when a hand landed on her shoulder. It was Mr. Oxford. Stella jumped as if coming out of a trance. Mr. Oxford looked into her eyes and was met by a cold, piercing gaze. As if by telepathy, he knew exactly what Stella was thinking. He whispered, "Stell, I felt the same way when I first met him. Don't let him hook you. We will get him legal—"

Before Mr. Oxford could finish his statement, the bailiff announced, "This court is called to order. All stand."

Stella took one more look at Mr. Clyde, and then she looked at Mr. Oxford and smiled. "Yes, Pops. That is about to begin."

Victor completed his morning appointments earlier than expected and decided to surprise Stella by meeting her at the courthouse instead of the restaurant.

On his arrival at the courthouse, Victor asked an officer to direct him to the courtroom where Mr. Clyde's hearing was taking place. The officer pointed him to courtroom number 9.

Victor walked in just as the judge was walking out of the courtroom and into his chamber. He was about to take a seat quietly at the back when the bailiff announced that the courtroom would be cleared for the next case. Victor started to leave, and then he abruptly turned around. He thought he saw someone he recognized.

Victor froze. It was him. The man in shackles was the same man he had seen and heard arguing with his parents a few days after his eighteenth birthday—the same man he'd thought he'd overheard blackmailing his parents. This was the man whose conversation with his parents had led him to the truth about his adoption.

Victor attempted to move forward. But the crowd from the front of the courtroom ascended upon him, and he could not move. Just then, Stella turned around and saw him. She made her way to his side. She held him by the shoulder and sat him on the nearest bench.

"Water," she said to an officer standing beside her. "Please get him a glass of water."

Before the officer returned, Victor spoke. "I have seen that man before. Is … is he Mr. Clyde?"

"Yes," Stella replied. "He is Mr. Clyde."

The officer returned with a jug of water and a glass that he had taken from the table where Stella sat. Close behind him was Mr. Oxford.

Stella poured water into the glass and lifted it to Victor's lips. Victor drank without touching the glass. His hands were shaking uncontrollably. When Stella removed the glass, Victor took a deep breath, and then sadly, he asked, "Was he my abductor?"

"Yes, Victor," Stella answered in a raspy voice. "Mr. Clyde was your abductor. I was going to tell you at lunch."

Without another word, Stella, Victor, and Mr. Oxford walked out of courtroom number 9 and then out of the courthouse.

"Leave the truck," Stella told Victor as he struggled to get the keys out of his pocket with his still trembling hands. "Your employer will have it picked up."

They drove to Stella's home, where Cook prepared a quick lunch for the three of them.

Victor tried to eat but could not. He was feeling both mentally and physically imbalanced. His stomach was churning. If he swallowed one bite, he would throw up. At the same time, his mind was racing as he wondered what unimaginable fate he might have suffered under the hands of that evil man.

Victor had seldom questioned the reasons for his inability to remember his life prior to his fifth birthday. As he sat silently at Stella's kitchen table gazing at the food in front of him, he realized that unlike Stella, who had been forced to forget her childhood, he had deliberately suppressed his. There had to be a reason. Victor ached within, and for the first time since he'd found out that Stella was his sister, he questioned whether he would have been better off not knowing.

Stella insisted that Victor stay with her. He would not. He wanted to return to work, in hopes that for just a few hours, the thoughts that now occupied his mind would vanish. Both Stella and Mr. Oxford begged him to stay, but upon his insistence, Stella drove him to his apartment.

On the way there, Stella joked about their first arguments, which he seemed to win all the time. There was no response. He sat motionless in the passenger's seat and looked straight ahead. Stella suggested that he take a few days off work to process all that had been heaped upon him in so short a period. Still, there was no response. Fearing the worst, Stella offered to spend the rest of the evening with Victor.

"No," he said abruptly. "I need time to think."

Not knowing what else to do or say, Stella reassured Victor that Mr. Clyde would suffer for his deeds. "Leave him to me," she said. "Today I won my first battle against him. He will be tried right here in Haileysville. His troubles have not yet begun. This was only the tip of the iceberg. I will make him pay dearly."

As Stella pulled up at the curb in front of Victor's residence, Victor said good-bye to Stella, and getting out of the vehicle, he closed the door behind him. Slowly, he walked toward the building without looking back.

By his silence, Stella could tell that his mind was buzzing with this newest revelation.

Stella and Mr. Oxford had told Victor of his abduction, but never had he imagined that Mr. Clyde was the culprit. When Victor had arrived in Haileysville at the beginning of summer, everyone had been speaking about Mr. Clyde and the atrocities he had committed against children. He had even seen a glimpse of Mr. Clyde in the newspaper but had not recognized him until he'd seen him in courtroom number 9.

Victor felt that even he had betrayed himself by not recognizing Mr. Clyde before now. He questioned whether he would have been able to unravel the connection between him and Mr. Clyde if he had recognized him earlier.

On entering his one-bedroom apartment on the ground floor of the three-story building, Victor paced back and forth, thinking of his deceptive existence. His entire life was a lie.

In one day, he had been faced with more questions than he could ever hope to have answered. Why had his adopted parents not told him that he was adopted? Why were they being blackmailed by Mr. Clyde? Why could he not remember his life prior to age five? What exactly had Mr. Clyde done to him after his abduction? How much did Stella know? Was he the reason Stella hated Mr. Clyde as much as she did?

Victor's head was spinning with what-ifs, hows, and whys as he tried to anticipate what lay ahead. He was happy to finally know where he came from, but he was afraid of the hidden demons that lay ahead. He could only imagine the horror he might have endured while in the hands of Mr. Clyde. He felt the urge to scream but could not. He wanted to hurt someone. But who could he hurt?

Slowly, Victor walked into the bathroom. Standing fully clothed underneath the showerhead, he turned on the hot water at its maximum.

He hoped to wash away the lies that engulfed his entire life. He wanted them gone.

That night, as Stella slept, a lady appeared. There was joy in her smile, and a bright light beamed all around her. She looked at Stella and the little boy as they played in the enchanted field of beautiful flowers. Then, slowly, she disappeared. Stella turned to the little boy, and for the first time, she saw his face. She was instantly awakened by the ringing of the telephone. She jumped from her sleep, wondering who was calling so late at night. She turned and looked at the clock on her nightstand. It was 9:30 a.m. Stella reached for the telephone.

"I could not wait until you got here!" the voice at the other end exclaimed joyously as Stella placed the phone to her ear. It was Dr. Solticix. "I had to tell you immediately." He paused as he tried desperately to be calm. Then Dr. Solticix said slowly, "Victor Chance is your brother. The serological test has identified biological relationship between you and Victor."

Stella jumped out of bed and started to scream. "I knew it! I knew it! I knew he was my brother."

Through those screams came tears of joy. Stella could not contain herself. She could not wait to tell Victor. But first she had to find Pops. He had to be the first to know.

Without saying good-bye, Stella dropped the telephone and rushed out of her bedroom, screaming at the top of her voice, "He is Eric. He is Eric. Yes, yes, he is Eric!"

On reaching the kitchen where Mr. Oxford was just finishing his morning coffee, Stella breathlessly informed him that Dr. Solticix had telephoned with news that Victor was indeed the long-lost son of Nelly and Hugo James. "I knew it all along!" she exclaimed. "I did not need any serological test to confirm it. I knew he was Eric."

With Mr. Oxford still beaming from the news, Stella made a phone call to Victor. There was no answer. She called CEGSC and was told that Victor had not shown up for work that morning. Neither had he called.

Stella's heart sank as she dialed Victor's phone several times and got no answer. "God," she whispered. "I just found him. I can't lose him again."

She quickly got dressed, and together, she and Mr. Oxford drove to Victor's apartment.

When they entered the apartment through the open front door, they found water everywhere. They frantically dashed through the one-bedroom apartment looking for Victor.

They found him fully dressed, sitting in a fetal position in the shower, and although only the hot water control knob was turned on, cold water was spouting from the faucet.

Stella screamed, "Victor!"

There was no answer, and her brother did not move. Stella reached out to grab him, but Mr. Oxford held her back. "Call for the ambulance. *Now*," he told her as he reached to turn off the faucet.

The ambulance arrived within minutes. Victor was alive but unconscious.

The paramedics rushed Victor to Haileysville General Hospital with Stella riding beside him.

Epilogue

One Year Later

"Wendy," Stella asked, "did Mr. Clyde's attorneys complete the transfer of funds from his offshore accounts to our clients' trust account?"

"All but the accounts in the US Virgin Islands," Wendy responded. "They were having some signing issues, but that was taken care of. All transfers should be completed within seventy-two hours. I have also received a completed report from the accountants showing that liquidation of all Mr. Clyde's assets has been completed. Based on our estimates, there is nothing left in his name."

"Marvelous," Stella responded. "We need a tally of everything before we can begin making payments to Clyde's victims and their parents."

Stella had completely annihilated Mr. Clyde in the civil suit against him. The jury had not only found him guilty; they'd awarded everything he owned—bank balances, stocks, bonds, real estate, companies, and stores—to his victims. They'd even made his victims beneficiaries of Mr. Clyde's life insurance policies.

At the reading of the verdict, Mr. Clyde, for the first time, showed some emotion. The smug and taunting expression on his face had vanished. This time, instead of looking directly at Stella, he'd bent over and cradled his face in the palms of his shackled hands.

His life as he knew it was over. Four weeks prior to the civil proceedings, the federal case against Mr. Clyde had ended. He'd been sentenced to twenty-five years to life, to be served at the end of his original fifteen-year sentence, with no possibility of parole.

His fate was sealed. Stella had kept her word. She'd turned him into a pauper. He had nothing left, not even a penny to bribe his cellmates with.

⟜

After receiving intense therapy, which included hypnosis, Victor had received a clean bill of health from his psychiatrist. He was fully recovered from the nervous breakdown he'd suffered after discovering that he had been one of Mr. Clyde's young victims.

Upon his recovery, Victor moved out of Stella's house in Haileysville and took up residence in his childhood home in Mount Pleasant. With legal help from Stella, he had his name changed to Eric James. He also decided to follow in his father's footsteps and continue the work he had started. With his engineering degree and Mr. Scuffey as his mentor and tutor, he embarked upon mastering the art of grafting.

⟜

One week after his official retirement from the law firm of Godfrey, Oxford, Smith, Jeremiah, & Associates, Mr. Oxford watched Eric walk Stella down the aisle and into the arms of Jeremy.

The wedding was held at Nelly's Cove, and in addition to the Oxfords, the Honigs, the Godfreys, and Theresa, every patron in the facility was in attendance. Stella's grandparents, her cousins, and even the Newtons were in attendance. It was one of the most elaborate weddings ever held in Mount Pleasant.

As the guests walked into the ballroom, they were greeted by a large portrait of Nelly and Hugo hanging directly over the entrance with a sign underneath that read "Welcome, All."